Praise for *What Doesn't Kill You*

"When it rains, it pours for Tee Hodges, the spirited, stiff-upper-lipped protagonist of DeBerry and Grant's latest. This is the anti-pity party: snappy, fun, and inspiring."

—*Publishers Weekly*

"*Essence* bestselling authors DeBerry and Grant (*Gotta Keep on Tryin'*) create a blueprint for restructuring your life in their new novel. This is a story that is sure to keep these authors' fans wanting more."

—*Library Journal*

"Witty commentary from Tee keeps the humor flowing, and the dialog rings true throughout."

—*Sacramento Book Review*

"*What Doesn't Kill You* has definitely made me stronger! I love this book!"

—Sybil Wilkes of the *Tom Joyner Morning Show*

Also by Virginia DeBerry and Donna Grant

Gotta Keep On Tryin'

Better Than I Know Myself

Far from the Tree

Tryin' to Sleep in the Bed You Made

Exposures

What Doesn't Kill You

A Novel

Virginia
DeBerry
&
Donna
Grant

A Touchstone Book
Published by Simon & Schuster
New York   London   Toronto   Sydney

Touchstone
A Division of Simon & Schuster, Inc.
1230 Avenue of the Americas
New York, NY 10020

First Touchstone trade paperback edition January 2010

TOUCHSTONE and colophon are registered trademarks of Simon & Schuster, Inc.

For information about special discounts for bulk purchases,
please contact Simon & Schuster Special Sales at
1-800-456-6798 or business@simonandschuster.com.

The Simon & Schuster Speakers Bureau can bring authors to your live event. For more
information or to book an event contact the Simon & Schuster Speakers Bureau at
1-866-248-3049 or visit our website at www.simonspeakers.com.

Designed by Carla Jayne Little

Manufactured in the United States of America

10 9 8 7 6 5 4 3 2

The Library of Congress has cataloged the hardcover edition as follows:

DeBerry, Virginia.
  What doesn't kill you : a novel / by Virginia DeBerry and Donna Grant.
    p. cm.
  "A Touchstone Book."
  1. African American women—Fiction. 2. African Americans—Fiction. 3.
Domestic fiction. I. Grant, Donna. II. Title.
  PS3554.E17615W47 2009
  813'.54—dc22
                                  2008007827
ISBN 978-1-4165-6420-1
ISBN 978-1-4165-6421-8 (pbk)
ISBN 978-1-4165-6621-2 (ebook)

For those who are trying to hold on,
even after the handle breaks off.

We gratefully acknowledge:

Hiram L. Bell III for way more than I could ever list—DG.

Gloria Hammond Frye, Juanita Cameron DeBerry, and the late John L. DeBerry II for the right stuff.

Alexis, Lauren and Jordan, Brian, Christine and Arielle, the future—which becomes more present with every book.

John L. DeBerry III and Valerie DeBerry, my brother and sister extraordinaire for their generosity, spirit and loving indulgence of their older sister's unconventional path—VDB

Our ART (Advance Reading Team): Gloria Frye, Juanita DeBerry, Keryl McCord, Valerie DeBerry and Elizabeth Opacity for taking time out your busy lives to plow through pages, give us feedback and remind us why we do this.

Tyrha Lindsey, Tracey Kemble, and Cheryl Jenkins for keeping 4 Colored Girls Productions moving forward while we toil over the keyboard and spend weeks on the road.

Victoria Sanders, our agent, for her wise counsel, unwavering support, enthusiastic encouragement and for her apparently endless cache of champers!

Our editor, friend and ally, Sulay Hernandez, who manages to keep us grounded, uplifted and oh yeah, laughing, throughout our entire process—often a pretty complicated task.

And all of our friends and family members—you are too numerous to name individually—whose continued love and support is surely the grace of the Creator at work.

What Doesn't Kill You

1

. . . all you can do is mop up the aftermath, dump it in a giant personal hazmat container and move on.

I shoulda known better. But I guess life would be boring if we had all the answers. How about half the answers? Maybe that would have kept my butt out of the gigantic sling it ended up in.

Who am I kidding? No, it wouldn't. Anyway, until the day after my daughter's wedding—and all that champagne—I really thought I had a handle on my life. Then it broke off.

But if you can't drink champagne at your daughter's wedding, when can you? Amber's wedding—it's been two years and it still seems impossible she could be married. My little girl looked so beautiful I had to pinch myself to keep from boohooing. That day she and J.J.—Baby Son-in-Law I call him, because he still has a face like his fourth-grade picture—made a whole bunch of promises to love, honor and put up with each other's mess. Then she wasn't my little girl anymore. She was J.J.'s wife. My own vows didn't hit me that hard.

In the limo after the ceremony I popped the cork on one of those cute little champagne splits to calm my nerves. Not that I was nervous like test-taking nervous, but your only daughter's wedding does fall into the major life-change category—those events that give us gray hair and stress us out, like moving, losing your job, grinning and bearing it while dealing with your ex-husband and his wannabe diva girlfriend for three whole days without slapping either one of them. Besides, I knew the bubbly would help me smile through all the picture taking even though my feet sizzled like raw meat on a hot grill, thanks to those very cute, very high shoes Amber talked me into because they looked so sassy with my lilac dupioni silk suit. And I looked damn good, thank you very much. Better than J.J.'s mother in that tired blue ruffled muumuu, and let's not even discuss that woman Amber's father paraded around. I mean, who wears a miniskirt and thigh boots to a wedding? Don't take my word. Check out the video. I looked great—way too young to be the mother of the bride. Except for that corsage.

I hate corsages. They're for old ladies who wear mink stoles and musty dusting powder. That will not be me. Ever. The last thing I needed was a big, sloppy orchid planted over my double Ds. Why do you think I wear this minimizer harness? But Amber just about had an ing-bing at the florist's—you know, one of those fits like she used to pitch when she was two and she didn't approve of my day-care wardrobe selection. Ever try explaining to a two-year-old that the pink flowered pants are in the dirty clothes and she should be thankful she has something clean to wear, since Mommy has been featuring the same tired black skirt every other day for two weeks and scraping together enough quarters to hit the Laundromat by the weekend because the check for the used-car-dealer jingle Daddy wrote is still "in the mail"? And that she needs to get her skinny behind dressed, since Mommy is ready to scream because she doesn't want to be late for work again? You can't. So somehow I'd manage to tease, trick or threaten her into her clothes and I'd wash out the pink pants that night by hand, which pretty much guaranteed the next day she wanted to wear her jeans with the stars embroidered on the back pockets. We sure came a long way from those days.

So I wore the corsage, because Amber has always had first-class taste, thanks in no small part to good home training, because I love her more than anybody in the world, and because arguing with my daughter can be like convincing a pit bull to let go of your leg—which isn't a bad quality. Early on I made sure she learned how to stick up for herself. Besides, it was her wedding. OK, their wedding.

It's just that I wasn't ready for anybody's wedding. Oh, I was used to the two of them hanging around the house, from the time they were in high school, and all through college, listening to the stereo, watching TV, playing games on the computer. By the time they were in tenth grade, he'd dropped the "Mrs. Hodges," and since he had sense enough to know not to call me Thomasina, he invented his own name for me. "Yo, Mama Tee, what's for dinner?" He'd ask this while taking inventory in my refrigerator, just as big and bold. "Did you ask *your* mother?" I'd say, but by then he'd be setting the table— placemats, silverware, napkin folded just so. He was always sweet, and I figured he'd be around until Amber chewed him up and was ready for the next flavor. Shows you what I know. Either he is the right flavor, or she hasn't chewed the sweet out of him yet.

Anyway, in the fall after they had both graduated and

found their first jobs, I was up early one Saturday, getting ready to go get my hair done, and the doorbell rang. Amber came flying downstairs, wearing the white blouse, tweed skirt and black leather Minnie Mouse pumps she'd put on when she was trying to look sophisticated. I knew something was brewing, since it was only a little later than the time she usually got home from Friday night. Before I could say anything, she yanked open the door and J.J. strolled in wearing a navy blue suit. A suit? On a Saturday morning? It made me dizzy. J.J. kissed her, handed me a box of still-warm doughnuts and a bouquet of red and white carnations wrapped in that shiny green tissue paper. That's when my knees went to Jell-O and I almost missed the seat of my chair as I sat down. The two of them plopped on my sofa, all bright-eyed and shiny-faced.

"What's wrong?" I said, which I know is not what you're supposed to say when somebody gives you flowers and doughnuts, but it's all I could think of. The next thing I knew, he was down on one knee, holding a black velvet box. "Oh no," is what came out of my mouth, which wasn't exactly what I meant, but really, it was. I dropped the flowers all over the floor. J.J. swiped at a tear on his cheek after he slid the twinkling half-carat diamond on Amber's finger. "Look at it, Mama!" Her hand was shaking when she showed it to me. Then she finally remembered to say, "Yes." And I ate six doughnuts—I don't know what flavors—then went to the hairdresser, because what else was there for me to do?

Later, when Amber and I were alone and I could speak in complete sentences, I sat next to her and took her hand. At first she thought I wanted to examine the ring, but I covered it with my other hand. "You two are so young to get married. You just graduated from college. Your whole life is ahead of you." I must have read that in *The Fools' Guide to Motherhood*, because those words never came out of my mother's mouth.

"Not as young as you and Daddy," she informed me and snatched back her hand.

So I pointed out the obvious. "You see how well that worked out." But the "case closed" look had come over her, like when she just had to have the Chinese symbol for luck tattooed on her left thigh for her eighteenth birthday. I said, "To my knowledge no one in our family is Chinese," and she informed me she was eighteen, she could vote, so she could decide what to do with her body. I said, "We used to be able to drink at eighteen too. There's a reason they changed it." Ultimately I let it go. Her left thigh was her business, and I guess getting married would have to be too. After all, J.J. had an education and a job. He had a good head on his shoulders and to the best of my knowledge, he wasn't a drug addict or a serial killer—these days you never know—so the rest was on her. One of the great jokes of life is that by the time you're old enough to recognize how little you know, all you can do is mop up the aftermath, dump it in a giant personal hazmat container and move on.

Next thing I knew, I was up to my eyelids in bridal magazines and sample menus. I had no idea there were so many banquet halls and bridal shops within a fifty-mile radius of home. Or that there would be so many decisions to make—calligraphied envelopes for the invitations or Mom's lovely penmanship? Edible, potable or savable favors? Tall, see-through or short, see-over centerpieces? Hotel choice for out-of-town guests? Rehearsal dinner, breakfast the day after or both? Or that it could possibly cost that much to get married. But it sure was fun, and it turned out just like Amber and I planned—picture perfect. I mean, J.J.'s parents are lovely people, but their idea of decoration was crepe-paper streamers and balloons, and my daughter's wedding was not going to be that kind of affair. Besides, his father had gotten transferred to Dallas a few years back, so it's not like they could keep up with all the details. I acquired some shiny new platinum plastic, with a limit high enough to pay for a very nice car, in order to sponsor the occasion. It would be the only bill in my long history of bill paying that would make me smile every month when I wrote the check. Isn't that why I went to work every day? So I could afford the nicer things in life? Anyway, whatever it cost to make my baby so happy, I was willing to spend it. Except it made me remember how happy her father and I looked that Friday we ran off to city hall, all hope and expectation.

I had shed my usual stonewashed Jordache for a green silk dress with bat-wing sleeves and shoulder pads the size of throw pillows and pulled my hair into a Jheri-curl ponytail with a big black clip-on bow. He had hair back then, long as mine, and it was cut in an Afro shag that bobbed when he played keyboard. Folks used to say he looked halfway like O.J., back when that was cute. He had rolled up the sleeves on his rented tuxedo and wore the ruffled shirt open so you could see his gold chains and the curly hair on his chest. Mercifully, there are no pictures, but we had it all figured out. He was the music man—the next Stevie Wonder. And I would be right by his side—his fan, his muse, his manager. We were gonna light everybody's fire. It made sense to me at the time. Love can make you a first-class fool.

But none of that mattered on Amber's wedding day. It was the most perfect October day I ever hope to see. We had made it through corsets, crinolines, upsweeps and the first big crisis of the day when they sent the white stretch limo instead of the white superstretch SUV I paid for. Amber got on the phone, turned into the Bride of Frankenstein, and thirty minutes later we had the right car.

By the time we arrived, the church was full. The bridesmaids arranged themselves in their six degrees of purple gowns. Dad, looking very dapper in his first-ever purchased tuxedo, was about to walk Mom, elegant in amethyst, to their seats when she reached up, patted my cheek and said, "You know, Tootsie, you're getting old." That's what I love about my mother. She captures those sentiments you won't find on a Hallmark card. After that, I gave Amber a kiss and a final fluff, trying hard not to look like I was losing my last friend, which is kind of how it felt. Anyway, I snapped out of it when she took her father's arm, because that made me mad. Why should he get to give away somebody I raised? But she wanted it that way, so before I got madder, I let the best man, Baby Son-in-Law's cousin Ron, escort me down the aisle. I squeezed his arm so tight I probably stopped the poor man's circulation, but he winked and smiled and whispered, "It'll be fine." And for some reason, I believed him. So I vaguely remember grinning as we marched in, but really I couldn't feel my face, or my feet touch the floor, because I couldn't figure out how twenty-one years had gone by, and my child—the one I grunted and pushed to deliver without the benefit of drugs so I remember every blasted, blessed moment—could possibly, legally, be getting married.

At the reception, people from the job just didn't know what to say. I couldn't wait for them to spread the word on Monday—tell the others how together Tee was. You know, some people think we don't have anything or know the proper way things are done. I wanted them to see that Thomasina Hodges was—and always would be—a class act, especially that snake in suede loafers. He sent regrets, but his assistant showed up and fell all over herself telling me how fabulous the wedding was. So I smiled, said my "thank yous" graciously, had another sip of champagne and watched as she took one more California roll from the passing tray. After that, Julie, who had been the receptionist on executive row, and the only other brown face, came up and said, "I don't know how you can look so calm." I told her sometimes the commercials get it right. Never let 'em see you sweat. We clinked our glasses on that, hugged and I buzzed off, ready for my next post receiving-line meet and greet.

My best buds from the neighborhood—Diane, Marie, Cecily and Joyce—our kids had been in school together—nodded their collective approval and congratulated me on throwing a stellar wedding. We called ourselves the "Live Five" and we toasted to my good taste. Twice.

Then I had to get through the first dance, and the song Amber's father wrote especially for her. All that ooohing and aaahing about how sweet it was just pissed me off because he always did know how to upstage me. I pay for the whole soiree, but he gets over with a song. OK, he offered to chip in on the wedding. I just couldn't bring myself to accept. I mean, he wasn't a deadbeat dad—just a deadbeat husband. I never had to hunt him down or get the states of California and New York involved in making him cough up child support. Sure, in the beginning he almost never saw her—LA was way more than a chunk of change away, and his monthly contributions barely kept Amber in juice boxes and sneakers, but it came regular as the IRT, which is to say sometimes it was late, but it always arrived eventually. After he finally started making some money as a musician, he'd take Amber with him during the summers when he toured—Budapest, Sydney, Johannesburg . . . And even though food on the table and new school clothes every fall doesn't leave quite the same impression as your very own frequent-flyer miles, a visit to the cockpit, getting pinned with your very own wings (which my darling child wore every day for six months) or seeing a kangaroo in its native habitat—at least the man was present in her life. But tattoo and all, Amber had been a great kid—not a nickel's worth of trouble—as long as I don't count her adoration of her father. So her wedding— exactly the way she always dreamed about—I wanted to give her those memories. All by myself.

But wouldn't you know it? After his serenade, Dear Old Dad presented the happy couple with a big fat check toward the down payment on a house—guess he must've sold a couple of songs—finally. That brought the room to its feet. Terrific. OK. I guess it wasn't like we hated each other. But it didn't take long after we parted ways for the reasons we got together in the first place to seem like they had been written in the sand. I guess we both loved each other once upon a time—that was a whole 'nuther happily ever after. The only thing we still had in common was that we both loved Amber, so we agreed to be civilized about our daughter and not to bad-mouth each other in front of her, and after I made it clear that as far as I was concerned it was not then, nor would it ever be, OK for him to have put his dreams first and his family somewhere farther down on his list, he gave up trying to convince me we could be friends. So the good thing about him singing was that I didn't have to dance with him, because I don't know if I could have managed to glide across the floor, like when we used to do the Hustle—

—so I sucked down another glass of champagne, kept my mother-of-the-bride smile firmly in place and watched from the sidelines. And even though I thought I was doing a pretty good job, my bad attitude must have been showing just a little, because both my mother and Julie came over to ask if I was OK—I assured them I was.

The maître d' kept my glass full. Frankly, he was supposed to. As much money as I laid out—including the coconut shrimp and mini lamb chops during the cocktail hour, beef Wellington and sea bass for dinner and the Viennese table with the chocolate fountain—he should have been at the door of my complimentary suite with a rose and a mimosa the next morning. But now we're back to shoulda, and that woulda killed me for sure.

Anyway, my problems started the next day when I woke up, and shoulda, coulda and woulda did not stop the train wreck in my head, or keep the elephant from tap dancing across my aching body. I mean, I'd probably had more to drink in one night than I had consumed in the last decade. My mouth felt like I'd been sucking vintage sewer water and I wanted to call room service or 911 for an Advil and orange juice IV because I could not remember where the bathroom was or imagine dragging myself to it and trying to find the pill bottle in my toiletry bag. That would have meant I had to open my eyes. I had tried that already. The little bit of light sneaking through the drapes made me want to vomit.

Then he coughed. And my heart about exploded out of my chest because I didn't know he was there. Or who he was.

I jumped up so fast my brains banged against the inside of my skull, and as I caught sight of those high heels, my suit and new purple lace bra and panties in a heap on the floor, I came to the horrifying realization that my lumpy brown body was bare-butt naked. So I snatched the spongy beige blanket off the king-sized bed, uncovering a king-sized man, and I suddenly realized HE was J.J.'s cousin Ron, the best man. And I thought, *Oh my Lord, what else don't I remember?*

"I didn't expect to hear from you before noon." He rolled up on his elbow and didn't seem the slightest bit surprised to be where he was. Or to be skin-side up.

Then he smiled that killer smile, the one I had been avoiding since he showed up at the wedding rehearsal and J.J. introduced him and I thought, *That's cousin Ron? The one who was like a second father to J.J.?* Second fathers are not supposed to have bulging biceps or voices like hot buttered rum on a cold day. At the ceremony he kissed my cheek before depositing me at my designated pew. I sat there, doing my best to look motherly and not think about how good he smelled and how good those lips felt on my cheek.

Ron was pretty popular with the ladies at the reception too—I saw more than one of the bridesmaids giggle at something he said, then bat her eyelashes as he obligingly twirled them around the dance floor. I swear I even saw my mother grin at him when he stopped by their table to chat—not that I was paying attention or anything. And when the time came, he gave such a beautiful toast about how he'd watched Amber and J.J. learn to love each other, from puppy love to grown-up love. How attending the wedding meant we would all be there to help them love each other for many years to come. And he was right. I had seen it, in my own living room. I glanced over at Mama and Daddy, who had finally left Brooklyn and moved to a retirement condo in Maryland. They had been so worried when Amber and I set out on our own, but I showed them I could take care of her and I could throw this wedding without anybody's help, thank you very much. Mom said I was crazy— "It's a wedding, not a coronation"—but they sat there just beaming. That filled me up too. I had a little speech planned, except there really wasn't anything left to say and I had no voice to say it with. So I clinked my glass, toasted to their future and washed down the disappointments of my past. Because suddenly, in the midst of a sit-down dinner for 220 people, I felt totally alone. I mean, I had my daughter to love, J.J. too, and my family, but who did I have, for me—personally?

Could I say I loved Gerald?

Of course, I did. In my way. He was the one and only man in my life, and we'd sure been together long enough. Well, not exactly together. You can't exactly be together with a man who has a wife and three kids—they're not even kids anymore. Yeah, I know that sounds bad, but I didn't think of it like that. We never talked about Annie; in fact, the only thing I knew about her was her name. I heard about his children growing up. He heard about Amber. The time flew by. We shared some pretty significant moments along the way. I guess you could say we reached an understanding. We could be together on my birthday, unless there was a recital or a ball game, but not his. Major holidays were out, but that left a whole lot of evenings, the occasional Saturday, whenever our calendars coincided. I wasn't staying home waiting by the telephone. He didn't have to lie to me. I didn't have stray socks on my floor, fuzz in my sink, toilet seats left up, anybody telling me what I could and couldn't do with my money and my time or expectations that would never be fulfilled.

Amber and I had also reached a kind of understanding about me and Gerald. Back when she was thirteen, she came home early from a sleepover—flew up the stairs, barged into my room to tell me all about the party and found him there. No, she didn't catch us doing anything, but it sure wasn't what she expected from dear old Mom. After that, they'd run into each other from time to time—until the day Amber and I saw Gerald in the mall with his family. I tried to act like I didn't see him and dragged Amber into a sporting-goods store, praying she didn't see him either. But before I could even pretend I was seriously interested in the teepee of aluminum baseball bats, she was in my face. "Wasn't that your friend? Who was that with him?" It was a game of Twenty Questions I'd rather not have played. Especially since Amber was not buying my answers. Anyway, our discussion progressed into a screaming match in the car that I, not so proudly, ended with "because I'm grown and as long as you live in my house and I pay your bills, what I say goes."

Gerald was not at the wedding.

But Ron was, and now he was pointing in my direction, if you get my drift. And he had to go.

"You have to go," I said. It came out somewhere between a shriek and a question. Then I got this flash that my hair must be smushed to the side of my head, so I kind of ran my fingers through it, casually, and wrapped the blanket around me like a super-sized tortilla.

"Don't cover up." He patted the bed. "Come on and relax. We can order in some breakfast, take a shower. And later I'll help you get those presents into your car."

I saw the tower of packages and had this vague memory of the bridal party cavalcade carrying them to the suite. Ron came last—carrying a silver-wrapped box that felt like his and hers barbells. I think the others were gone. I hope the others were gone. I prayed the others were gone. I remembered looking at all those beautiful boxes and starting to cry, because the day had been overwhelming—the whole week, really. Ron surrounded me in a hug and I remembered that it felt so good. And then I was standing in the middle of the floor, in my tortilla, crying again, which made it worse, because I do not cry. I'd rather shoot staples under my fingernails than snivel and whine. But there I was, sniveling like a champ, and I couldn't stop. "Please don't tell anybody." I was begging. "I'm so embarrassed." It was pathetic. I was pathetic. A spectacle. I was just grateful there was no mirror where I could see myself.

He hopped into his tuxedo pants and brought me some tissues. "No need to be embarrassed."

That made me snort. "Oh, of course not," I said. "The mother of the bride traditionally sleeps with the best man."

Which made him laugh. Me too, for a moment. I wiped my face and tried to get my head together.

"We're all single adults here." Ron folded me in his arms again. Those arms—against that strong chest, which, I realized to my horror, now smelled more like my perfume than his aftershave. How much had I rubbed up against him? Couldn't the floor just open up and swallow me? But I wasn't getting off that easy. He kissed my eyelids and said, "Last night was great. And once you get to know me, you'll realize I would never disrespect you in any way."

Get to know him? Was he crazy? And what exactly had made last night so great? Other than the obvious? I yanked myself out of his arms, kind of like a fly coming to its buzzing senses just before the Venus flytrap clamps shut. The fact that I slept with a man I had known for all of two days was already too much for me to process. Now he thought I was ready to exchange vital statistics? I hadn't found myself in bed with anybody but Gerald in twelve years, and I can count on one hand with fingers left over the times we woke up together.

And when was the last time he told me it was great? On top of that, I didn't even know how old Ron was—somewhere north of J.J., but definitely south of me. And he was J.J.'s cousin and godfather. End of story. It was going to be hard enough trying to pretend this never happened when we both showed up at christenings, Thanksgiving dinners and other family get-togethers.

I guess Ron read the near-hysteria on my face because then he said, "Would you be more comfortable if I left?"

I babbled something that ended in yes, then headed for the bathroom, dragging my blanket behind me, because at that moment the suite felt very small and I did not want to see whether he was annoyed or relieved.

I took a long shower by the red glow of the heat lamp, letting the water rush over me, even my hair. I'd figure out what to do with my wet naps later. Clearly, I had stepped over some invisible boundary and needed to wash myself back to the other side of the line, where I belonged. I closed my eyes, let the water stream over my head, my neck, my shoulders, my back. I tried to let my mind go blank, but scenes from the day before popped in and out of my head like a slide show— Amber and J.J. scouring each other's faces in wedding cake, me floating down the aisle on Ron's arm, the Olympian prowess of the single women leaping and diving for the bouquet, the speech Amber made before she and J.J. left for their bridal suite at another hotel. She thanked me for being her mom, every day. Not just on special occasions, but during bad dreams, scraped knees, report cards—good and bad—acne breakouts and tattoos. She said she hoped one day she could be as good a mother to her children. Well, remembering that only prompted more waterworks. Somehow tears feel different from shower water, and the hot drops traced down my face, but enough was enough. I blew my nose in my washcloth and felt around for the soap.

When I got down to my feet there was a tender spot on my baby toe and I knew it was a blister from all that dancing. The Hustle, the Electric Slide, the Booty Call—ironic, huh? I hadn't grooved like that in years. My dad even took me for a turn around the floor, calling himself waltzing. And I danced with Ron, at least I remembered that part. Now, I would never have agreed to a slow dance, but it was one of those sneaky ones where the band starts off with some boogie music, then slides into a slow jam before you have a chance to make a graceful exit. Next thing I knew, I was cheek to cheek, smelling that good cologne. It didn't hurt that I caught my ex's eye. That made me snuggle a little closer, and you can see where that got me. You know as well as I do there's no fool like an old fool.

Then the lightning hit me right between the eyes and I dropped the soap. What did I drum into Amber's head whenever we talked about sex? Not the "sperm and egg, isn't it a miracle?" talk when she was young. But later, when boys' names started creeping into her conversation and one of her little girlfriends turned up pregnant. Yes, I did everything short of beg and bribe her to wait until she got older, which led to lots of eye rolling, heavy sighing and bolting from the car, which is where I usually arranged these intimate tête-à-têtes so she couldn't escape. I also told her that if ever, whenever—I could barely say the words, but I made myself clear. She had to promise me to use a condom. "I don't care where he tells you it hasn't been or how much he says he loves you—no latex, no sex." That wasn't just for Amber. Even after all these years, Gerald had to live with that rule too. But I had no idea exactly what we did last night, much less what we used, which only compounded my complete mortification.

I didn't even dry off. I snatched the terrycloth robe from behind the door, kicked the blanket out of my way and charged out of the bathroom. How in the world was I going to ask him if he had put a sock on it?

But Ron was gone. Damn. Just like he said he'd be.

I yanked open the drapes, turned on the lights and got on my hands and knees. Crawling around on the carpet like an insane crab, I found an earring back, somebody's long dried-up contact lens and a three of clubs, but not that little square wrapper. The panic was rising as I tore the sheets off the bed, but still nothing and I couldn't tell if I was shower wet or if I'd worked up a sweat. I wanted to scream, but the last thing I needed was hotel management showing up at the door. "Oh, I'm sorry. I was just looking for a used rubber. Do you think you could help me?" There is no tip big enough for that. So I sat on the bed for a second to collect what was left of my wits. That's when I saw his business card on the night stand. Ron owned an auto body shop. I don't know what I thought he did, but it wasn't that. He didn't look or act like any mechanic I'd ever seen. Anyway, he had written his cell number on the back, so I could have called him to ask, as casually as I could, if either of us had had the good sense to make at least one smart decision that night, but I was sure he already thought Amber's mother was crazy. A conversation about whether he'd used a raincoat was more humiliation than I could handle. So I took one last sweep of the suite—felt under sofa cushions, moved the coffee table. I was digging around in the trash can with the hotel ballpoint and bingo! Securely wrapped in layers of tissue was the evidence I needed. Hallelujah!

Then I was completely through. I called for a pot of coffee and started throwing clothes, lilac suit and all, in my bag because I had to go home. And there was not one doubt in my stressed-out, hungover mind that none of this foolishness would have happened if I hadn't lost my job the week before the wedding.

2

"Don't tell everybody your business, 'cause then it's theirs."

Correction.

I did not *lose* my job. Why do people say that? You *lose* your wallet when you've got too much on your mind and fifteen errands to run and you leave it by the coffee machine at the Wawa after adding six sugars to your twenty-four-ounce dark roast to keep you going. Five stops later the cashier has rung up a week's worth of groceries. You're in a panic because you've dug to the bottom of your purse, only found lint, and you can hear the rumble in the line behind you. You rush out, knowing you're on top of the "idiot of the day" list and that it's time to go home and notify the credit-card companies that it wasn't you trying to buy a yacht with your VISA card. That's *lost*. It's careless and you had a hand in it. When Fido digs under the back fence and takes a hike people say you lost your dog, but I say if he can't find his way home he lost himself. And as for losing my mind—I am not going to let anybody make me crazy, but this job situation came pretty damn close.

No, I didn't lose my job. I was never careless with it. I walked into Markson & Daughter twenty-five years ago—before there was a logo, a corporate headquarters, a factory or a staff. I *was* the staff. I mean, at the beginning it wasn't even like a job. It was some crazy experiment that became bigger than I could imagine. I'm not sure Olivia could imagine it now either.

It was 1980, and I was nearing the end of my twelve years of mandatory servitude. Thirteen, really—kindergarten counts. I was not thrilled with the idea of continuing to subject myself to teachers, boring classes and grades. But one day, after a borderline report card, Mom said that unless I won the lottery—big time—I was going to have to work for the next forty years. Her point was nobody can afford to pay you what eight hours of your life is worth, but as long as you've got to spend your time to get a check, you might as well get the most for it. And college would definitely increase the value of my hours. It was cold for her to lay it out like that, but that's my mom, bless her heart, and it got my attention.

When my guidance counselor asked what I was interested in, I said making money. Since there was no degree in that per se, he suggested business administration. Sounded good to me, like I could wear nice outfits, sit at my desk and supervise my staff. Hey, I was eighteen. What did I know, other than I didn't want to wear work boots and climb telephone poles like Daddy or clean bedpans and patients' behinds like Mom? Nothing wrong with that. Just not for me. So I went to Manhattan Community College, first off, because they accepted me, and because my parents could help me swing the tuition. The school's whole mission was to teach you how to work. I mean, back then they didn't even have a real campus. Just floors in a bunch of office buildings in Midtown where real people were working all around you, and you could imagine yourself doing the paycheck polka along with them. And I liked the idea of getting my associate's degree in two years so I'd have something in a frame to keep me motivated for the next two.

First semester my parents let me get the hang of college life, but one Friday during winter break, Daddy was counting out the contents of his pay envelope. I slid over, waiting for him to peel off my usual handout, and he said, "You know, you are too old to be getting an allowance. Nobody's gonna take care of you forever, including me." I was hurt, but I got the hint.

I made my way to the placement office at school and searched the board for a part-time job. Nothing heavy—enough to keep me in pocket change and a few used textbooks to show my folks I was down for the cause. Waitressing was out. I'd have told somebody off because a tip did not mean I would put up with ignorance. So were jobs that required prior experience. I didn't have any. I happened to be there when new postings went up and one caught my eye. "Assistant to fragrance entrepreneur. Typing, filing, phones, etc. Flexible hours. West Side location." Right part of town for me to scoot in after class. The hourly wasn't bad either. I swiped the card.

It took until the next morning for me to screw up the nerve to call, so I was disappointed to hear an answering machine with wind chimes in the background and a cheery voice saying, "You have reached Markson & Daughter, purveyor of creams and lotions crafted from nature's finest botanicals." I got the beep before I figured out if I liked the sound of purveying botanicals, but as soon as I said my name and why I was calling a winded voice broke in.

"Don't hang up. Can you come right now?"

I wasn't prepared for the impromptu interview, so I told her

I didn't have my résumé with me—like I actually had a résumé.

"Doesn't matter. You'll tell me what you can do."

Couldn't argue with that, and she sounded desperate, which improved my chances. I didn't look bad for a student that day, so I said I could be there by one. She told me the address and that her name was Olivia, and as I trudged along West Fifty-fifth Street trying to keep the gritty wind out of my eyes, I wondered what my desk would look like. And how soon I'd get paid. And how much further I had to walk. I didn't even know there was an Eleventh Avenue in Manhattan. Finally I got to the squatty red building. It looked so dilapidated I almost left, but I was too cold not to go inside, so I buzzed and she buzzed back before I changed my mind.

The job was on the third floor, up six long flights. Maybe that's why Olivia was winded on the phone. By midway I was dragging. Then there was all this weird art on the landings, like the photo of a woman's hand covered in bees. She was holding a rose. That still makes my skin crawl. I was about to turn around when I heard this "Yoo hoo," like she was Heidi and these were the damn Alps, so I kept climbing and concocting excuses why this wasn't going to work out.

Judging by her voice, I expected Olivia to be petite, like a pixie. And the chimes made me think she'd be some kind of leftover hippie. I was half right. She was a hippie from the bottoms of her red hightops to the tips of her fat pigtails, her lame attempt to control a mess of curly black hair. In between there was the denim shirt covered in hand-painted flowers and what looked like a lace tablecloth wrapped over her jeans like a sarong. And I was worried how I looked? Olivia was definitely out there but petite she was not. I looked up and this six-foot flower child was galloping down to meet me, fringes waving behind her.

"I'm Olivia and you just saved my ass! I didn't get one call until you. Destiny, huh?" I didn't bother telling her destiny had a lot to do with the listing being in my pocketbook.

Her loft was like Paradise Island meets Manhattan Island—plants and flowers hanging from the ceiling, on shelves rigged across the windows where sunshine spilled over them and onto overflowing terra-cotta planters on the floor. It made me forget winter was outside. And it smelled alive, like cut grass or Christmas trees—better than Mom's air freshener. I guess I looked stunned because Olivia explained she grew a lot of the herbs she used. "You make your own corn flakes too?" I shouldn't have said it, but I did. She laughed. "If I had time." She brewed raspberry tea with Tupelo honey and told me she did make the blue earthenware mug. I laughed and took a sip—it wasn't like Lipton's, but it was warm and sweet and I was freezing. It hit the spot.

I could tell by the piles of toys that had taken over the pea-green corduroy sofa that this wasn't just a business. Markson, her daughter and whoever else went with the package lived there too. It wasn't like anybody's home I'd ever been to. Then it occurred to me I'd never been to a white person's home before, which explained why I was feeling a little jumpy. And this didn't look like the ones on TV, but it was kind of cool. I'd only known Olivia a few minutes, but it suited her.

She shoved books and magazines to one side of the wood-plank table, and we sat on mismatched chairs while she made up some kind of interview. When she got to the part about what I wanted to do after graduation, I had learned enough not to say "make money," so I said, "I'm undecided," which was definitely the truth. Olivia nodded her head like she could relate and after a few more questions, she led me to the kitchen—her laboratory.

It was kind of industrial—no teapot collections, cookie-cutter displays or flowered dish towels. But it was as neat as the other room was chaotic. A stainless-steel vat and a scale sat at one end of a metal worktable, with wide-mouthed apothecary jars lined up nearby. Olivia reached into a carton on the floor and handed me a jar filled with shiny white cream. "Try some."

Definitely different from the ninety-nine-cent, no-name brand I used. The cream was smooth and thick and it smelled good enough to eat. She told me that when she and her husband lived in a village outside of London, there had been a field of lavender growing near their cottage. Cottage? She said it turned her on to the amazing scents in nature and she lost the nose for the toxic chemical perfumes in so many products. Olivia was the only person I ever met who could say stuff like that and make it sound normal. It also explained the sort of English accent she talked with, but there was something else in her voice I couldn't quite place. Anyway, I was wondering how she felt about Jovan Musk, since I thought that might be natural, when she told me how she started making creams while she was pregnant. They had moved back to the States and she detested the stuff in the pink bottles. I had to agree with her. Baby lotion always made me kind of gag too, but it wouldn't have occurred to me in a hundred years to make my own. Nobody I knew just *made* things like that—it was like making water. I said her cream was great. She told me to keep the jar, which I thought was really nice. People don't just give you stuff.

Then she passed me a stack of labels and a mug full of pens. She printed something for me to copy and explained she'd been so busy making cream to fill her first order that she forgot about labels. "Don't know what your handwriting is like, but it's got to be better than mine."

Now, I was never the greatest student, but people used to borrow my notes to copy when they were absent because they were always so neat. Handwritten labels sounded old-fashioned, but if that's what she wanted . . . So I sized them up, figured out where the words should go. Then in my best script I wrote, "Markson & Daughter, Almond Ginger Body Crème, 8 ounces."

"*Brilliant.*" Olivia practically hugged me, but I'm sure I looked at her like *I don't know you that well.* "Definitely destiny. Keep writing. I'll go fill jars. The order is due tomorrow."

So I wrote and thought how this job was a piece of cake so far. Olivia worked in the kitchen and told me how she had made diapers, crib sheets and baby food for her daughter Hillary too, so I knew for sure she was a little off. That, and she didn't eat meat, fish or anything with eyes. I told her I loved my burgers and fries and she didn't hold it against me—said she'd make me a veggie burger one day. A few weeks later she did, with some soy cheese. It was nasty.

I didn't say much about myself. What was there to tell? I lived with my parents in a semi-attached house in Brooklyn. I didn't make anything interesting or dream anything big. Not much to find exciting, especially for somebody like Olivia. Besides, I could hear my mom. "Don't tell everybody your business, 'cause then it's theirs." And she *was* my boss. Or at least she ran the place. Dad always said people can supervise you on the job, but don't let anybody boss you.

Anyway, around five minutes to three Olivia jumps up and says she has to get Hillary from school. I get my stuff together too and she says, "You don't have to leave now, do you?" like she'd lose it if I did. I assumed she'd want me to go. Daddy wouldn't have let the mayor stay in our house with nobody home. She said she'd be right back, and I didn't budge from the chair. Now that I know Olivia, I'm sure the thought that I might take something never occurred to her.

Hillary, who looked about nine, wore a blue pleated skirt and cable-knit sweater—pretty much the opposite of her mother's getup. But they both had dark curly hair and talked faster than the speed of sound. It was Hillary who told me her father lived in London and that she missed him a lot. That's when Olivia went to get oatmeal cookies, but not before I saw a look that said she missed him too. Later, she told me she and Eliot Markson were divorced, but she kept his name—because it was Hillary's, and because it sounded better than Schaeffer on fine botanicals.

By the time we labeled the last jar it was after nine o'clock. Olivia took me down on the freight elevator and showed me how to operate it, which improved the job 100 percent. Then she hailed a taxi, gave me cab fare home to Canarsie, since it was so late, and said she'd see me tomorrow.

I could tell the driver was pissed—probably never been to my neighborhood. He rattled over the Brooklyn Bridge, and the blur of city lights made me giddy, or maybe I was just excited after day one with Olivia. I looked forward to day two way more than I did to Intro to Economics.

When I told my father about my job experience, he chuckled. "Sounds like a Looney Tuney to me. Let's see if the check clears." It did. And a few months later, when a local weekly named Markson & Daughter's Almond Ginger Crème as one of its skin-care must-haves, it mentioned the special touch added by the handwritten labels. I started Olivia's book of press clippings with that article. I still have a copy too. And when the time came to switch to printed labels, we had the type specially designed to look like I wrote it.

Working for Olivia was never exactly a regular job, especially in the early days. She needed me to reassure her for the whole week before she took samples to the "Open See" at Bendel's, which was pretty funny since I couldn't have sold ice to a bunch of strangers, even in August. When she came back with an order, I was so psyched. She taught me about eucalyptus, rosemary, lemongrass, and that nasturtium flowers add color and spice to salad. I taught her principles of accounting. She never exactly got it. I kept her organized and on schedule, purchased the practical things like a typewriter, staplers and eventually our first computer—which neither of us knew how to use. When I made a suggestion, she listened, like I had some sense. I was starting to believe I did. Olivia had better instincts about marketing and sales than my professors. And I was pretty good at accounts receivable—people should pay what they owe. How else was I supposed to get a check? We made a good team.

In a way I was sad when the business got big enough for Olivia to move into a floor-through on Riverside Drive and make the loft her business address. I was in my last semester, and she said she wanted to keep the company small—exclusive but homegrown, she said. Still, she had to hire people to help with bottling, consult with chemists. But my desk was near the window, next to hers, which was still the big old table. I even brought in my own plant—a philodendron in a plastic pot the size of a teacup. Not even I could kill that. Olivia brought me samples of whatever she was working on. When I suggested Apricot Sage, she gave it a try. It's my favorite and it's still a Markson & Daughter best seller. And when I received my associate's degree in business administration, Olivia announced she was taking me to London.

I didn't even have a passport before then. Daddy didn't believe it until I showed him the round-trip ticket with my name on it. My mother, always one to take lemons and make a sour puss, asked if I was sure I wouldn't be the baby-sitter. I told her Olivia was going to deliver Hillary to her father for the summer, which had nothing to do with me, and kept right on trying to figure out what to pack in my borrowed American Tourister. England seemed formal, so I took clothes I would wear to church. Even got a new hairdo for the occasion—the infamous Jheri curl. I sort of wanted it to look like Olivia's hair—and Chaka Khan's. Nobody saw the resemblance.

Anyway, I, who had never set foot in an airport, was served a four-course meal with cloth napkins in business class. I never thought about how much money Olivia had, but hippie girl was not hurting. We checked into a swanky two-bedroom suite in Mayfair. I mean, the place had gloved doormen and chauffeured Bentleys out front. Olivia looked way more polished than usual in a slim white pantsuit and matching black luggage. And I'm sure I looked like cousin Mabledene from Doozerville in my plaid polyester A-line dress and powder-blue suitcase. I promised myself that day I'd never go anywhere looking so homely again.

We spent the afternoon riding double-decker buses past Westminster Abbey and Buckingham Palace, which bored Princess Hillary. She'd seen it all before. I tried not to walk into bass ackwards traffic. And that night I met Eliot Markson.

I wouldn't have put the two of them together if there was nobody else to choose from. Olivia must have been part of some phase he grew out of, but it sure explained Hillary's fondness for Fair Isles sweaters and tartan skirts. Eliot was pure Savile Row, and Hillary was Daddy's girl. "He's a bit of a prig," Olivia had whispered on a trip to the ladies' room after dinner. I had a few other choice names for him after I overheard him ask why she brought the nanny out to eat.

Transfer complete, Olivia and I were on our own. It was a little odd at first, hearing her snore in the bedroom down the hall, figuring out who was going to be first in the marble bathroom. I mean, it wasn't like we were running buddies or anything, but she kind of taught me things about the world outside of Brooklyn. But it was all so foreign, even the language, and they were speaking English. Once I relaxed I had a good time, and I think playing 'enry 'iggins took her mind off missing Hillary. We prowled the stalls at Portobello Market and she bought me antique garnet earrings. We sniffed and fingered our way through about a million plants at the Columbia Road flower market. In Harrods we fantasized about the day Markson & Daughter would have a counter there. And we took a train about half an hour outside of London to a town called Dorking, where Olivia got weepy walking by her beloved field of lavender. It was nice, but I think the tears were mostly because we were near that cottage she used to share with Eliot.

Everywhere we went Olivia had me take notes, since this was a "business" trip, therefore tax deductible. She learned that strategy from Eliot, who was involved in his family's wholesale jewelry business. Right. I never saw Olivia wear so much as a diamond chip. It would not be me.

And as if showing me a new country wasn't enough, when we got back, Olivia offered to help with my tuition at Baruch, where I transferred for the next two years. It wasn't some fancy school with a hefty tuition, but I still said, "Are you crazy? You are not my mother or the United Negro College Fund." And in an accent I knew quite well from my neighbors but never heard from Olivia, she said, "I know a little something about being a Brooklyn girl who's undecided about her future." Then she winked. Olivia Schaeffer—from East New York? Who knew?

That's when I entered my seriously studious period—or tried to. Truth is, I could never get as worked up over solving problems for hypothetical companies in class as I did negotiating booth rates for trade shows or finding the best way to ship to Palm Beach. At that point, we were mostly in boutiques and pharmacies, but business was growing every day. Olivia spent most of her time showing the line, checking out suppliers and developing new products. I held down the fort. I liked that. I felt useful, and I had reached a reasonable work-school balance.

Then I met my ex. It was one of those April days that make you believe winter is really over. I was booking it up Broadway when I heard this voice behind me saying, "You are looking positively hypnotic on this polyphonic afternoon." What?! Well, I *was* feeling cute so I was glad somebody noticed. I was all set to give whoever it was a hard time when I realized that a brown-skinned beanpole with a floppy 'fro, a shredded jean jacket and big black motorcycle boots had fallen in step beside me. Now, I was not in the habit of picking up strange men on the street, but everything he said seemed like poetry to me. What is it they say about birds and bees and spring? Probably the same thing they say about too much champagne and weddings. Anyway, by the time we hit Forty-sixth Street he had talked me into stopping at Howard Johnson's, at least for coffee.

Two hot dogs and a shared black-raspberry sundae later I was severely in something—like, love, lust? Who can tell at twenty? I asked what made him pick me to talk to. He said I had a beautiful vibe, and I got all tingly and tongue-tied. He was a musician—played a lot of instruments, but mainly keyboard—and although he wasn't with a band, he said he did lots of session work. DeBarge was planning to record one of his tunes. It was a big whoop at the time. He was heading to a gig and invited me to stop by the studio after work. I debated all afternoon until finally Olivia said, "Nothing good ever happens if you don't take a chance. If he's a creep, you'll come to my place." Well, I wanted something good, so I went for it.

Whatever happens in springtime happened to me while I sat on a lumpy sofa in the corner of that dark, crowded studio, smelling cigarettes and sweat and watching them lay down the music. It was the instrumental tracks for a ballad, but I didn't need words to make me swoon. In the booth he was all business and he sounded great—like "I'd buy his record" great. I was killing myself acting like I did this every day, and I couldn't believe somebody that talented had walked into my life. By the time we left I was under some kind of spell—probably lack of oxygen. It was late, and I knew I should call home, but what for? My parents wouldn't get anything about this and I wasn't about to wreck the mood so they'd just have to be mad at me. Wasn't the first time.

He drove me home in the beat-up yellow Opel Kadett he called Sunshine. It had no backseat so there was room for his Fender Rhodes. We parked around the corner from my house and talked until the windows fogged up about life, about the future, about all the songs he had written. "Music that will make things better. Songs that bring the world together." He spoke a lot in rhyme. Back then I used to think it was deep. And speaking of deep, when we kissed I felt like he touched my soul and showered me with stardust. I talked like that when we were together, heaven help me, and that was just a kiss. I mean, many had knocked on that door—nobody had come in, but I was ready for him to ring my bell.

I always thought I'd be nervous the first time, but with him it was like I had found a seventh sense, way past the five I knew. Beyond intuition, inner vision, superstition, all of it. Those were the days of his hole-in-the-ground apartment on West Nineteenth Street. It was three steps down from the street, and from the front window we could watch people's ankles go by. But it was our private universe. We'd eat baguettes and butter, bowls of grapes or Alpha-Bits, smoke a little herb sometimes, laugh, dream . . . oh yeah, and do it 'til I couldn't hardly walk. I could listen to him fool around on the piano for hours, making up songs about anything—pizza, sneakers, everlasting love. And the closer we got, the more the balance in my life went straight to hell.

We'd go to Monday-night jam sessions at dive bars so he could play and maybe connect with a musician looking for a sideman or a record label A&R person out to discover the next musical genius. We'd drag in late, I'd end up skipping class and feeling guilty, like I was letting Olivia down. But I always went to work. For once I had plenty to talk about. Him. His energy and creativity, the places we went, the people he introduced me to—everything about being with him made me feel special. In no time, he let me keep his life organized the way I did Olivia's. He let me—first sign I had lost my mind.

My parents lived on my case, said I could not march in and out of their house when I felt like it. I told them I was grown. Where have I heard that lately? Anyway, Mom suggested I move, since there couldn't be but one grown woman in her house and she had that covered. Daddy said a grown man ought to have a job. I said music was his job. He said the fools playing accordion in the subway could say the same thing. Clearly, we were having a failure to communicate.

None of that mattered, though, because we were in love. I knew it because he wrote a song that said so and put the tape in a Walkman he gave me for my birthday. I was dumbstruck when I heard it—*dumb* being the operative word. I think he got carried away too, because next thing I knew we were headed to city hall. Sounds stupid, but I can't even remember whose idea it was to get married. One day we were sitting in Sunshine, parked in a Jack-in-the-Box lot eating burgers and watching a wedding at the church across the street. He said something like, "Can you imagine us getting married?" And I must have said, "Yes." By the last slurp of my vanilla shake he had tied the straw wrapper in a bow around my ring finger and we were engaged. I still have that stupid thing in my jewelry box somewhere—keep meaning to toss it. Next thing we were exchanging "I dos" and chunky silver rings that looked more like car parts than jewelry. A guitar player he knew named Melvin and his girlfriend, whose name I never did know, stood up for us. Guess I could have asked Olivia, since she was in on it from the beginning, but that felt kind of weird. I mean, I didn't tell anybody, including Mom and Dad. Anyway, our honeymoon consisted of a romantic trip on the A train out to Rockaway Beach, where we walked hand in hand in the sand—avoiding cigarette butts, pop-top tabs and broken glass, and celebrating our new lives together.

"We're married! Surprise!" After my parents moved beyond shock, I think they were relieved. I was officially off their watch. They gave us the double mattress and box springs I asked for. It was all we could fit in the apartment, and the twin bed was getting a little too cozy. Then they bought themselves a new living-room suite in honor of their empty nest.

Olivia spied my ring soon as I walked in the door. She was unusually subdued. I figured she was hurt that I didn't confide in her before I took the plunge, but maybe she saw the writing on the wall. She and Eliot had eloped too. She did come around though, gave us a hand-blown glass vase. I still have it. She also understood when I said I wanted to leave school for a while. That's when she invited me to come on full-time. She had moved manufacturing to a small plant in New Jersey, and she was having the loft remodeled to make room for a sales staff. She couldn't pay me benefits yet, but she'd started talking with lawyers about how to structure her kitchen-table company into a corporation. If I hung in a little longer the company would turn that corner. I never hesitated. I wasn't about to give up my spot as first employee. That's a once-in-a-lifetime thing. It was a relief, finally being out of school. I wasn't exactly a dropout, since I had some kind of degree, and the extra money was right on time.

Unfortunately, the reality portion of my marriage set in pretty soon. The part about What's for dinner? Who's doing the laundry? And, What time are you coming home? Still, life was more *Newlywed Game* than *Divorce Court*. We even drove his piece-a car to Key West to salute the sunset for our first anniversary. Sometimes I hung out when he played, but I headed home early so I could get up and go to work. After I nudged him a little—OK, a lot—and made a few phone calls as his "manager," he started hustling commercial jingles, which he informed me were artistically beneath him. I said I'd be happy to cash the checks if it was too painful. But he was tickled silly first time he heard a jingle he did for a local tire chain on the radio.

Amber was as much a surprise to me as she was to her

father. One morning I slapped on my Apricot Sage Crème as usual and promptly washed it off because the smell was making me sick. When I got to work the smell of everything including Wite-Out made me want to puke, and Olivia said, "Bet you're preggers." I said she was nuts. That's why I never gamble.

After several days of needing a clothespin for my nose, I swallowed my pride, which always sticks in my throat, and found a clinic. It was filled to the rafters with women and wiggling children and strollers and crying babies and overworked nurses—it sobered me up from my bohemian romance in a heartbeat. When I got the official word from a doctor that I had company, I wanted to go cry to Mom and Dad, but I distinctly remembered telling them I was grown, so that was out. Papa Bear was so excited he stayed up all night writing a lullaby. I stayed awake too, worrying about paying for college, baby food, and a car with a backseat. Then the arguments started. I wanted him to look for a job, at least part-time. He said a job would waste the creative hours he needed to compose. Right. I reminded him he wasn't Ashford or Simpson yet. Then he decided we should move to LA, since more recording was coming from the West Coast. I ended that when I said the one of us who did have a job worked in New York.

By my fifth month I craved sweet potatoes, and I wasn't real happy with my marathon prenatal clinic visits, or that we were searching in Salvation Army stores for a crib. I told Mom we didn't want to waste money on something the baby would only need a short time. That's how he explained it to me and I halfway bought it—maybe a third of the way. But she was not interested in having her grandbaby sleep in a used crib. "You got a new bed, didn't you?" So she bought one, which made me feel

about two feet tall. And worry about what kind of life I was—
we were—bringing a baby into.

I didn't talk about the bad stuff at work—my misery did
not want company—but I'm pretty sure Olivia knew I wasn't
a happy camper. She never said anything directly, incorporat-
ing M&D Enterprises moved to the front burner and Olivia
arranged for hospitalization. When she told me, I didn't know
what to say, for once. I just hugged her. We got kind of gushy
for a second, then we laughed because her boobs and my belly
took up so much space we couldn't get very close. I wasn't the
only newly covered employee, but I sure was relieved to cross
that off my worry list.

During that same time Olivia was having her own family
trauma. After a long bout with Eliot and Hillary, she relented
and agreed to let her daughter enroll in an exclusive boarding
school in Switzerland. So my child was coming as hers was going. One afternoon a little after she shipped Hillary off, Olivia
was repotting my philodendron, which by then was a six-foot
vine I nicknamed Rapunzel, and she suggested I bring the baby
to work with me, the way it used to be when Hillary was small.
I think it made us both feel better. And it meant Mr. Music
would not have to be Mr. Mom. I was never too sure how that
was going to work out.

Amber arrived a week early, and from the moment we met
I was in love. And I loved my little family trio. My six-week
maternity leave was the happiest time in my life. I was his baby,
Amber was our baby, and la la la la la la la la la means . . . the
song couldn't last forever.

Reality, round two: bundling Amber in the quilted snuggle
sack Olivia made and carting her to work, mightily pissed because he was still laid up in bed. Problem was, I wasn't seeing

any record deals or hearing any Top Forty tunes, and it just didn't look like he was trying that hard. I mean, I watched Olivia build a company out of stuff she cooked up in a pot in her kitchen. I was willing to help him, but we had a baby to support and I was doing most of the supporting. And I used to keep Amber up later than I should when he was out because I was lonely. And worried. His rhymes were getting on my nerves and I wasn't about to admit any of it. My parents may have bought the mattress, but I made my own bed. I was going to sleep in it—or burn it.

Then I came home one day and he was wearing a jacket and tie and said he's got a job teaching piano, at my old alma mater, of all places. Oh happy day. It was perfect—for a few semesters. I liked the way it sounded too—professor—OK, he was an instructor, but the students called him professor. I was executive assistant to the president and CEO of a corporation. That was my title after the reorganization. My salary got fancier too. But after a while he'd come home mad. Nobody in the department knew what they were talking about. They were mediocre musicians infecting students with their lack of creativity—he was always dramatic. The longer it went on, the more frustrated he got. I'd tell him to chill. It was just a job. He'd blow up and tell me music was never just a job. Then Amber would cry, so we'd stop fighting—at least at first. And we'd play Old Maid, or ride the horsey, and her little grin was enough to keep us in check.

By the time Amber got to pre-K we had the scheduling down pat. I'd drop her off in the morning. He'd teach his classes, then pick her up and keep her until I got home. Then one day he said he had a fight with the department chairman and quit. You what?! I told him he'd better kiss and make up. But he had a plan. He and one of his students, a talented sax player, were going to drive to LA in Sunshine. They'd share expenses and make the record company rounds. That was a plan?! Well, I went off—told him to grow up. He said if I didn't believe in him, why were we together? You can feel where this was heading. He went west. Said he would send for us when he got settled. I was through. I had stuck my neck out to be with him and he left us. Period.

My folks said we could always come home, but I knew I'd lock horns with Mom over Amber. Besides, Nineteenth Street was home. Life was simpler without having to worry where we could park the car and not get a ticket, or whether we were disturbing the genius at work. And I was handling my business— working, taking care of my child. I did not need my parents or my ex, and I was way too busy for moping and hoping and sorry songs. Except for those nights I cried until I fell asleep, but that didn't count. Nobody saw it. He kept sending tapes of the stuff he wrote about breaking up and making up. Seems like our marriage was just a source of material, and I was tired of hearing my life in C major. I sold his precious Fender Rhodes. He left that too and it was in my way. That got a rise out of him. I'm still waiting for the song about it.

In the meantime, I had a life to live. Money was tight, but Amber never knew it. I spruced up the apartment, then moved to a bigger place when the man upstairs left. I took computer classes so I could at least pretend I knew what the consultant was talking about when it was time to set up Markson's system. Amber was as smart as they come and I rode her teachers to get her in every enrichment program they had going. We took advantage of all the city had to offer—museums, plays, concerts— you name it, we went. For a while Amber even took riding lessons at the stable near Central Park. Hillary's old boots and helmet fit her great, but Amber wasn't into horse manure. Neither was I, which is why I went ahead and divorced her father. He wasn't too keen on my vibe when I had him served, acted all surprised. Well, I was surprised when he tossed his duffle bag in the car and took off, so we were even, but I never bad-mouthed him to Amber. Promised Daddy I wouldn't. Besides, she knew who was there for her every day. Truth was, my ex gave me the best gift I ever got—my daughter. She was my rock, my strength, my happiness. Amber kept me focused.

And Olivia had given me a job to grow into. She was growing too, traveling the world—Zambia, Nepal, Ecuador—looking for local suppliers of the natural ingredients she used. She hired a PR firm and spoke out about nurturing the planet. That brought us more attention, and Markson & Daughter products became available in more high-end outlets. She dressed more like a grown-up, got a better haircut. Me too. There was still something special between us, especially when nobody was around and we shared one of those "Can you believe it?" moments, but the days were mostly full, and they were more about business. So I hadn't exactly hit the lottery, but it had become a pretty great gig. On our fifteenth anniversary I had the card I swiped from the placement office framed and gave it to her, which cracked her up. "I still believe it was destiny," she said.

Finally, we outgrew the loft, but when we'd been looking at new space for a while she shocked me—said the tempo and hustle of the city was wearing her out. After a factory visit she had gone for a drive, stumbled on a farm for sale, fell in love and made an offer. So she was moving our headquarters nearby in central New Jersey. New Jersey?! Was she kidding? All I knew was the stinky part between the Holland Tunnel and the airport. Why would anyone want to live there? But she took me to the farm, showed me the wooden house plopped in the middle and where the lavender would go. Then we drove to the steel-and-glass office park where she had decided to move Markson & Daughter.

What the hell was I going to do? Commuting was out. There was no train down the block from the office. There were no blocks in Princeton Junction—just big parking lots. Driving from Manhattan was out—the tolls, the traffic, the hide-and-seek parking when I got home—it made no sense. And I wasn't about to look for another job. What could compare to the one I had?

Amber took it better than I did—especially after she saw the place I found—a duplex with a fireplace and patio. The complex had tennis courts, a pool, and the rent was less than what I'd paid on Nineteenth Street. We were both excited when I bought my first car—a used white T-Bird I named Aretha because it was classy and flashy—and it had a backseat. Amber liked her new school, she met a boy named J.J. You know the rest.

And as for Gerald, I met him at a car dealership when I decided to trade up. He leased my starter Lexus. I can't exactly explain what attracted me. First thing I noticed was that he looked so precise—from the crease in his trousers to his shirt sleeves rolled up just so, like they were pressed that way. And his mustache was trimmed an eighth of an inch above his lip—always looked exactly the same, not a hair out of line. Gerald looked sharp, a little like my dad. I was feeling pretty happy with myself that day—living in the suburbs, picking out my first new ride. I don't usually like salespeople following me around, but it felt more like he was keeping me company. It was gorgeous out when we went for a test drive and he directed me down windy little roads I'd never seen before, past houses with horses grazing and mums in autumn colors lining the walkways. I swear, we were gone an hour.

Yes, I kind of knew I was flirting. For years I'd put myself on lockdown, being Amber's mother. I hadn't used that muscle in so long—it felt good. Besides, he wasn't wearing any identifying jewelry. Gerald called all over North America to locate the coupe I wanted—shiny black with black leather interior. And I think he called me at work every day until it arrived. I started looking forward to it. When I picked up the car, he took as much time as I needed explaining all the levers and switches. Then, when he handed me the keys, there was a little silver *T* on the key ring that I know was not standard issue. Oh, and a card with his private cell phone number. Said he'd be happy to show me some more of those back roads and unexpected places. I don't know, Gerald was smooth and steady, not artistic and crazy like my ex. I felt like he could actually *do* stuff, not just write songs about it.

We went out a few times before he told me he was married. I swore I would never talk to him again. Except it's like when you've gone all day without eating and you think you're not hungry until you put a stick of gum in your mouth. Then you could chew the shrubbery. After a while I decided that in a way, his being married was a plus. I could have a snack now and then without turning my life—or Amber's—inside out.

Anyway, the offices of Markson & Daughter still had lots of greenery, but now it was maintained by a plant service. Rapunzel took to her new home—the office next to Olivia's—and over time became a blanket of green on my credenza. Olivia got feelers from companies wanting to buy her out, but she wasn't interested. "It would be like selling my child." And speaking of children, Hillary never did come home. She married Viscount

Somebody, became Lady Hillary and took up residence in his drafty castle. By the time Amber was in high school I'd bought a place that impressed even my mom, complete with landscaping and a lawn service, since I was living in the Garden State. That's not too shabby. For years everything went great—until the morning Olivia didn't show up.

In all the time I'd known her she'd never been more than a few minutes late for anything, but that day she had a nine-thirty meeting scheduled, and when I hadn't heard from her by ten o'clock I called her home, her cell—nothing. By ten-thirty I was on my way to her house.

From my car I could see Olivia sitting on the porch in her pajamas, head propped against her rocker. The newspaper had slid down her legs. A breeze tinkled the wind chimes and had blown some pages against the railing. I remember thinking, *Wonder if she still snores?* I'd give her grief about that. It all looked so normal, but then I got closer, and I realized she wasn't breathing. That couldn't be. We'd said our good nights the day before. She was excited about going to get her teeth whitened. "So I look young and perky. All right, middle-aged and perky," she told me. I said I'd be sure to wear my shades. They were on my desk, so I could pop them on when she walked in, but right at that moment I had to grab hold of myself, because I had to do something to make this go away. I was trembling so bad the emergency dispatcher had trouble making out the address. And I've never felt more empty and helpless, waiting to hear the ambulance siren. I had my eyes closed, praying. I couldn't look at her like that.

They called it sudden cardiac death—that about summed it up. Her heart was broken and it stopped. You'd never have known it to look at her, but I knew how sad she was that Hillary had become so distant. I'm no doctor, but that's what I think wore her down. Olivia had two grandsons she saw only on state occasions. I watched how she was with Amber, so I know she had mounds of love stored up to give them. But confidences shared with an assistant amount to what? Part of my job description? Certainly not the basis for an official diagnosis. Nobody was interested in my theory anyway, but you'll never convince me otherwise.

I went through the funeral in a hazy limbo. She was still so young, not that much ahead of me, really, although I never thought of her as an age. Olivia was never big on birthdays anyhow. "Why celebrate one day? Rejoice for them all," she used to say. Hillary acted like she barely knew me, didn't introduce me to her family. So after all the prayers and eulogies, I drove Amber back to her dorm room. She was pretty shook up and she talked nonstop about things I didn't even think she remembered. Then she hugged me, hard, before she left the car, told me she loved me. I hadn't heard that much since she entered her teens, and I sure needed it that day.

After that I went home and lit some ginger-almond candles. The smell reminded me of the loft and the first day we met. I didn't know what to call Olivia. My employer? My friend? A little of both, I guess. I'd probably spent more time with her than with anybody else in my life, and my every days would never be the same.

Olivia was barely in the ground when Hillary started entertaining offers to buy Markson & Daughter. How could she just ditch a company her mother built from scratch all around her? She was the damn inspiration. She saw what we went through. I mean, if it had been left to me . . . Let me not even start. It was Markson & Daughter, not Markson & Tee, so it was hers to sell. She could take the money, add a wing to the castle, buy a ladder for social climbing. Hillary wasn't even interested in her mother's personal things. She told me to crate the ones in the office and ship them. Why? So she could stick them in her royal attic? I took the framed job posting home. That was ours.

Then I was a lame duck—executive assistant to the dead president. That made me what? In the way? There was no one there who understood how far we'd come. And who was *we*? *I* was on my own and it was time to jockey for position in a race I never expected.

Didier Lowe, Olivia's senior VP for operations, became interim president. When he joined Markson it was a big deal—a coup, they called it in *Cosmetics News*, since he came over from a bigger company and he was supposed to be some kind of boy wonder. I didn't like him from day one, with his black patent hair slicked down over his little pea head, his great big superiority complex and his signature black suede loafers, no socks, even in January. He wore them with everything: suits, jeans, probably his pajamas. I was through when he sent the memo requesting that staff call him Monsieur Lowe, so we spoke as little as I could arrange. The feeling was obviously mutual since almost immediately he had HR tell me I'd be moving to another office to make way for Monsieur and his assistant. So with my computer, the pen mug Olivia handed me that first day and Rapunzel, I moved downstairs to Marketing. I think they had an empty office. I answered to the marketing VP—I think they flipped a coin and she lost. Anyway, she made up projects for me, like reading entries in the annual high school essay contest. I proposed compiling a corporate history. No one had been there long enough to know it all but me. I'm not sure she got what they'd use it for, but she approved. At least I'd be out of her hair for a while. It would be my last gift to Olivia for all she did for me. Didier would probably use it as an executive doorstop.

Around the time Amber got engaged, Markson & Daughter became a subsidiary of a mammoth cosmetics conglomerate traded on the New York Stock Exchange—so much for homegrown. New rumors spread daily, but not much changed for a while. Then the pinstriped vultures from the home planet started touring the offices, interviewing various people. Nobody said boo to me, which should have been a clue, but I was happily engrossed in wedding plans.

Then I got a memo from human resources asking me to schedule an interview. Do you know they had the nerve to make me reapply for a job? That's what it amounted to. The woman who interviewed me looked about Amber's age, and she was definitely wearing a fragrance from one of the other subsidiaries. It made my eyes water. She assured me it was standard procedure to reevaluate employees when they were unifying the workforce. Oh, that made me feel a lot better. I wanted to get up and tell her this company wouldn't exist without me, but I tried to keep my cool, act like a dignified professional. She flipped through my file, asked if the associate's degree was the only one I held. I wanted to say that what I did for this company had nothing to do with degrees. It was about ingenuity, persistence, and dedication, but I answered, "Yes." I explained that I was Olivia Markson's first employee. She looked underwhelmed. Then it was over.

Nothing happened for a month and a half. We had Amber's shower, the final fittings. Then it was Friday morning, my last workday before the big event and I was summoned to HR again, this time by the director. As soon as I sat down, he started this speech about appreciating my loyal service, eliminating redundancy, blah, blah, blah. He stared directly in my eyes like he was trying to hypnotize me. It sounded like he was speaking under water, but I caught the upshot. "You're firing me." He said some stupidness about outplacement and I snapped, "Will I have a job with this company after my vacation?" He sputtered and tried to find a delicate way to say no, but that was the answer. He babbled about papers to sign, a separation package, and not removing company property, but before he was done I walked out—

—and straight into my escort, a wide-bodied guy in a blue blazer who would accompany me to my office and out of the building. I was outraged. Olivia Markson herself left me in her apartment alone the very first day she met me, and this goon was supposed to make sure I didn't steal anything?! Like there was anything I wanted besides my job—but that ship had sailed.

Nobody looked at me as I walked through the halls, Bulldog trailing behind me. When I got to my office, I laid my head on the desk. It was too heavy to hold and I was getting a migraine trying not to cry. Then Bulldog says, "Do you need a box for your things?" which I guess is corporate speak for hurry up and get the hell out. I raised up and glared at him and he shut up and stepped back. Then I looked around. What was there to take, really? I dumped the pens on my desk and put the mug Olivia had made in my purse. Then I looked at Rapunzel and remembered that tiny white plastic pot, and Olivia repotting it, and the twenty-five years . . . next thing I knew, I had snatched it and started feeding forty feet of philodendron to the shredder. The loud buzzing and grinding—that's exactly how I felt, what I wanted to do with what they had made of Olivia's company. And oh, did I happen to say that while that was going on I accidentally on purpose shredded the neatly arranged and carefully annotated index cards I had been using to organize the Markson corporate history? It was so easy—they were right in my top desk drawer, exactly where I'd left them before my trip to the guillotine. If they wanted to know how it all started, let them come ask me.

The flower pot fell and dumped dirt and leaves all over my shoes, the carpet. Then Bulldog got tense. "Hey, what are you doing?" I shot back, "What does it look like I'm doing?"—like that made some sense. He kept eyeing me like he wanted to make me stop but couldn't figure out how. I didn't stop until I got that high-pitched whine and the shredder teeth clogged.

By now people had gathered around my door to see what the commotion was. I pulled off the shredder lid and started tossing the green bits up in the air like confetti. I had been spending money on Amber's wedding like confetti and I kept seeing the gown, the flowers, the limo and all the bills—and me with no job. "Bye-bye!" I said and the leaves were all in my hair and I know I looked like a crazy woman, but at that moment I was. Then Bulldog had had enough. He snatched my purse and my arm and dragged me out to the applause of my coworkers.

And I decided right then that nobody needed to know about this until after the wedding.

3

I didn't need advice and I was not collecting pity.

So there I was, seventeen days into my little hiatus, as I called my *outplacement*—I hate that word. Anyway, I was having myself a personal ball, making discoveries every day. Like how great it feels pouring a second cup of coffee and ignoring the traffic report. And how civilized the supermarket is on Tuesday afternoons—not like the Friday night crash-cart derby. Who knew the Super Shop carried canned eel? I'm still not sure what you do with it. Eel salad? I don't think so, but in all my years of grabbing a four-pack of Albacore so I could cross it off my list and race to the salad dressing, I never noticed it. I learned the names of the people at the dry cleaner, took advantage of Monday discounts at the car wash. I was seriously getting into life in the leisure class.

So this one morning I hit the drugstore to pick up vitamins, which I take religiously, and my monthly supply of feminine necessities, because that visitor was due the next day. Another advantage of the day shift—no teenage boys on the cash register so we don't have to pretend we're not embarrassed. Then, around eleven, I dropped in at Ten & Ten, my nail salon—they cost a little more, but they use the best products, not that no-name crap some places try to pass off on you. I pulled into the space right in front, which never happened during my standing Thursdays at seven. The midday dress code featured jeans and sweats, not business suits with twelve-hour wrinkles, the uniform of the after-work crowd. I could actually hear the smooth jazz playing above the massaging whirlpool pedicure chairs, and I could take my time picking a polish without somebody wrestling me for the Peek-a-Boo Pink. Not that my color changed a lot from week to week, but I like to look. I keep it simple—no tips, wraps, jewels, rainbows or butterflies, thank you very much. I have nice hands, like my mother's, no need for overkill.

So I'm cuticle deep in warm moisturizing cream, eyes closed and really looking forward to the hand massage, when I'm snatched out of my peaceful trance. "Mom, how come you're not at work?" Uh-oh, snagged by my own daughter, sounding just like me. And I felt like I was playing hooky since I hadn't bothered telling her I'd been kicked to the curb by my employer. Excuse me—former employer. I wasn't too worried about her trying to catch up with me on the job. Everybody who knows me knows I do not like email. It's for work, period. Don't send me forty-two forwards of the same joke that wasn't funny last week, because I will delete them. And I've got better things to do with my spare time than follow the blinking cursor, so I don't have a computer at home. If you want to tell me something, call me—at home, not at work, which obviously doesn't matter any-more. And don't call on my cell phone because it's probably not turned on. The charm of having my purse ring is highly overrated. And don't get me started on the losers who aren't content to annoy everyone around them with a chorus of "When the Saints Go Marching In" every time their phone rings. After that they have to share a detailed description of little Timmy's first time going to the potty by himself or a blow-by-blow account of Jane's divorce-court nightmare with everybody who's in earshot.

From the time Amber was little I told her jobs were for work, not for personal business. I mean, she could always call me when she needed to, but we never spent a whole lot of phone time. And once she got her own job she still followed that rule. We spoke in the evening, usually on her way home, because unlike me, her cell was always on. Or when she was trying to cook dinner for J.J., and she'd ask me how to tell when a steak is medium rare, or if you can substitute skim milk and butter for cream, bless her heart. They had come back from their honeymoon all glowy and drunk with love. How could I throw cold water on their wedded bliss with my rotten news? Life would do that soon enough.

Besides, I wasn't broke. No need for a news flash. Those people at Markson had sent me some kind of mail, but I tossed it in the fruit bowl with the pears I wasn't eating. Whatever they had to say could wait until I was ready to hear it because the time for cranberry sauce and cornbread stuffing was right around the corner and I'd already been to the Trim-a-Tree shop at the mall to pick up a few things for Amber's first Christmas on her own. Nobody changed jobs before the holiday bonus checks went out, and thinking about that was a booster shot to my pissed-offedness since they were going to get away without giving me one. Hell, my severance agreement—which sounded to me like they were planning to slice off my right arm, which is a lot like how it felt—was supposed to give me one week's pay for every year I worked. Except the cheap fothermuckers only counted the years *after* Olivia incorporated. You know that's just wrong. I was there before any of them. That should count for something. Anyway, I wasn't about to let that nonsense ruin my holidays. I'd been working since I was nineteen, and I deserved time to enjoy my freedom while I had it. As a matter of fact, I went ahead and paid for the cruise I was planning to take with the Live Five in the spring. Diane and Marie would be celebrating one of those birthdays with a zero in it and I had no intention of missing the fun. I booked my own cabin, because this was not camp—I was not sharing a bunk. And I got one with a balcony because, why take a cruise if you can't see the ocean? When I took a new job, they would just have to understand I had a prior commitment and needed that week off.

In any case, Amber didn't need to know about my change in job status until I started looking for a new one.

Actually, besides Gerald, nobody knew. I definitely hadn't told my parents. They were all settled into their active adult community—I think that's what the brochure called it. There was no point worrying them. I also didn't need my mother talking about, "I knew from the beginning that woman wouldn't treat you right." Like Olivia died just to mess with me. And after twenty-five years, I was not convening a committee of friends to discuss what I should do and what so-and-so's hairdresser's daughter did when she got canned. I didn't need advice and I was not collecting pity.

The day the axe fell I called Gerald, and after I finished picking plant flakes out of my hair he took me to lunch. He didn't say much, just that it was their loss. Like I didn't know that already? But he listened to me rant, which is really all I needed.

What else could I expect him to do? It was kind of nice, seeing him in the afternoon. That didn't happen too often. Afterwards I went home and pulled myself together for the surprise bridal shower Amber's coworkers were throwing that evening, because those corporate monkeys were not about to stop our show.

Anyway, I could feel Amber waiting for an answer, so I opened my eyes real slow and said, "I might ask you the same question," to buy myself a few seconds to get my story straight. She presented exhibit A—her left hand. "Nail emergency." I could see the broken tip on her index finger and I knew she could not tolerate any flaw on the newly banded hand. The child had been obsessed with her nails since she was eleven and asked for a manicure for her birthday. I thought it was cute and innocent enough considering some of the CDs she'd been asking for. Clearly, she was transformed by the experience, because the next thing I knew the girl was saving her allowance to get her nails done once a month. Since then I know she's spent a fortune on tips, wraps and whatever else would strengthen the short, soft nails she obviously got from her father's people.

Amber put her hands on her hips, talking about, "I'm on lunch. Your turn."

I told her I was having a mental-health day. It wasn't a lie—not exactly. Then she told me I deserved it, kissed me on top of my head, like she was the parent. I felt relieved—like when you were a kid and you got away with something. But I was so wound up I barely even remember the hand massage.

Afterwards I met my fellow Markson outcast, Julie, for lunch, which wasn't exactly relaxing either. She spent most of the time chugging Chardonnay and moaning about how hard it was going to be to find a job. Unlike her usual sunny self, Julie was sounding the alarm before the first flame, but I wasn't going for it. She had hardly looked yet. Besides, I knew I was good at what I did. I would be an asset to anybody who hired me. Then Julie couldn't believe I hadn't applied for unemployment. So I didn't tell her I hadn't gone for my outplacement counseling session either. "After all those years and the way *they* treated us . . ." We had stopped using the *M* word. It was all "us" against "them" and Julie thought *they* should pay. "They owe us." She had already gotten her first few checks and was looking forward to her twenty-six weeks of assistance—said it would keep her in wine, which was obvious, and out of trouble, which was not. Julie felt we were entitled, but I was not interested in taking a number and singing the blues in exchange for a handout. If I didn't need one when Amber and I were first on our own, I surely didn't need one now.

But by days nineteen, twenty and twenty-seven I realized my little run-ins with Amber and Julie were the least of my problems. Each day I checked my date book, counted on fingers and toes, but it added up the same, which meant I was late—for a very important date, and for me, that was unheard of. It had been thirty-three years, and you could time a Cape Canaveral shuttle launch by my period, except when—I couldn't even finish that thought. I cleaned behind my refrigerator, planted tulip bulbs, sorted my pantyhose drawer—anything to distract myself from what hadn't happened yet. But hard as I tried, I kept coming back to Ron and our impromptu wedding celebration. I still couldn't call up the teeniest flash of a kiss, the feel of his hands, nothing. I don't know. Maybe I didn't want to. But whether I remembered or not, it happened—I'd found the evidence and thought I was home free. I mean, I'd gotten through twelve years with Gerald without even a scare. Now I was expecting to be a grandmother, not to be expecting.

As day twenty-nine of my permanent leave rolled into day thirty, my house was spotless, but I was a wreck. I dragged out of bed before dawn, made coffee—not that I exactly needed fresh brewed caffeine. I was already wired. The morning news, complete with grizzly headlines and flash-flood warnings, did nothing to distract me from the soap opera that played in my head all night. "Amber, honey, remember when you were little and you begged me for a baby sister or brother?" I couldn't imagine forming my lips to say those words, or what she would answer when she found out who the daddy was. Then I had this horrifying thought that it could have been Gerald too, which made matters worse. That's when I had to get out of my house and do something or I was going to peel my skin off. So I tucked my nightgown in my jeans, pulled on a baggy sweater, my raincoat and my favorite hide-everything hat, and walked out—

—into a monsoon. It was so dark the streetlights were still on. The rain came down sideways and the wind was strong enough to rock my car. If I had good sense I'd have gone back inside, but crazy people don't care about storms. I wasn't sure I could drive the mile and a half to the drugstore—the one I don't usually go to—without running off the road, but I also couldn't sit home starting a list of girls' and boys' names.

Who knew there were so many home pregnancy tests? When I had Amber, there were maybe three. Now there was a wall of pastel boxes. How many styles do you need? I made sure no one was looking and picked one up. *"A plus sign means you are pregnant."* Not on this day—middle-aged, unmarried, unemployed and pregnant was definitely not a plus. I didn't have the patience to stand there reading labels like I was comparing laundry detergents. So I snatched the only box that wasn't a sweet baby color because I was not feeling pink or blue. It looked like medicine and I needed to go home and take mine like a grown-up.

I seriously considered leaving a twenty on the shelf and shoving the test in my pocket, but I would have turned to stone if I walked out and the alarm went off. So I plowed up the aisle, filling my little red basket with tissues, chips, cough medicine, lightbulbs—whatever was within reach—to keep my secret safely hidden. And when I got to the register, I rifled through a plastic tub of nail clippers to avoid looking the white-haired clerk in the eye, although I swear I noticed a little twinkle when Mrs. Claus handed me the bag.

I went in my door pulling off soggy clothes, down to my wrinkly nightgown, and headed straight for the bathroom, where I soon realized that no amount of squinting and holding the directions up to the light was going to help me read them. Then I had to dig around for the dollar-store glasses I only needed because they squeezed too many words on a piece of paper the size of a Post-it. *"For best results test should be taken first thing in the morning."* Like I could wait one second longer. So I peed on my hand, my leg and the toilet seat before I got my aim right and hit the strip. Then I watched the second hand creep around the face of my watch and prayed the line wouldn't turn blue. After seven minutes I couldn't tell what color it was. Gray? Lavender? Mauve? Now, I'll admit I wasn't seeing anything clearly at that point. I'd gone past worrying about telling Amber, to imagining what I could say to Ron—and/or Gerald. I already felt like I'd cheated on him, which, under the circumstances, didn't make any sense, because Gerald went home to his wife. But when I showed him wedding pictures, I felt guilty every time Ron's smiling face appeared. Not crazy enough to confess, but I did feel sorta bad, and somehow announcing I was pregnant by another man was not the way I would want to end things.

Lucky for me, the test I bought was a twofer. Clearly, they expect you to screw up the first time. So I drank three bottles of water and did the whole thing again. This time the line seemed rosier. I was almost happy, until I checked the instructions. They specifically said *not* to drink three bottles of water and repeat the test because the results would not be accurate, which meant I was back at the starting line, and I still didn't know what color it was.

So I did what any woman in my predicament would do. I begged my doctor's office for an appointment. After much sighing and clicking of computer keys the receptionist told me the doctors were booked solid, but a nurse practitioner could squeeze me in in an hour or so, if I could get there. If I had to flag down a police car I was going to get there. And when she said squeeze me in, she wasn't kidding. The office was jammed with women of every size, shape and trimester, and they all seemed to know each other. I hoped not to be pledging their sorority—Sigma Gamma Round.

After giving up my seat three times to women who were sitting for two and trying to find magazines without "baby" or "maternity" in the title, they finally called my name.

Margo—we'd agreed to first names—had spiky blond hair and wore a white cotton jumpsuit like a mechanic's, minus the grease. When she asked the reason for my visit, it came shooting out like a hot, shaken soda. But she stayed cool, flipped through my chart, asked my age, and then whether I still used my diaphragm. I mumbled something like, "Most of the time." But for Amber's wedding, it never made the suitcase. What for?

I wasn't planning to need the love dome. So much for planning.

Margo did an exam, drew some blood, said she'd call with results the next day.

I almost leaped off the table. "Tomorrow?!"

She said the pregnancy-test results would take a few hours, maybe longer. There was no need to wait. I assured her I didn't mind. Right then, I didn't want to be by myself. So I resumed my vigil in the waiting room, every second hoping that in the next one I'd hear my name. Three hours and fifty-four minutes later I did.

Margo quickly put me out of my misery. "Well, you're not pregnant." I have never been so happy *not* to be something. But before I got to feeling too good she announced she was waiting for more test results to confirm the likely cause of my missing cycle. It was a symptom of perimenopause. Was she talking to me? I could not be old enough for menopause—peri or otherwise. I guess she'd seen the blank stare before, because she launched into a song and dance about changing hormone levels and the irregular periods, night sweats, mood swings and other fun that could be coming my way. It almost made me wish I was pregnant—not just old. Margo stressed that I shouldn't slip up on birth control or be having unprotected sex. Just what I needed, sex ed for seniors, but at least I could skip the Lamaze refresher course. The bad news—most of my eggs were scrambled, but there were still enough good ones to fry my behind. I wrote a check for my copay and left with a handful of pamphlets about my "new stage of life" and a nonspecific bad attitude.

So the last thing I wanted to see when I turned into my block was a crowd in my driveway. Not just neighbors—there was a fire engine out front, behind the squad car with the slow-spinning red and white lights. The news van was around the corner. Didn't they have some corruption to cover? My blood pressure was normal when Margo took it, but I'm sure it shot up in the high triple digits as I stepped out into the murky mist to find out what was going on at my house.

Soon as I walked up, the crowd parted, giving me a prime view of the gigantic Norway spruce that had towered over my backyard, the tallest tree in what I considered my own little piece of forest. During my absence it keeled over—fell diagonally across my property and left a gaping hole where the roots used to be. I couldn't believe it. The top reached out to the street where it was bound in yellow police tape.

After determining I was the home owner, the sergeant proceeded to tell me how lucky I was. "That thing coulda come down on somebody's roof, a car. It even missed your lawn furniture. Rain musta loosened it up and the wind just took it." A lot like Dorothy and Toto. Then he said I had to clear it out of the road in forty-eight hours or face a summons.

I thought I was pretty lucky too, until I called my insurance agent. Even though it made the storm-damage review on the evening news, she said that since there was no property loss, the removal was on me. Then she offered to review my coverage to see if I was adequately insured. Great. Do you know how much it costs to cart off a forty-foot tree? My lawn guy asked if I wanted it split for firewood, but soft wood makes smoky fires, so I just had him take it away. I'd buy some cherry when it was time to throw a log in the fireplace. Yes, it could have been a lot worse. It just wasn't in my budget for the month. But I could handle it. And guess what showed up three days later—like I needed cramps and water retention on top of everything else.

I managed to keep myself out of trouble for the next few weeks, did some things I'd been meaning to do—like get the car detailed, finish my Christmas shopping, organize the photographs I'd been stuffing in boxes for years. I arranged them chronologically in matching red leather albums so they'd look nice on the bookshelf in the den. And I gave in and got my eyes examined—bought some cute glasses too, because if my perimenopausal self needed reading glasses, they had to be cute. I never knew glasses could cost as much as jewelry. Good jewelry.

A couple more pieces of Markson mail arrived, but I couldn't bring myself to read them. I tried. I'd decide to rip open the envelope on the count of ten, but by nine I'd be too upset, so I'd chuck it back in the pile. I mean, normally I am very organized with my mail—sort it as soon as I walk in the door. Junk mail goes straight in the trash. Bills I file, and catalogs go in a basket by my bed for further browsing. Markson mail was none of the above. I wanted to write "Return to Sender" across the front but finally I decided I'd deal with it at the beginning of the new year. Out with the old, in with . . . something surprising. I loved surprises.

And then Amber started asking me for Nana's sweet-potato casserole recipe because she wanted all the traditional dishes at her first Thanksgiving dinner. There was never a recipe. I watched Nana make it, then Mom. Guess Amber was watching the Macy's parade. You bake the sweet potatoes, mash them up and add butter, brown sugar, a handful of chopped pecans, crumbled bacon, pineapple, vanilla, cinnamon, nutmeg . . . then you taste it to see if it needs something. I had to make one to figure out amounts I could write down. It would have been easier to just bring the thing, but Amber had to do the whole meal herself, so I wrote it on an index card, had it laminated, then gave it to her in the casserole dish from her china pattern. I was passing on something precious, in something precious. That made me feel good.

What wasn't sitting so well was the prospect of Ron as a fellow dinner guest, but I decided not to sweat it. After all, they won't convict you of a crime if you're mentally incapacitated. I committed an indiscretion while suffering from stress-induced, champagne-assisted insanity. I'm sure it's a defense in somebody's court of law. Anyway, I figured I'd see him and wonder what in the world I could have been thinking.

Wrong.

Before he arrived I was perfectly relaxed, looking sharp in a cranberry knit-pants outfit I hadn't been planning to buy, but it was too "me" not to. There was hooting and hollering from the football game in the background and I was sipping cider, talking to friends and family and staying out of the kitchen, per Amber's request. But it sure smelled like Thanksgiving. Hadn't seen Baby Son-in-Law yet. He was on a supermarket odyssey, trying to find the fresh pearl onions Amber had left off her shopping list and just had to have, bless him.

I was feeling proud and, I'll admit it, a little weepy, celebrating with my daughter and her husband in their first apartment. The folding tables they borrowed—since their dining-room set hadn't arrived in time—were set with new china and linen, and they were starting traditions of their own. Mom and Dad didn't make the trip since they'd been up for the wedding, but I was sorry they weren't there to see it. Neither were J.J.'s parents, but the newlyweds were heading to Texas for Christmas.

Then Ron came strolling in with a bouquet the size of an end table. And that smile. I made a break for the bathroom while he took off his coat, but I could still hear him so I turned on the faucet, squirted some mouthwash and started gargling. Don't ask me why. After a while I was relaxed by that minty fresh feeling and composed enough, I thought, to speak to him like a rational adult, so I came out. Guess who's waiting to use the facilities?

He said, "That's where you've been hiding." For some reason my eyes fastened on his left eyebrow where the shiny black hairs stood up against the grain and I had the strongest urge to smooth them, but I knew better than to touch him. Instead I said, "What makes you think I'd be hiding from you?" and exhaled as I slipped by, but I still caught a whiff of that cologne. Damn.

I thought I was safe back on the couch, but then he stood somewhere behind me, talking to one of J.J.'s buddies. It was like I could feel him smouldering back there and then I was having goose bumps, which made me mad after all I'd been through on his account, so I got up and moved closer to the TV. Somebody asked him if he was still driving at Pocono Speedway, and I blurted out, "You race cars?" before I could shut myself up. He kind of swaggered, shook his head. "Used to." Now I knew the man was crazy. Then he said, "Racing stock cars was my passion, but I gave it up about a year ago. Still do some customizing. Restoring classic cars is my main business." Like I wanted to know about his passion. He added something about the good old days and his Demon Dodge, but by then I had tuned him out and glued my eyes to fourth and goal—stupidest thing I ever saw. Grown men crouching like bullfrogs in the snow, then slamming each other into the ground. For a ball? I couldn't tell you what happened, but some folks cheered, some booed, and next thing I knew Ron was at my side talking about "Falcons or Lions?" I said, "What difference does it make?" I seemed completely unable to speak to the man except in the form of a question. Anyway, I wasn't interested in the zoology quiz so I squeezed between two folks sitting in folding chairs to get to the crudité platter on the coffee table.

I don't know what got into me that day. I mean, the apartment was only so big, but whenever he was close enough for me to smell him, I had to move. After a while I felt like Ms. Pacman, eating whatever was in my path and trying to stay ahead of the Ron monster. The only place left to escape to was the kitchen, so I went for it—

—only to find Amber, in tears, standing next to a gargantuan, golden-brown turkey. "Baby, it looks beautiful," I told her, doing my best not to notice a tornado had hit the kitchen. Every pot, colander and melon baller she got as a wedding present was in use. I counted three pans of rice, ranging from scorched to paste. The collards looked a bit . . . al dente, and the peas, waiting for their pearl onions, looked a lot like soup. But she'd made a lovely salad, and the sweet potatoes looked just like Mom used to make 'em. Then she blubbered, "The turkey is still frozen. I thought it would thaw out in the oven."

I wiped her tears, like I used to when she skinned her knees and needed mother's touch to make it better. Then I said it would probably be fine if she turned the oven up to 450 and covered the bird in a foil tent. Except I poked it with a meat fork. A harpoon would have been more useful. That's about the time J.J. arrived with a bag of shallots because he thought they looked kind of like little onions. I got my hug and kiss, and I guess he never got the "no email" directive because next thing out of his mouth was, "You know, Mama Tee, I sent an email

Turkey-gram to your job, but it bounced back saying 'addressee unknown.' What's up with your IT people?"

Busted. And at that moment my brain was as frozen as Big Bird. Sure, I could have blamed it on techno trouble, but that was more lie than I wanted to keep straight. All I could think of to say was, "I don't want to talk about it," which pretty much said it all.

Except my child would not let it go, so I finally blurted out, "They laid me off, alright?" which was the first time those particular words came out of my mouth. It was a total shock to me. I mean, my chest felt tight and I wanted to disappear, just melt into a corner where I couldn't see the two faces looking at me in total disbelief. But I didn't have time to dwell on the full meaning of my revelation because Amber started having a meltdown. She's always been on the emotional side. I used to call her my water girl—99 and 44/100th percent pure tears, which is exactly why I was not about to have this little chat before the wedding. Now, when I walked in the kitchen, I could tell she was already stressed. My child likes everything just so and dinner was looking like a page from a "how-not-to" guide. Anyway, hearing I got fired seemed to send her circuits one volt over the maximum and the sparks started flying. First, she snatched the bag of shallots and screeched, "What am I supposed to do with these?" and flung them into the sink full of dishes. Ker-splash! Then she just started sobbing. Between gulps she'd say stuff like, "How could they fire you? You practically started the company with Olivia." Just what I needed to hear right about then. I tried to assure her I'd be fine, but that just made it worse, so I told J.J. to take her to the bedroom and let her calm down. I could finish dinner.

Ha! Who was I kidding? I was vibrating like a mad woman

and on the verge of chucking it all and ordering pizza. That's about the time I realized how quiet it had gotten in the living room. Clearly the action in the kitchen was more interesting than some old fourth and goal, so I guessed my cat was out of the bag. I was going to have a hard time being thankful about that. Then Ron poked his head in the kitchen. He looked at me. I looked at him, and then I said, "The turkey's frozen," and burst out laughing because . . . I don't know why. At that moment it seemed hilarious. Ron said he had a blowtorch back at the shop, which sent my brain someplace it shouldn't have gone, so I directed it back to dinner. Turkey Lurkey was way too big for the microwave, and if he went back in the oven he'd have been done just in time for a midnight snack.

Then I saw the lightbulb come on over Ron's head. "The grill." It was the first home furnishing J.J. purchased. Amber was looking at armoires and ottomans, but as long as J.J. had a bed and his 36,000-BTU, stainless-steel, three-burner gas grill he'd have been fine. Baby Son-in-Law comes from a long line of men who cook—with fire—and sell big wolf tickets about secret sauce, so I guess Cousin Ron's suggestion came pretty naturally. I wasn't sure how we were going to get twenty-five pounds of semipolar poultry on a grill, but then he took off his leather sport jacket, rolled up his sleeves and went at it with the meat cleaver. He worked up a sweat, but he actually cut it into semirecognizable pieces, kind of like the nine-piece buckets of fried chicken where you can't tell a breast from a thigh from a back. Next thing I know he's on the patio firing up the barbie.

I persuaded J.J. to persuade Amber not to return to kitchen duty. Then I dug around for the pressure cooker the happy couple got as a wedding gift and filled it with the greens, because chewy collards is more fiber than anybody needs. I wasn't sure what kind of secret sauce went with barbecued turkey, but I whipped something up. The hardest part was leaving the kitchen. Having all those folks looking at my jobless self, I couldn't have felt more exposed if I was naked—OK, that may be an exaggeration, since I had not forgotten the last time I saw Ron. Anyway, the only way to get the turkey parts to the auxiliary cookery was to pass through the living room, so I threw my shoulders back and came out talking—about the slight menu deviations, the football game, whatever came to mind.

By the time I grabbed my coat and the tray of underdone bird, Ron had the grill cranking. I watched while he adjusted the flame and the height of the racks. He had big, strong workingman's hands, but there wasn't a trace of grime under his fingernails, and I could see he had used lotion to smooth the skin on his scraped knuckles. Which I know has absolutely nothing to do with the story. Anyway, let me tell you, it was cold out there, but the frosty air was quiet, relaxing in a way. And I was surprisingly warm by the fire—I will not give him credit for that, except I felt kind of weird, holding the tray, not knowing what to say, wondering what he was remembering about me. After the bird was on the grill, he turned to me and said, "The name's Ron. Nice to meet you." Then he tipped his imaginary Kangol and disappeared inside. Guess he was giving me a second chance to make a first impression. And as much as I wanted to say, "Who asked you for one?" given my position, it was best that I shut up and take it. We would have made a pretty baby, though—OK, I need to stop.

Princess Puffy Eyes emerged from the bedroom eventually—kept trying to talk to me about what I was going to do without a job, but I was having none of it. I even sat at the opposite end of the table so she couldn't bring it up. Nobody else did either.

I think Amber's maid of honor's boyfriend was about to, but he got the evil eye and a kick under the table, and he asked for the stuffing instead. And you know what? Barbecued turkey is really pretty tasty.

At the end of the evening I told Ron it was good cooking with him . . . on the grill, and to drive safely. It felt a little less weird, but I sure was worn out. And as I left, I asked Amber not to mention about the job to her grandparents. I'd tell them when the time was right.

But that night I could not sleep. Don't know if it was the excitement of the day, insufficient hormones or too much sweet-potato casserole, but I rolled around, wrestled with the sheets, knocked pillows on the floor, and all I kept hearing, over and over, was myself yelling, "They laid me off, alright?" It bounced off the walls and hit me right between the eyes. Those people had taken my job, like I was some shiftless, lazy, half-steppin' loser. I didn't deserve that. I figured one day I'd retire, on my own terms, when I was good and ready. There would be a luncheon and speeches, then maybe Olivia and I would make a return trip to London. Except then I'd see her on that porch, dead, and me in the HR office with that man and his condescending attitude and irritating voice telling me about my loyal service, and my security escort off the premises. By dawn I could have taken the Grinch in a steel-cage smack-down because my usual championship Christmas spirit was out for the count.

And as December rolled along it only got worse. I was not interested in decking a hall, singing a carol or jingling a bell. I couldn't bring myself to address Christmas cards I'd already bought, open the ones I received or accept invitations to parties I always attended, because when people asked how I was, I didn't want to tell it and they wouldn't want to hear it, so what was the point? I didn't want to see Santa's workshop store windows, a sugarplum fairy or a Christmas pageant, and for the first time in my life I didn't put up a tree because I didn't feel like celebrating. And to remind me why I was in such a foul mood, I had finally gone through my last paycheck and the one they cut for my vacation time, so December's bills came directly out of my pocket. Ho ho ho.

Gerald and I didn't usually see each other much this time of year, which always made me blue, but this year it was a relief. It was all I could do to spruce myself up on Christmas Eve eve, our traditional night together—dinner out, a few drinks, then back to my place for dessert, if you get my drift. Tell you the truth, that didn't even cheer me up and it always does. Oh, and he gave me a very generous gift card. I had him stop shopping for me years ago—never did get the sizes right. So I'd add to whatever he gave me and get something I really wanted— usually eighteen karat.

Then one night Amber shows up, full of fire, to tell me she and J.J. had a big fight after she told him she wasn't going to his parents' for Christmas because I'd be all alone. I sat her down right that second, told her that job or no job I was still the mother, that I was fine and that she needed to go pack and get on that plane to Dallas with her husband. It was an award-winning performance, since I was feeling sad and sorry and would miss them both like crazy, but that was not her problem. She need not be fighting with her husband on my account.

So Christmas Day I watched old movies in my pajamas, had a tuna sandwich for dinner and kept the answering machine on. The kids and my parents, who were all sure I was out having a little extra eggnog at somebody's house, left me messages because I didn't have the energy to fake jolly.

So one afternoon I'm hanging out, counting down the days 'til the new year because I was too through with the old one, and my doorbell rings. I saw the postal truck, so I figured it was a late Christmas arrival, but the mailman hands me a letter I have to sign for. When I saw three names on the return address my knees got wobbly. Whose lawyer had something certified to tell me? It sure wasn't an inheritance—I don't have those kinds of long-lost relatives. I stared at it a long time, like it was going to speak to me, but when I finally ripped it open I was stunned. Attorneys for Markson were demanding I return property that I removed or destroyed—namely the corporate history I shredded accidentally on purpose—or risk forfeiture of my severance payment and possible prosecution. For something I'm sure they were planning to bury in an archive? I didn't know whether to be mad or scared first, but it did make me open the other correspondence in my fruit bowl in-basket.

Most of it was about their so-called stolen property, each one nastier than the last. Who did they think they were talking to? A criminal? Then quick, fast and in a hurry I needed to arrange for something called COBRA. Reptile family—it figured. Anyway, without it I'd have no health insurance, just like before Amber was born. Poof, twenty years of progress gone, one snakebite at a time. And I couldn't believe the size of the payments—every month? But that's all right, I'd only need coverage until my next job. Then there were pension papers, which didn't mean jack for another twenty years. I shoved the whole wad back in the bowl since I couldn't shove it where I wanted to, but I had to give them some kind of answer to let them know I was not to be messed with. Right. The mind is a terrible thing to lose.

Being mad gave me momentum, so down to the basement

I went to excavate my house-closing papers, since that was the last time I needed legal advice. Hint: try not to need an attorney during the holidays. They're either skiing or in the Caymans. After a lot of phoning and referring I found somebody who could see me New Year's Eve.

Basically she charged me $325 an hour to tell me Markson could do what they threatened. Great. Well, I didn't have the files, which is basically what it said in that very expensive letter from my shark to theirs. Nor did I recall what happened to them, which I believe is lawyerese for, "I'm not going to tell you because it makes me look bad." If they wanted to be hard-assed about it, I suggested I could re-create them, given some time and access to Olivia's old records. I was sure we could come to some civilized understanding, which also meant I declined my attorney's offer to be put on retainer. That basically meant I was supposed to give her $2,500, just to hold in case I *might* need her services. Do I give my doctor extra money *in case* I have a heart attack? No. I figured I could hold my money as well as she could. Besides, I wasn't looking to buy the company. Just get their attention so we could be done with each other.

On the way home I picked up a plate of takeout barbecue, with cornbread and black-eyed peas on the side for luck. The clerk gave me a noisemaker too—like I looked like I wanted to party. I never cared much for the whole lose-your-mind, party-like-it's-1999 thing anyway. It was amateurs' night out. So I fluffed the sofa cushions and stared at the TV, doing my own personal countdown until it was time for the ball drop. Given my state of mind, I would like to have seen the ball explode into a million pieces, but I at least wanted to see the year out to make sure it was over. I was counting on a clean slate, a new page to start the next phase of my life.

Around eleven-thirty the phone rang. I let the machine answer, but I heard Mom's voice. I was kind of surprised—thought Daddy would have found someplace for them to shake a tailfeather, as he would say—so I decided to pick up. "The perfect way to end my year. Talking to my mother," I said with all the energy left in my tank. She said, "I just wanted you to know I'm leaving your father."

4

Ignorance is not bliss.

It was 1:07 a.m. by the clock on the microwave, and my lang syne was already old by the time I convinced Mom not to take the bag she had packed and get a cab to the Ocean City railroad station. What train she was planning to catch in the middle of New Year's Eve night, I don't know. And I didn't ask where she was heading because "your house" was not a good answer. I had enough happening in my life without plopping her in the middle to do play-by-play commentary—like she was really going someplace.

According to her, she could not live under the same roof with "that man," meaning my father, one minute longer. Now, I'm not saying they didn't have their share of arguments in forty-some years of marriage, but it was always more fussing than fighting. And if they ever came close to calling it quits, I wasn't in on it, so I admit I was having trouble taking Mom's announcement with the proper degree of seriousness—with any degree of serious-ness. When I asked where Dad was, she sucked her teeth and said, "At the clubhouse with all his new friends." I don't know. Seemed like a good spot for a party—no driving involved, plenty of room for dancing and a whole wall of windows that looked out on the water. People pay good money to spend their vacation in places like that. All they had to do was go down the block, except I made the mistake of asking if they had been out together. I mean, Dad likes to party as much as the next guy, and he's not usually the one wearing the lampshade, but we all have our moments—no need to remind me. Maybe he was having one of those high-voltage nights and she got sick of him and came home. Well, she about came through the phone telling me about *those* people he had taken up with. "All up in your face grinin' and tryin' to act like they known you forever." Huh? So she was mad because the residents of The Seasons at Shoreline were too friendly? This would only make sense to my mother, and you can see where Amber gets her flair for the dramatic. After an hour's worth of trying to talk her into rolling up her hair and going to bed, I realized the only way to tame the hot in her tamale was to pay an impromptu visit. Definitely not on my to-do list, but I promised I'd arrive before the Rose Parade was over if she would just stay put. "Suit yourself," she kind of sniffed and informed me she would be sleeping in the guest bedroom, which by the way hadn't had any guests since I helped them move in, not that she was keeping track or anything.

Happy New Year to me. I dumped the rest of the black-eyed peas and cornbread—clearly they had not brought me luck. Then tossed some clothes in a tote bag. I figured I could smooth things out and be back on the road before I needed the third pair of panties, because I still had to straighten out my little misunderstanding with Markson and get myself reemployed, which was way more than a resolution.

I caught about ten winks and headed out before dawn. By the time I hit Route 1 I had convinced myself this trip was a good idea. I mean, what made me think I could go the whole holiday season without seeing my parents, at least long enough to eat some sweet-potato pie and unwrap my annual slippers? Mom must have thought I wore them hiking—something I would never do even in the proper footwear—because every season she bought me new ones. After I got married I informed her I did not need any more fuzzy bunny scuffs, but I would appreciate something slinky, maybe with marabou feathers. Talk about somebody with their lips poked out, but she came through. They were white, with come-catch-me heels, kind of like the pair I found under my parents' bed when I was ten and nosing around where I didn't belong. It wasn't until I was grown I realized that meant she didn't always sleep in flannel nightgowns—which I didn't exactly need to know. Anyway, I still have those slippers. Sad to say, these days they don't get as much use as the scuffs, so I was about due for another pair.

Thought about lots of old stuff like that while I drove, singing with Luther on the CD player. In the middle of "A House Is Not a Home" it came to me that Daddy was the one who said they'd be alright on their own for the holidays. I don't remember Mom speaking on the subject, which I guess was her silent protest—unusual tactic for her. And since Amber wasn't around, it was kind of like making them go family-free cold turkey.

It felt strange taking the turnpike south to see them. The car practically knew the way home to Brooklyn, but now that was somebody else's address. Well, they had earned a sweet retirement. Lord knows, they clipped enough coupons, scrimped, saved and made do long enough building their nest egg—which is what I thought I was doing at Markson. But I had to stuff that subject in the glove compartment until I got back.

By the time I was belting out "Any Love" I was squarely focused on the fact that Gerald hadn't called with our regular phone signal—two rings, hang up and two rings again—just a way to say he was thinking about me. On New Year's he usually called in a quiet moment, after the midnight madness, so I decided maybe I didn't hear the click while I was on the phone with Mom. Anyway, when "Don't Want to Be a Fool" came on, I switched to Teddy and a little "Love TKO." Then we were into "Bad Luck," and I could see Daddy and my uncle acting like they were the Blue Notes singing backup at a backyard cookout. Mom shook her head and smirked, but I could tell she was having a good time, which isn't always easy.

When I drove up to the brick-and-wrought-iron archway with the brass plaque announcing I was indeed at The Seasons at Shoreline, I was thinking about crab cakes and where to take my parents for lunch, since I was sure everybody'd had a good night's sleep and was back in their right minds. Somehow I'd forgotten I had to stop at the guard house before entering the complex. I have to say the place was pretty grand—not Beverly Hills grand, but a world away from Ralph Avenue. I had to tell the guard whom I was visiting, then she activated the camera hidden in the bushes before the gate slid open—very high tech. She asked if I knew how to find the address. "Of course," I said. How could I not know how to find my parents' house? Right.

The trees and shrubs along Shoreline Boulevard looked like they had been planted longer than the year since sections one and two opened. I mean, I live in a nice neighborhood. And mine was a planned community too. It was just planned around

1968. Nothing about this place screamed old folks' home, and I thought, *Wow, good for them,* while I was trying not to think, *Will I ever be able to retire?* Those thoughts were supposed to stay in the glove compartment. My immediate problem was that sections three and four had been completed since I'd moved them down in August, and nothing looked familiar.

I eased into a cul-de-sac called Dolphin's Way with a Chesapeake on the corner—that was the two-story shingled salt box, but it wasn't the right street. That led me to another circle, past an Annapolis, the duplex brick-front town house. I had been through all the models with them—Tidewater, Edgewater, Beacon Hill . . . They settled on the Dorchester, a center-hall ranch. Mom had no interest in stairs, and Dad loved the big bay window and columns out front. It was larger than the house I grew up in, and I remember thinking their stuff looked old and small when we got it inside.

Anyway, I was on my fourth trip past Sandy Lane, Sea Shell Court, Shark Tooth Drive—names that sounded like you were on vacation, which I guess is what retirement communities are about. Life's a beach. I still couldn't find their house and that made me aggravated, and I had to pee, and I thought about heading back to the guard house, but I didn't leave the bread crumbs so I wasn't sure I could find that either. I veered left at the fork by the gazebo in front of the pond, and there was Terrapin Way, their little corner of coastal heaven. Daddy's old Camry sat in the driveway. And I do mean old. My father did not believe in new cars—always said, "They charge too much for that new-car smell and I never did like it." Not me. I have never been interested in anybody else's mileage. Anyway, I pulled in behind him. Before I got to the walkway he swung open the door, reading glasses parked, as usual, in the middle of his forehead. I gave him a big hug and he kissed me on both cheeks and the tip of my nose, like when I was little, and said, "What a surprise."

I said, "Mom didn't tell you?"

He paused a second and said, "She's not telling me much these days."

Uh-oh. He nodded down the hall, "She's closed up in there." That's when I saw her tan suitcase outside the guest room door. Mom was taking this charade a little far. I wanted to say, "OK. You guys can stop. I get the message." But Daddy looked sad and mad and through with the whole thing. "She doesn't like nothin', won't do nothin'. Can't even get her to help me unpack. I'd do it myself if she'd tell me where she wants things. I don't know what's wrong." And for the first time in my life I believe he didn't. "Maybe she'll talk to you." That didn't sound good. He went back in the den.

That's when I noticed all the boxes stacked in the living room, exactly where I left them months ago. The furniture still sat where the movers put it down. Now, when I was growing up my mother would mop the kitchen floor at midnight because she couldn't sleep if it was dirty, and heaven help you if you left a wet ring on the coffee table. How could she have been walking around with this mess in her house? And nobody said diddley to me? I admit I'd been preoccupied, but still . . . When they first moved in I had lined shelves, put away pots and kitchen crap, assembled beds, hung curtains. Mom said she could handle the rest, but nothing had been handled, and now the beat-up A&S boxes with the Christmas balls sat on the floor next to a naked pine tree, obviously Daddy's attempt to encourage holiday cheer. I got that choked-up pull in my throat, because all of a sudden this was serious and it just couldn't be.

I didn't even stop for the bathroom, headed straight for the guest room and knocked. No answer. "Mom?" She finally said, "Come on in." She was sitting on the side of the bed, dressed in a gray pantsuit, hands folded in her lap. Her purse sat on a box marked "Pictures." I was expecting her to look different since she was acting so strange, but she didn't. Maybe wound a little tighter. "I thought it was *him*," she said. *Him*? She'd called him Daddy, Leon, your father, but never *him*, like he was the enemy.

I scooted up close to her on the bed. It was like trying to cozy up to a brick wall. Based on the neat stack of old *TV Guide*s on the bedside table and the trash can half full of tissues, catalogs and an empty jar of hair grease, I knew last night wasn't the first she had spent in this room, but I decided it was normal for older people. They get tired of each other's tossing and turning, funky farts and morning breath, right? I know I would. When I asked what's up with the boxes, she started in. "He can throw 'em in the bay for all I care 'cause I'm not stayin' here." She informed me her friend Dolores down the block from their old house had an extra room and she was going to rent it. As far as I remembered, she and Dolores weren't even that tight. When I tried to find out what was the matter, she said she didn't remember having to answer to me. Either I could take her to the train or she'd call a cab like she'd said last night.

It was time for a distraction, so I said, "How about some lunch?"

"I'm not hungry." She sounded like a five-year-old before nap time.

"Well, I am, and I need you to show me how to get out of this complex and find a restaurant." I figured I'd fight five with five.

"Ask your father. He's always in the street. Acts like he don't know when to come home."

Alrighty then. I have never worked so hard to get somebody to let me buy them a meal, but finally she huffed and sucked her teeth and put on her coat while I ran to relieve my bladder. And to call Amber's cell and tell her where I was. She and J.J. had come back from Texas in time for a party at Ron's Pocono chalet. So he skied too. Did the man do anything slow? I decided to drop that line of questioning. Anyway, I made up some excuse why her grandparents couldn't come to the phone—no point starting Amber's year under a cloud too. I could handle this. And with the proper training I could handle a cage full of lions with a whip and a chair, but I didn't take that course.

Gerald had left a message on my answering machine, and hearing his voice made me really want to talk to him. Not that he could do anything. I just wanted to tell somebody what was going on because it was getting a little heavy to carry by myself. Well, I put that thought right back in my hip pocket because truthfully, I was just glad he was able to squeeze out a minute to let me know I was on his mind. I knew he'd be in the middle of his annual Hair of the Dog Party. I've heard it was quite the happening, even saw pictures once. He was smart enough to take out the ones of his wife, but still there were a whole lot of folks I didn't know, in a house I'd never been to. We skipped the Polaroids after that, although every now and then I'd fantasize about throwing the party with him—at my house. I had better taste in furniture.

At lunch I jabbered about nothing in particular—especially not about having to look for a J-O-B. Mom picked at her fried shrimp, but at least she wasn't looking at the train schedule.

Then she put down her fork, leaned over to me and whispered, "Your father is messin' around with somebody."

I almost choked on the coleslaw. Not my dad. He was a hardworking family man who brought home his pay, kept his promises, was always there when we needed him . . . Sounded a lot like Gerald, which didn't make me feel too good. Frankly, I had never spent a whole lot of time thinking about my situation from the wife side, and I didn't want to be having those thoughts right at that moment, so I pressed Mom for details. Had she seen them together? Did he smell like the wrong perfume? Did Mom get her number from his cell phone? I was sure that wasn't it. She didn't want one. Didn't know how to turn one on, and when Dad handed her his, she would touch it like it had cooties. My mother didn't offer any tangible proof. All she would say was, "I just know." Then she folded back up into her pinched silence.

I couldn't believe this was happening now. I mean, they weren't exactly out to pasture, but they were supposed to be contented. I dropped Mom off at the house, told Dad I needed him to ride with me to find a gas station. While we rounded the drives, past the neat new homes in this pensioner's paradise, I wondered where the hussy lived. Or was she tucked away in some other enclave—a Crown Victoria driving vixen looking for a playmate? I pulled into the empty parking lot of a closed dental office, still not sure how to put this. I was not in the habit of confronting my father about anything, much less his extramarital sex life. I gripped the wheel, looked straight ahead. "Mom says you're cheating on her."

"Oh, for cryin' out loud! Is that what she thinks?"

Music to my ears. Now, I realize people lie about things like that—I had not exactly been a pillar of truth with my own daughter when it came to my . . . situation. But my father can't lie worth dirt. Not to me—never could, not about the tooth fairy, or the Easter bunny, and when I asked if he was happy I had gotten married, he said, "If you're still happy in a few years, I will be too." Guess he and Mom knew a little something about the long run. And truth is, I figured I'd be like them when I got married, but I think that brand of love has been in short supply since the '50s. Or maybe I hadn't figured out where to look for it.

When we got back to the house, Daddy barged in the guest room and started in. "I've been with you all these years, Bernice. Why in hell would I wait 'til I went bald and got arthritis in my knees to go tippin'?"

"'cause you got old and foolish—wearin' plaid pants and callin' yourself playin' golf." Mom sucked her teeth, got up and walked past him, just as nice as you please, but he followed. They fussed about where he went and what he did when he got there. Then he said she had gotten boring and stuck in her ways. It was like watching two old opponents in the ring, and I didn't want either one to win or to lose. Eventually they retreated to their neutral corners, but at least they were fussing, which was better than the silent treatment. And that evening Mom thawed some of those homemade TV dinners she fixes and keeps in the freezer. The only conversation at the table was when Daddy asked the blessing and we both said, "Amen." But we ate together, and slept separately, me on the old squeaky sofa bed, since the guest room was still occupied.

Next morning I started tackling boxes. I liked having something to do—sorting, folding, arranging, making lists of what they needed. I'm good at getting things organized. Soon Mom came in to supervise, still not saying she was planning to stay.

They got into it again right before lunch. Dad had taken to going to the clubhouse dining room in the afternoon and Mom went off—didn't know why he, all of a sudden, had to go out for lunch when she'd been fixing it for him all the years they'd been together. Then there was the real sore point: he played bridge after lunch. Seemed Dad had become a regular card sharp. When he said, "Why don't you come play with me?" she told him he already had a partner, and besides she played bid whist, then went back in her room and slammed the door. Bingo. So in my role as Dr. Tee, PhD of daughterly reason, I went to investigate.

Yes, he did indeed have a partner, a widow from Cincinnati named Marge, who was a decent bridge player, with very low hussy potential. Homewrecking hussies do not wear argyle sweater vests and black lace-ups with white anklets. I'm sure she was only interested in my father's cards, so I had to hip Daddy to the fact his wife was jealous. "Of Marge?" He looked surprised, but he got a little sparkle in his eye too, like he was proud Mom still got jealous over him. That evening he came walking in with his and hers track suits, with their names embroidered on the jacket. Not my idea of romantic, but Mom perked up some. Guess nothing says love like matching, monogrammed clothes.

There were enough activities at Shoreline to keep you busy from morning 'til night, and my mother had not participated in any of them, so next day I dragged her to an aerobics class. I was more winded than some of the retirees, which is pitiful, but during cool-down several people said they hoped to see Mom next time. Then, before she could object, I drove to the clubhouse for lunch. She was about to catch an attitude when Daddy pulled up next to us, looking so happy to see her. So she ate, and talked to people, even Marge. Mom admitted the food wasn't half bad, which from her was a rave, and she stayed afterwards to watch Dad play bridge. I took the opportunity to slip away. Mr. Ferguson, a former plumber from Indianapolis, was a little too anxious to know about my plans for the evening, and I just wasn't ready to date a man with Geritol on his breath.

After a few days I knew things were better. They both started asking me when I had to get back to work. I said not to worry, I had some time. Oh yeah, I had *lots* of that. But as long as I was playing matchmaker and social director, my own clock wasn't ticking so loud. And it was kind of nice having Mom ask me, "What are we gonna do today?" while she poured me coffee. So we explored the malls—Mom needed new duds, and I was tired of washing out those same panties. I picked up a few other items too—on sale. Had to keep up my image for Mr. Ferguson. We even found a beauty shop where she got an acceptable relaxer, which she swore was impossible beyond New York City, and a haircut that was more flattering than anything she had worn in years. And while I was under the dryer it occurred to me that part of my mother's problem was that she didn't drive. In the city Mom had buses, subways, gypsy cabs and my father. Now she was down to the Leon Express, and I know she didn't want to be in his pocket all the time.

Ever try teaching your mother to drive? Don't. She challenged everything I said, like she knew reverse from park. Pretty soon I remembered that it didn't work for Amber and me either, which may say something about the patience level of the teacher. In any case, I found a little driving school that specialized in novice seniors and signed her up. Dad was delighted—started surfing the classifieds to get Mom a little putt-putt. Another problem solved.

I knew they'd be alright after the night they went out on a date. Mom got all dolled. She'd even gotten the hang of her new hairdo after I showed her how to set it. They put on their Barbie and Ken track suits and went for dinner and a movie. And when they got back they were holding hands, and Mom said I could take the guest room since my back must be killing me—like my aching bones had anything to do with their little reunion. But it meant my mission was accomplished, which should have meant I took my butt home. Which I planned to do the next day. And the day after that. I don't know—it was nice being in a place where there was no rush hour, and around people who were not stressing about why they didn't get a promotion or what the new boss wanted. And the place was so beautiful. We did some furniture shopping, picked out a closet system and arranged to have it installed. I even went to the driving range with my father and Mr. Ferguson—Andy—who was very sweet and mostly harmless. He just liked to flirt—guess it keeps you young, at least at heart.

Except while I was teeing off, Amber was blowing my cover. This time it was Mom who flung open the door before the car stopped rolling. Those arms laced across her chest meant somebody was in trouble and I thought, *What did Daddy do now?* except she was after me. "When were you going to tell us you got fired?" Oops. Amber told me later that she figured since I'd been with them so long I must have said something. At the time I was too PO'd to appreciate her logic and before my head caught up with my mouth I said some pretty hot things about minding her own business. But I'm ahead of myself. First, I had to deal with my parents. Testifying before Congress would be easier. At least they let you take the fifth.

Now you have to understand, my parents were not unemployed for ten minutes in their adult lives, so this was the equiv-alent of being struck by lightning—twice. I had to backpedal my way through the whole sorry saga, while talking them down from the edge of hysteria. Mom kept moaning about how they shouldn't have sold the house because then I could move in with them. I assured her I didn't need to move anywhere and frankly I'd sooner pitch a tent in the woods than move in with my parents, and you know how I feel about indoor plumbing. Dad kept asking if I needed money. That took me straight back to the kitchen table and him telling me I was too old for an allowance, which is how I came to work for Olivia in the first place. Some days life paints a funny picture when you connect all the dots. Anyway, I promised them I'd be just fine, better than ever, but it was clear this little bubble had burst, and it was time to rejoin my regularly scheduled life.

So eleven days into January I packed my very spiffy new purple velour slippers, my after-holiday markdown wardrobe acquisitions and a couple of Mom's frozen dinner specials, be-cause you have to leave with a care package, and I headed due north. Before I left Terrapin I glanced in the rearview mirror at Bernice and Leon, still standing in the driveway. Daddy's arm draped over her shoulder, and Mom leaned, ever so slightly, into his side. Did they always fit together like they were made for each other, or did that happen over time, like erosion? I don't know, but it was a nice picture to drive home on—Humpty and Dumpty back together again, no king's men required, although I like to think I had a hand in it. Except you and I both know I should have played my hand faster and taken my behind home, but at the time you wouldn't have known that either. We're all geniuses when it comes to playing the cards other people are dealt.

Truth is, I was ready to go home. OK, I wasn't exactly looking forward to applying for unemployment and looking for a job—that's the understatement of the year. And I wasn't thrilled about the pile of mail that would be waiting on my front-hall floor, unless it included my first "separation" payment from Markson—sounded a little like alimony, and I deserved it. I was faithful in that relationship and they abandoned me. Anyway, I missed my house, my bed, and despite the fact that we talked on the phone half a dozen times and I probably would have only seen him twice anyway, I even missed Gerald. I don't mean *even* Gerald, but I missed him too.

At another time I would have said I missed going to work, missed Olivia. In the early years we were a little mismatched family in that loft. She would close the office between the holidays and on the first morning back we were like kids, catching each other up on our vacations. Olivia started the tradition of everybody bringing in a dessert they wanted to get out of the house before the I'm-gonna-get-skinny-this-year calorie counting started—cookies, cakes, rugelach, strudel. It was the last hurrah, and we would fly around the office on a nine-to-five sugar high, followed the next day by salad and the latest "lite" food. That office family mattered a lot to Olivia, just the way her real family did. Which is what made it so hard to watch Hillary treat her mother like she didn't matter. And the rest of us obviously weren't worth a tallyho either.

Anyway, thinking of Hillary reminded me that my last conversation with Amber was pretty shabby. It's hard to admit your child makes more sense than you do sometimes, but it happens, and she was right. I should have 'fessed up about the job. And now I really missed her most of all.

Talk about withdrawals—we were a team most of my life,

and I still couldn't get over how quiet my house was since she moved. I know it used to make me crazy when she put the empty milk carton back in the refrigerator or borrowed my favorite earrings and accidentally lost one. I mean, I was really happy for her. I truly believe she and J.J. love each other, for the long run, like my parents. Then, while I was concentrating on keeping the car between the lines, I could see my folks in my mind's eye, holding each other, waving, getting smaller as I drove away. It made me feel full—my heart, my head, my stomach—like I might explode. But I felt empty too, like there'd be nothing to spill out if I did burst wide open. That's when the musical selection cycled around to "I'm So Tired of Being Alone." I stabbed the radio button so hard, I broke a fingernail.

And without intending to, I found myself pulling into Amber and J.J.'s parking lot. I wasn't planning to stay long. Just time enough to say I'm sorry, get a hug, maybe share some frozen dinners if they hadn't cooked yet. Yes, I should have called, but I was still getting the hang of manners for mothers-in-law. I did ring the buzzer instead of using my key—at least upstairs. A man carrying a bowling bag held the downstairs door. If I had been a puppy I would have been wagging my tail when I heard footsteps in their apartment—I'll admit, I was that excited to see Amber. Then the door opened—

—and there was Ron, wearing blue coveralls that looked custom tailored and holding a screwdriver—Phillips-head, not vodka and orange juice. I was thinking, *What the hell are you doing here?*, but I got this simple grin on my face and said, "What a surprise," to quote my father. Clearly, I was tired and having some kind of brain-circuitry overload.

"Right on time. I got a shelf that needs holding. Come on in." I swear, his smile was as big as mine, which meant what?

Neither one of us had good sense? Well, I wasn't expecting any from him, but I should have known enough to run the other way. Instead I let him usher me inside, but when his hand touched my back I all of a sudden felt warm and gooey, like grilled cheese. Then I was remembering how it felt dancing in his arms. Well, I could not be mooning over this man like a damn teenager. Especially since for the first time since we woke up in the same bed, we were all alone. So I sat in a straight-backed chair on the other side of the room and crossed my ankles—very proper.

It seemed Baby Son-in-Law was putting in some extra hours, Amber was at the dentist, and I had come for a hug from my daughter, not to hold anything of Ron's. Except it was really the newlywed's entertainment center he was assembling. J.J. was great with a hard drive, or a motherboard, whatever that is, but useless with old-school tools. The unit looked at least half built—too traditional for my taste, but it wasn't my house. Then I noticed there were knobs and wingnuts all over the coffee table, right next to the directions, still sealed in their plastic sleeve, so I said, "Are you planning to read the instructions?"

He said, "When I come across something I don't know how to do."

The arrogance—but truth is, it looked pretty sturdy. We chatted about his skiing and my parents. I left unemployment off the discussion topics. Ron had a really nice voice—very soothing, like a late-night DJ, but not the ones who try too hard to sound studly. It made me want to listen more than talk, if you can believe that. Anyway, after a while I went to the kitchen to find us some snacks and when I came back all the doors, shelves and wingnuts were accounted for, but he was flipping through the instruction booklet.

"All of a sudden you don't know how to do something?"

"Yeah. How to get you to let me take you to dinner."

Guess I walked straight into that. I mean, don't get me wrong. The man was very appealing, but my life was complicated enough and Gerald and I were, I don't know—established? I was going to say like an old married couple, but that was definitely not true. Anyway, we understood each other. Our little thing worked for both of us. This just wasn't the time to be sampling new flavors.

So I was in the middle of my very sensible explanation of why it would be too complicated for us to go out. That's when my daughter walked in, still lazy-lipped from the Novocain.

And Ron cut to the chase. "Would you have any objections if I took your mother out to dinner sometime?"

Amber smiled sideways. "Num b'at d'all," she said, which I knew meant "None at all," which blew my cover yet again. Would she have been so quick to second that emotion if she knew how I'd spent her wedding night? I didn't know, and I wasn't about to find out, but I knew it was time to collect my hug, say my piece and leave.

I led my rubber-lipped baby to the kitchen where she accepted my apology without rubbing it in—probably because it's hard to gloat when your mouth doesn't work. Then Amber announced, as best as she could, that she and J.J. were starting to look at houses. I remember my little girl playing house and now she was talking about buying one. At least she'd have a place to put her own Barbies, bikes and other remnants from past phases that had taken up residence in my basement.

Ron walked me to my car, said he'd be in touch. I didn't doubt it. He stood on the walkway, waiting until I drove off. I guess to show me he was a gentleman. It was like I could feel him watching me and I fumbled with my keys, the seat belt, the gearshift, the lights—like I had never driven before, worse than my mother the first time she sat behind the wheel, which made no sense. But finally I managed to drive off without running into anything.

Which meant there was absolutely nothing left for me to do but go home.

I saw the letter from the Markson attorney as soon as I walked in the door, like it was glowing red or radioactive or something. I picked up everything around it. Tossed out old sale circulars and filed my bills in the rack on my desk in the den, where I keep them organized according to due date; writing checks would accompany my morning coffee, since I needed to catch up with the front of the month. No big deal if they were a little late—I always paid on time. I had unpacked my suitcase, watered my plants and changed into my nightgown before I sat down at the desk with my attorney mail.

Bottom line: they were giving me a week to produce the aforementioned corporate history. That ended three days before I got home, which I would have known if I had come home when I should have, or if I had forked over my lawyer's retainer. Let me tell you, ignorance is not bliss. It just means that when life slaps you upside your head you can say, "Where'd that come from?" and halfway believe yourself. Anyway, without said document I would be in default of my separation agreement and thus ineligible to receive any monies under the terms of the agreement. *What the . . .* They could not be telling me they weren't paying for my twenty-five years of service, minus the five they were too cheap to include. I went and got those glasses I forget to wear, just to make sure I read what I thought I did. I got real quiet. And I think for a moment my heart stopped. Then I could feel my pulse beating hard and slow in my neck, like war drums.

I must have read that letter a hundred times, and even though he didn't write it, I could smell Didier in every word. He had the office and the big title, but I did more for that company and Olivia than he could begin to understand, and all I was going to have to show for it was a measly check. Now he was taking that away. Yeah, I knew I shouldn't have shredded those index cards, but that was just an excuse to cheat me out of what I had coming.

Needless to say, I didn't do much sleeping. I laid in bed, steaming, thinking about how much I had done for Markson & Daughter and how unfair this was. By morning I was breathing fire and I was ready to burn somebody's office down. There was no point wasting money on legal representation. It didn't do jack the last time, so at 9:01 a.m. I called the Markson lawyer who was handling my case—a Ms. Benson, Bertrand, Bernard, something. I've got a mental block about the name because she was so cut-and-dried, mechanical, methodical that I might as well have been arguing with a computer.

Every word hurt when I said it, but I offered to re-create the history, which I had pretty much done all night in my head anyway. Ms. B, which could have stood for something else I wanted to call her, said that window of opportunity had closed. I wanted a window to shove her out of when she went on to inform me that the company had generously opted to forego further prosecution as long as I did not pursue the matter. Generously? So now they were doing me a big favor? We had nothing further to discuss, so I hung up before I said something very unprofessional, and I was not going to give her a lunatic story to tell over lunch.

So all ties had been officially cut, hacked, mutilated—we were done. Twenty-five years flushed, and right then it left a really bad smell. I could hardly think straight the rest of the day, but I made myself do normal stuff—run some laundry, change my bed, sit down and write checks. I don't know what made me madder: the fact I didn't have the money I was counting on or that after taxes it wasn't going to buy me much time anyway. But that was the past and I wasn't going to get anywhere looking backward. Maybe this was a blessing in disguise. Right. They say sometimes you have to burn the forest to save it. It works in the end, but first you have to go through hell.

5

. . . time stands still when you're running out of patience.

Next morning I was mad as hell—but it made me feel like I could lick the world. I got up early and put myself together like I was heading to work, because I think clearer when I'm dressed for success. And I'd be ready when I found out where to go file for . . . unemployment. Even at home by myself the word made me feel about two feet tall. I could hear Julie insisting, "They owe us," except it still felt like charity and I didn't want to need it. Not exactly need, but without that separation payment . . . Let's just say it's amazing how fast your money goes out when there's no in-come. But this was only a temporary setback. I wasn't going to need anywhere near the twenty-six weeks you're allowed.

So I rifled through the section of my closet where I kept the clothes with the tags still on—my security stash, because I like to be prepared for all occasions. I settled on the tweed suit I bought while I was shopping with my mother, because I wanted to look like the competent, capable employee I had always been. I must say, I'd have looked at me and been impressed. Then I tacked a new calendar to my bulletin board, sat at my desk, cleaned my glasses. Maybe after I was done I'd give Julie a call. She'd been wanting to get together for lunch. That would feel almost like the old days, and since she was in the same boat I was, I didn't have to pretend changing course wasn't pissing me off.

First surprise—there was no actual unemployment office to go to. I was all ready for battle, with my sword to cut through red tape and my BS deflector shield. I started grumbling when I found the Department of Labor in the phone book and they didn't list an address. Now they were going to make me climb some endless phone tree just to figure out where to go. Except the phone was it. Or I could go to their website—youlostyourjob.com or whatever the heck it was—like this was some damn game. But this was my life and I had played by the rules. Except the rules changed, and nobody told me 'til I struck out.

Anyway, I told you how I feel about computers—I no more had one in my house than I had a copier, a fax machine or a key to the ladies' room. And who in their right mind would type in all their confidential information and then press send? How was I supposed to know where that ended up or who could get it? So I stuck with the phone and pressed 1 to file a new claim.

Who actually makes up those application questions? *Are you presently ready, willing and able to work full-time?* No, I'm leaving for my bungalow in Tahiti, but can you forward the check? *Do you have more than 5 percent interest in any company for which you worked?* I should, but I don't and if I did, why the hell would I be bothering you? And do you know they have the nerve to ask if you want taxes withheld? You don't have a job, but they got to make sure you're right with the IRS.

Then, after I told them everything but my shoe size, I found out how much the check would be—didn't know whether to hit the floor or raise the roof. Yeah, it was the maximum, but *before taxes* it wasn't even a third of my salary. I made more than that twenty years ago. What was I supposed to do with it? Sure as hell not pay my bills. Clearly, they do not mean for you to be comfortable in any way, shape or form. That's probably why it's so easy to arrange direct deposit. So your mail carrier can't keep track of the pitiful little checks you're getting. As it was, he'd see my "Notice of Benefit Determination." I know he knows what's in those envelopes. If you think about it, who knows more about you than your mailman?

Anyway, I was never one to balance my checkbook to the penny or keep to a budget. Long as I stayed a step ahead of the minimum payment I was good to go. But now I had COBRA to worry about on top of my regular monthly nut, and the dread of adding all those numbers from all those "invoice enclosed" envelopes arranged neatly on my desk, and seeing how much I was in the minus column, propelled me toward my next challenge—the Help Wanted section. No postings on a bulletin board this time. I sorted through the newspapers my neighbor took in while I was away and found the Sunday classifieds. That's when it hit me: I didn't have the slightest idea what to look for. I suspected "assistant to company founder" was not a category.

I crossed out the New York listings right off the bat. I wasn't about to move back, and commuting is like a part-time job with no benefits. Then I checked out the big ads with logos and artwork—if they spent more on their ad, they could afford my salary. No itty bitty startups for me—been there—and I wasn't signing on for anybody's growing pains.

Some positions sounded glamorous, like interior designer. Or director of major gifts—that had a good ring until I realized it was convincing rich people to put your charity in their will. How do you ask somebody that? There were lots of health-care jobs. Mom always said there'd be a steady supply of patients. And I'm still not sure what a milieu supervisor does, but I decided to skip it. They only accepted faxed or emailed résumés, like two-thirds of the other ads, which became problems two and three. No fax. No email. Whatever happened to a stamp? Or an interview, in person? Guess that changed when Personnel became Human Resources. But at this point my number-one problem was no résumé. Never did go back and write one after Olivia said not to bother. Never needed it until now.

So I got a pen and a fresh pad—then stared at the blank page, trying to figure out how to describe my work history. After a while I wrote my name and address, the company name, number of years employed, my degree—all two years of it. That left a whole lot of space. I put down my job title: executive assistant. What did that mean? How was I supposed to describe what I did to help build Markson & Daughter from kitchen concoctions to fragrance empire? Typing, filing, phones, et cetera. Yep—did that from day one. Performed duties of a guinea pig, cheerleader, stock clerk, graphic artist, therapist, defender, advisor, peacekeeper, negotiator, project coordinator, mother hen, personal shopper, stenographer, event planner, marketing consultant, strategist, comedian, purchasing agent. By then there was smoke coming out of my ears because I shouldn't have to explain this to anybody. Except now I had to find somebody to pay me to do it again. And I didn't know what to say or how to organize it, and the longer I sat there the more it felt like my nose was being rubbed in something I didn't do. So I took off on a field trip to the bookstore for some how-to résumé help. Left a message on Julie's cell too. Suddenly, I understood why she was sucking down Chardonnay at our first lunch.

Clearly, this résumé writing was no simple task, and lots of other folks didn't know how to do it, because there was an overflowing section on the subject. Reference books, workbooks, ring binders and pocket guides, some complete with CD-ROM templates to give your résumé that custom touch. I never realized how much of a science there was to "packaging" yourself, because that's what they called it. Not cheap either. They mean for you to invest in your future. I found an armchair and thumbed through the stack I had collected, which didn't exactly make me feel better—sort of like the store brand in a premium world. But each guide promised to show me how to go from cut rate to first class.

I had narrowed it down to three when my phone rang. Julie said she'd meet me in the cosmetics department at Nordstrom's—as good a place as any. And after weighing the options, I bought all three books. They had different strong points and I was doing this once and for all.

First off, all that résumé research made me realize I needed a computer to compose it on—part of my marketing efforts, because Tee, Inc., had to be outstanding. Guess I could have used Amber and J.J.'s, but then I'd have had to deal with my daughter standing over my shoulder worrying me to death. Besides, the world was changing—correction: had changed—and it was time for me to get with the program. My Brother portable typewriter did not have changeable fonts or graphics. So I stopped in one of those computer megastores, just to look.

I liked the laptops right away—nice and neat. Yeah, they cost a little more, but if they did the same thing as those big machines, who needs the excess sprawl? Now I know Baby Son-in-Law would want me to shop around for six months, compare prices, wait for the sale, but I didn't have time for all that. And of course I got the color printer—with the copier, fax and scanner, a surge protector, cables . . .

Spending money I didn't exactly have sure took my appetite, so I wasn't real hungry when I got to Nordstrom's. Julie was in the cosmetics department all right. Behind the Markson counter, wearing the white smock with navy piping I helped Olivia pick because it looked so crisp and fresh. Julie broke into a big smile when she saw me. I was horrified. Working with the enemy? With *them*? First words out of my mouth were, "How could you?"

At lunch I barely touched my burger. Julie said she started as holiday help because she had been steady job hunting, nothing turned up, and she was going crazy. I was sure she hadn't invested in the proper tools. Anyway, I asked why she couldn't have worked in leather goods. Except she knew the Markson product line upside down and backward, so they hired her right away. Turns out she sold everything but the display counter, so they asked her to stay. And she actually looked happy. Said she never realized how much she liked working with the public. Right. I told her I was working on my self-marketing plan. Not sure yet if I was making over my professional profile or counting down thirty days to the career I craved, but this time I wasn't falling into the first job that crossed my path.

Julie was glad to see me looking good, sounding so positive. Just hearing her say it made me feel better. Then she told me how impressed she'd been when she came to work at Markson and heard how I started part-time as a college student and worked my way up. That was one of the nicest things said to me by somebody I wasn't related to, but at the moment all I could think was, *Up to what?* Then she was off and running, about how she was investigating courses in merchandising so she could advance in retailing or maybe open a store one day and . . . Her enthusiasm was exhausting, and frankly she was not about to sell me on the idea that getting fired was the best thing that happened to her. I think being around all those fragrances had made her dizzy.

I told her it wasn't necessary, but Julie insisted on treating me, since she was working. I told her next time would be on me. To celebrate my new job.

The rest of the afternoon I spent with manuals, USB cords and cartridges. And with Cablecast. As long as I was moving into the digital age I might as well get myself online too, so after a return visit to my new best friend, the salesman at the computer store, I allegedly had everything I needed. Problem was, I didn't know a USB port from a DVI connector, and if that wasn't bad enough, there was a stack of software I was supposed to load. And a wireless router so I could surf the web from any room in my house or from up on the roof, for that matter. Except this was all very different from that first computer I got for Olivia's loft and installed myself. And now you're supposed to put it all together by following these diagrams with arrows and six words of explanation in ten different languages, like that's going to tell you what to put where. I had some suggestions for where they could put things.

Fortunately, good old Gerald arrived just when I was ready to light a match to the whole setup. I meant to slip into something a little less corporate, but time stands still when you're running out of patience. Before I knew it, he was ringing my doorbell. And no, he didn't have a key. Did I have a key to his house? Although I must say, since shortly after Amber moved he had made himself quite at home—brought slippers, extra underwear, clothes to change into. I blinked and ended up with a drawer full of his stuff—and socks under my bed. It wasn't so bad, though. I kind of liked not going out all the time.

For years we had nowhere to be *but* out, at least two turnpike exits from either of our towns—the Ironbound in Newark, down the shore, only off-season, the city occasionally, but that made me nervous. Anybody might be in the city. Usually we'd end up in some out-of-the-way spot that had seen better days, which cut down on the potential for chance sightings. Now it was nice having him build a fire, snuggling on the couch or in my bed with the pretty sheets and the bedspread I wasn't afraid to touch because who knows what's on there. I mean, at this point it's not like we were swinging from the chandeliers. Through the years, Gerald went from salesman to sales manager at the dealership, and his profile went from lean and mean to where's-the-belt. But he could still hit the spot. I was past looking for gymnastics, or Prince Charming, because at this point the frogs had turned to toads and most of those were horny. It's just that back doors and sneaking around gets old. Sometimes you just want to settle in, read the paper, talk about what color to paint the den, not worry about what time it is— regular stuff, like folks do.

Anyway, Gerald showed up, and I'm not sure if he was happier to see me or my computer boxes. In any case, he took over the installation, which suited me fine. The bad news was I had to listen to his version of the history of the microprocessor, binary logic, tech stocks he wished he'd bought and every other thing he knew about computers. The good news is I learned to selectively ignore him years ago. As long as I nodded in the right spots and kept Scotch on his rocks, he was perfectly content. Except right after I ordered Chinese food and was slipping into velour lounging pajamas, the phone started ringing.

First it was Diane, one of the birthday-cruise crew, talking about "Wouldn't it be nice to have a presail soiree?" That meant wouldn't I like to plan one—that's how those things got done. Well, I wasn't about to tell her I had more pressing matters than party planning. We were friends and all, but I wasn't confiding anything I didn't want to hear repeated. Within minutes she'd have been calling people I didn't even know telling them I was out of work. So, I said I'd think about it. Which I would. After my first paycheck. There was lots of time before bon voyage.

Soon as I hung up, the phone rang again. I was sure it was Diane remembering something she meant to tell me, probably about somebody else, so I answered, "What'd you forget?"

And he said, "Thomasina?"

The inside of my ears started sweating when I heard my name—my whole name, in that voice. I mean, my head was spinning from the day, Gerald was laid out on his belly trying to reach the outlet behind the love seat, and I'm flutterated because Ron said my name over the phone. This made no sense. I don't know why, but I kept feeling like Gerald would be able to tell I was talking to another man, not that I didn't have every right to, especially since it was just J.J.'s godfather.

Then I remembered I hadn't said anything yet, so I eased as far away from Gerald as the cord would let me and I said, "Yes," like it was one of those people taking surveys who manage to call when you've got a mouthful of string beans. I knew I couldn't keep up the charade for long, so I made my answers short, which meant that when he said, "How about dinner next Saturday—say seven-thirty?" it was easier for me to answer, "That's sounds fine" than to explain why it wouldn't be a good idea. Or to ask why in the world he kept after me. Truthfully, there was younger, cuter talent out there—maybe not cuter, especially when I really got myself together. But I hadn't exactly been cooperative. I could not figure out why he kept on coming. Guess I'd have a chance to ask him, on our . . . get-together. I wasn't prepared to use the *D* word. Dates imply romance, and we weren't having any of that.

So I hung up, straightened out my face, freshened Gerald's drink and made myself pay attention to his lecture about spyware and firewalls. Great, the easier things get, the more I have to worry about. Anyway, before the General Tso's chicken and shrimp lo mein arrived I was hooked up. While we ate, I told Gerald about my day—except for the money part. We never discussed finances, although I wouldn't have minded if he slid a couple of bills my way when the delivery guy showed up, not to be petty. Soon I realized that the tuning-out thing works both ways. He had turned on the TV and entered the basketball zone. At least until after we ate. Then he nodded off on the sofa with his head in my lap. I was actually glad. I wasn't really in the mood for chit chat or even doing the do. My mind was on composing my résumé, what bills were due, how strange it was going to be working for somebody else . . .

Next thing I knew I was waking up to an infomercial about

making millions buying property with no money down. Maybe I should have listened. Anyway, I shot up like somebody on fire, which was usually enough to get Gerald rockin' and rollin', but sleepy head was slow to get it in gear. Guess none of us move as fast as we used to, but I certainly was not interested in his getting busted for breaking curfew, which was usually midnight. Beyond that it would take more than "It was Bruce's birthday . . ." or "Roger sold fifteen over projection . . ." to get him off the hook. So I got Gerald together, checked for makeup and sent him home—never my favorite part of the evening. I was always closest to admitting it wouldn't be bad not to wake up alone and wondering what he said to his wife when he got in their bed. But I had plenty to think about without dragging a dead horse into anybody's Spine Align Comfopedic.

So I threw myself into mounting my career campaign— sounded a lot like war. I realized later it was. I worked to assess my on-the-job strengths, analyze my skills, define my objectives—it felt a lot like I was back in the guidance counselor's office, and I wasn't sure I had any more idea what I wanted to be when I grew up than I did then. I did exercises to uncover my natural talents. Seems I'm detail oriented, but so's a brain surgeon, and I didn't see med school in my future.

You're supposed to arrange your work experience in chronological order, starting with the most recent. First, last and in between it was all the same, so I went to a chapter called "Rev Up Your One-Company Credentials." They make it sound like you're some kind of trifling, unambitious deadweight if you work for the same place more than two years. But to avoid looking like one, they suggest you break up your service by describing the growth in your responsibilities, using Dynamic Words—*was* or *did* will not do. Why see when you can observe? Only a wimp would suggest, when you can innovate, formulate and transform. Made me want to leap tall buildings in a single bound. Then there was the tricky question of salary history. To me, it was a no-brainer—I wanted people to know up front what I was worth. But all three of my guides suggested leaving out the specifics, so I followed their advice.

After I worked out what my résumé should say, I came to the typeface dilemma—did I want to be dependably serif or innovatively sans serif? The font should speak to the position. Now, really, what does that mean? But I worked at it—must have tried every one on the machine including different languages. The Cyrillic alphabet is very attractive as letters go, and frankly I wasn't sure it was any more confusing than whatever mumbo jumbo I had written to describe twenty-five years on the job in short, punchy sentences.

I must admit I was feeling very efficient, setting up files on my own computer, creating my own system, the way I did for Olivia. She would never have known where anything was without me—stop it. Anyway, I'd be at my desk by nine, dressed at least for casual Fridays because finding a job was my job. I was laying the foundation. In a week or so I had several printable and scannable versions of my résumé and I was trying to decide whether to tackle the text-only and email versions—because I found I needed four résumés, not just one. But it was time for a break, so I went in search of the perfect paper. That involved shopping, something else I'm good at. By the time I got home with my deckles and linens and laids, oh my, in a neutral array from ice-white to banker's gray, there was a dingy number-ten envelope waiting for me with the startling news that I would receive only ten weeks of unemployment. Ten?! Oh no. We were nipping this right in the bud. You let a mistake hang around, next thing you know it's gospel.

So I hit the phone, and I was not filing a complaint with some automated, humanoid programmed to say "please," "thank you" and "have a nice day" like it gave a rat's rump. Somebody was going to speak to me. I hit "0" until I got a living, breathing, person, Ms. Cavanaugh, which I knew because I took her name and her supervisor's and everybody else's who tried to tell me the twenty-six weeks of eligibility started from the date of unemployment, not from the date of filing. You mean I'd be penalized for being a conscientious citizen and not using taxpayer money until it was absolutely necessary? Yep. That's exactly what they meant.

You want to talk about upset? I was ready to march on Washington, but who was I going to tell? Not my family—they were worried enough already. Gerald would say something like, "You'll be alright, baby," which was either a vote of confidence or a prerecorded announcement. I was not ready to turn this into some kind of soap opera for my friends. *The Middle-aged and the Jobless? All My Bills?* I don't think so. And what could I expect from Julie except "I tried to tell you." So I kept my protest to myself.

Needless to say, as the weekend approached, I was not in a social frame of mind, so I tried concocting a halfway reasonable excuse to back out of my "appointment" with Ron. That's when I found out he had told J.J., who told Amber, who called to let me know she knew, sounding so excited you'd have thought she won the lottery. She asked where we were going, what I was planning to wear. She never asked what I was wearing when I went out with Gerald—she'd barely look at me. And I didn't push it. Nobody likes to see disapproval in her daughter's eyes, or hear disappointment in her voice, so it became easier just to go get it over with.

For wardrobe I went with basic black—slacks and a sweater, nothing fancy because I didn't want to look like I was trying. But I didn't want to seem like I didn't care either, so as a last-minute touch of pizzazz I draped a purple silk scarf over my shoulders. A glance in the hall mirror confirmed I looked perfect for a nondate with my daughter's husband's godfather. The one plus: for the first time in years, it didn't matter who I ran into.

Then I was out the door. None of that waiting on pins and needles for *him* to ring the doorbell, like a schoolgirl on a Saturday night. Of course, he offered to come get me—even sounded disappointed when I said I'd be coming from an appointment so it was easier for us to meet. Which was *technically* true—after we'd spoken I made a six o'clock at Ten & Ten for a change of polish. Just like I'd convinced myself that by not using the *D* word it was *technically* not one. I mean, it wasn't a date if I met Julie, or Amber and J.J. at a restaurant. Why was this any different? Except deep down I knew I was *technically* full of it.

Ron chose Fujiyama—I'd driven by the place a thousand times but never eaten there. I mean, I'm from New York. I grew up ordering egg foo yong and fried rice from the local greasy wok, then discovered Szechuan dishes in the '80s when we all did. As for Japanese cuisine—I may have had tempura once, but raw fish, soybeans and horseradish? Right up there with canned eel. A little exotic for me, and for Gerald ravioli was a walk on the wild side. He liked his beef big and well-done, his chicken roasted, fried or smothered in cheese, hold the curry and chipotle, and vegetables required lots of butter. Besides, the restaurant was in the forbidden zone—less than a mile from my house. Yes, I keep mentioning Gerald; he'd be present whether I liked it or not. And even though I told myself that going out with Ron was *theoretically* not cheating on Gerald, it was hard to shake the feeling it was wrong, which I understood was *theoretically* the basis for my relationship with Gerald. But there was something uncomplicated about Gerald and me. We were honestly dishonest. I liked it that way. I know it sounds pretty screwed up, but it wasn't if you really think about it. I didn't know what Ron was about. So between *theory* and *technicality,* I convinced myself Ron was just about dinner.

The only space in the lot was between two SUVs, and I squeezed in, trying not to feel overwhelmed—by the behemoths on either side, by my jobless, soon-to-be checkless state, by my shrinking bank account, by this evening. Did I look OK? What if he was late? Should I wait at the bar? Did they have bars in Japanese restaurants? What would I order? What would we talk about? The engine idled, burning gas I couldn't afford, so, after a final check of the mirror—yep, exactly the same as when I left home five minutes ago—I counted down: four, three, two . . . and launched myself into orbit.

The rock-and-roll beat hit me before I opened the door. Good. There would be no whispering sweet nothings. Ron, standing watch at the bar, flashed me a "come to Papa" grin soon as I walked in. Damn. He intercepted me in three giant steps, said, "Nice to see you—on purpose" and planted a welcome kiss on my cheek before hello got past my lips. Then I inhaled. I was almost toast. He said I looked great—one worry off the plate. Normally I'd have said, "So do you," because he did—gray slacks with a navy turtleneck that eased over his chest, hugged those biceps—stop. I was keeping this platonic, which is kind of hard after you've already slept with a man, even by accident. So I just smiled and said thanks, which proved I could still talk.

The hostess in her red kimono led us across a bridge over the indoor pond. Ron rested his hand on the center of my back and explained that the hibachi room offered a wider selection than the sushi bar—which I only half heard because I was trying to keep the tingle that shot up my spine from making me fall in the water.

Seating in the dining room was communal—eight guests and one chef to a table. Whew! Saved from a cozy corner table for two where I'd try to keep the conversation light while doing my best to convince Ron that his interest in me, though flattering, was misguided. That I appreciated it, really, but his efforts would be better directed toward some PYT who'd be happy for his attentions and to be his wife, then make him lovely babies that they could raise together and live happily ever after. Isn't that how it's supposed to go? Anyway, our side-by-side chairs between the party—and I do mean party—of four women who were on at least their second round of apple martinis and the couple who looked like they'd been married thirty-five years and run out of things to say didn't leave me much wiggle room. Ron thanked Erika, our hostess-san, and greeted Jason, the hibachi guy, who said, "Good to see you." Clearly, Ron was no stranger here. Then I was wondering who a man I didn't want to be out with in the first place had brought here to dinner the last time. Me, jealous? Is that stupid or what? It used to happen years ago, when Gerald would say something about his wife, a place they had been, a movie they had seen, and I would feel hot and prickly—upset because it wasn't me. Clearly, it was time for my handy dandy bud nippers, because this was not taking root.

Seats, menus, cocktails—no champagne this time. I was keeping my wits, and all my other stuff, firmly under control, so I ordered tea. Ron asked for the usual, which turned out to be sake—served chilled, the way he had it in Hokkaido. *Hokkaido?* He'd been to Japan? Before I could ask, Jason commenced our dining experience in a blur of flying knives, spatulas and flaming food. I remembered the Thanksgiving turkey-cue and Ron and J.J.'s charter membership in the Brotherhood of the Blaze, so a restaurant with fire at the table made perfect sense. I conveniently ignored the heat waves wafting up from the grill, just like I was ignoring the ones radiating from him. No need to fan the flames.

Jason entertained the tipsy quartet by flipping chunks of sauteed zucchini into their open mouths like they were seals at the zoo. My lips, on the other hand, were sealed. Ron leaned over and whispered, "The show is pretty tacky, but the food is actually good." Then he made a few suggestions, which I gladly accepted since I didn't know a sunomono from a gyoza, I couldn't see the menu, and I wasn't putting on my glasses. That spelled, in no uncertain terms, what I was going to spell out later—that he and I were chronologically challenged. Meaning Ron was too young for me—not that I was too old for him, but glasses, even cute ones, said the next word on our spelling test was AARP.

While our tablemates kept up the hibachi hijinks, Ron asked about my job hunt. Guess Amber filled him in on that little detail. I said it was fine. Period. What was I supposed to say—I was scared out of my mind? I wasn't admitting that to myself. Then he caught me fiddling with my scarf and told me how much he liked it—said purple was definitely my color. That's when I remembered my wedding outfit. Did he think I wore purple as some kind of "let's get it on" signal? Luckily our appetizers arrived before I threw myself on the grill. Cute little dumplings for me and raw fish for him. Shumai and sashimi. Ron unwrapped his chopsticks, saw me pick up my fork and said, "Let me show you how the natives do it." I was afraid he'd done that already, but then he was sliding his chair back so he could slip his arm around me, put his right hand around mine and balance the sticks in our hand with his left. Ah man, since when is eating a full-contact sport? Then he stroked that little valley between my thumb and forefinger, said that's where the bottom stick was supposed to rest, but it was like the fire from the hibachi passed through him directly up my arm, down into my chest, and I couldn't breathe. So I dropped the chopsticks—told him I was probably a hopeless case. His lips were right next to my ear and I could feel his breath when he said, "I seriously doubt that." Double damn. Now, I was too grown to be beside myself, over what? A nice smile and some cologne that probably had sex hormones in it or something. They do that now, you know. If you ask me, it took him a few seconds too long, but he finally moved his arm back where it belonged. The problem was, Ron made me feel like—like a girl—and I didn't care for it one bit. Last time that happened, I found myself coming out of city hall hitched to somebody else's dreams.

Fortunately, there was still Jason and his corny jokes as a cover—making the shrimp dance, shoveling rice, noodles and veggies onto plates. And I recovered enough to ask Ron about Japan. Yes, he had been there, as well as China, Turkey, Mali, Ghana, someplace called Burkina Faso, Argentina, Brazil and most of Europe. What kind of mechanic traveled the world like that? But there was quite a bit to learn about Ron.

He was a Jersey boy—his word, not mine—born and raised.

His father and J.J.'s were brothers and when he was thirteen, his dad, an auto mechanic, died. He latched on to his uncle, a newlywed with a brand-new baby boy. He got so attached to his little cousin, John Jerome, he passed up a top engineering program in Michigan and headed to college in Philadelphia because it was close to home. I never thought of auto mechanics in college. Shows what I know. Well, five years later, armed with a master's in automotive engineering from Drexel, he landed a hotshot job in Motown, hog heaven for a car guy, and this time he went.

In spite of my best efforts, I found myself leaning in, playing with the ends of my scarf, wanting to know what came next. Which meant I had to lean back when he held up some of his tako for me to taste. Not only was octopus not about to pass my lips, I had no intention of nibbling little tidbits from his chopsticks. I knew where that could lead. Anyway, he was supposed to be a star, rise up the ranks, maybe even head his own division one day and of course become a credit to his race. But on his way up the corporate ladder, Ron discovered he liked old cars better than new ones, and that he hated being a desk jockey. He was spending three out of four weekends visiting tracks and speedways—at first for work, then because he loved it. He asked if I knew how it felt to hang a curve at 150 mph. I said, "Do I look like I don't have good sense?" Thankfully, he didn't know me well enough to say yes.

So six years ago, he quit the executive suite, moved back to Jersey and used money from his 401(k) and savings to open First Class Custom Restoration, a shop that specialized in classic cars. And he started racing a 1970 Dodge Charger he'd rebuilt himself.

Quite a story, but it didn't feel like he was ego stroking. You know the people who say stuff like, "That reminds me of the time I had lunch with the Pope at the Vatican," with the sole purpose of making you feel like a loser. It wasn't that. Ron's stories were matter-of-fact, funny, interesting—kind of like him. And listening to Ron's escapades gave me a chance to do a little biographical math. I figured he was nine years younger than me, which I added to Gerald, minus the fact that Ron was family—sort of—and the equation did not compute, which confirmed my hypothesis: I needed to leave him alone.

By the time I had all this sorted out, my green-tea ice-cream had turned into pea-soupy slop, our fellow diners had gone, the hibachi had been scrubbed, and Ron was handing over his credit card. I grabbed my purse and offered to split the check. Not because I was ignoring my shaky finances and showboating. And I'm definitely not one of those women always scrambling to look equal—I'm still retro enough to like it when the man pays. But I was hoping my gesture might shift the balance of the Date Weight scale. Ron smiled, ignored me and paid the bill.

I got a frosty jolt when we went out to the parking lot—just what I needed to rev up since we were now at the moment I'd been prepping for since I agreed to go to dinner. But he beat me to the punch. More accurately, he took both my hands, before I even got my gloves on. Skin on skin was definitely not part of the plan. That shot enough volts through me to melt an iceberg. Then he said my name—I hate the way I get all tingly when he does that. It took a lot of focus to keep all that energy from traveling south. That's when he tells me he likes me. Yeah, I guess even Stevie Wonder could see that. And even though I knew he'd never mention our postwedding encounter, I still didn't want to hear whatever he was going to say next. So reaching for my trusty bud nippers, I told him I was sure he had plenty of young women calling his cell phone or whatever it is young people do these days—I emphasized the *young* part. Then I managed to shiver so it looked like taking my hands away to button my coat was necessary.

That's when he told me he knew how old I was—and it didn't matter. Guess I should have figured he'd done some homework, and that a man who likes driving 150 mph doesn't scare easy. Then he pulled my collar up around my neck, said that most of his life he'd known what he wanted, but it hadn't been easy for him to express it. That's how he stayed in a job he hated five years too long and in a relationship he knew was headed nowhere long before it crashed. Now he knew he wanted to get to know me. If I had been seven, I'd have put my fingers in my ears and made loud noises, because I did not want to hear this. So I did something equally mature—blurted out, "I'm seeing someone."

Ron rocked back like I slapped him. Then he shoved his hands in his pockets, said he didn't know. Of course not. Amber wouldn't tell it. I'm not even sure J.J. knew about Gerald. And I wasn't up for true confessions, so I looked down at my shoes, told him it was a long story. He got real quiet for a moment, then cleared his throat, said he was sorry to hear that. For a split second I thought, *Yeah, me too.* That's when I knew I had to stop thinking and get out of there. So I said I was sorry, I should have told him sooner, like an apology made me look less like a trampy, two-timing, middle-aged nymphomaniac, which by now he had to think 'cause it's how I was feeling. Then I thanked him for dinner. He said I should tell my guy how lucky he was. Right.

That's when it happened. Ron leaned over to kiss my cheek.

I turned my head just the teensiest bit. And his kiss landed on my neck, right below my ear. As soon as his lips touched my skin, and his breath warmed inside my collar, I was back in that hotel suite. And I remembered exactly how we ended up together, how he hugged me that night and I wouldn't let him go, how his hands felt caressing my back, how I was tired of holding myself together and I wanted to feel like I used to when I believed love would last forever . . .

That was quite enough remembering. The vibration started someplace so far away I couldn't have found it with a map, and before he could see me trembling, I willed my legs to get me out of there—instead of what they wanted to do.

I went straight to the computer when I got home—made myself finish the text-only version of my résumé, because that was something tangible. A reminder that this was not the time to lose my head over some foolishness. I let a man come between me and what was good for me once before—got a wonderful daughter, but not a BA. I was too grown for that BS now.

Next morning I got busy on my cover letter, since according to my manuals, if it's not catchy, the résumé gets dumped. So I worked on creating a uniquely expressive but concise way to say I'm here, your search is over. When I heard Amber's voice on the answering machine, I wouldn't pick up. I knew she had checked in with Ron and she was hot. She'd get over it. One day she might understand. In the meantime, I didn't want to hear it.

After two days of writing and deleting, all I had was Dear _____. Not that I'm opposed to tooting my own horn. Just couldn't find the balance between tuba and kazoo. And it didn't help that at the most inconvenient moments I'd get these flash-backs of Ron's lips brushing my neck. Then I'd be in the parking lot again, and I'd have to get up and water the plants, brush my teeth, pinch myself—anything to get my head back in the groove. Or was it a rut?

Anyway, I finally got all my materials together and buried myself in the help-wanted ads determined to find my dream job—excuse me, career opportunity. According to one of my books, jobs are about time clocks and hourly wages. My parents had jobs. They also had a pretty nice house by the bay to show for it. I, on the other hand, was a salaried professional. Right. So I skipped over the administrative assistant, receptionist and secretary positions—too junior. After lots of circling and crossing out, I narrowed my focus to five choices—all of them mail-ins. I still wasn't too keen on making a cyber corporate connection. And I wanted to see how sharp my layout looked on the dove gray paper I'd picked out. First thing Monday I went to the post office feeling quite pleased with myself. I figured the phone would start ringing by Wednesday, I'd have a few interviews, then decide which opening was the best fit.

So I was jazzed to get a call Tuesday morning to schedule an interview the next day. Even better, the company was conveniently located fifteen minutes from my house. Not exactly destiny, but it looked like my $75 worth of advice—plus equipment and supplies—had bought me instant results. This was going to be easier than I thought. Not that I was exactly worried—just anxious, not sure what to expect. See, that's what I get for letting Didier and those people make me doubt myself.

My hairdresser worked me in that afternoon. Got my nails done too, then spent the rest of the day researching my prospective employer online, another pointer I picked up in my reading. They manufactured generic drugs—something I certainly never thought about, but I never thought about Ginger

Almond Crème before I walked into Olivia's loft either. Oh, and while I was online, I couldn't stop myself from surfing for information about Markson, which was a mistake. An article about Didier's prowess in adding to their product line made me mad. Kept me up that night too. Or was that because I was rehearsing my interview answers like I'd be making my Broadway debut?

Well, it was show time alright, and I was dancing like a damn Rockette about how excited I was by this new opportunity. But the interview could not have gone better. Seemed my expertise and polish were exactly what they were looking for. I was brought in to meet the chief financial officer—a short, doughy man with an off-the-rack blue suit and twelve hairs arranged across the top of his head like some kind of musical instrument. That's who I'd be assisting. He complained how hard it was to find applicants with the proper degree of knowledge, strong work ethics and good sense. So true.

My last hurdle would be those references upon request. I was holding my breath, daring those Markson people to bad-mouth me. And I breathed a sigh of relief when I was offered the job. Guess I wasn't a big enough fish for Markson to fry, so at least they had thrown me back in the employment pool without ripping my fins off. Actually I wasn't a bit surprised when I got the offer, after all the fuss they made over me. It was the salary that threw me—$25,000 less than I'd been making. I told them, as tactfully as I could manage, that I couldn't possibly accept such a dramatic cut, instead of blurting out "Are you crazy?"—my first impulse. After much conferring, they coughed up another $5,000, but our negotiations ended there. Too bad. They seemed like decent people, but truthfully the offices were a little bland—too much laminated woodgrain and fake ficus. It occurred to me later that of course they were cheap—the whole business was based on it. But it wasn't a bad start. The enthusiastic welcome settled my nerves, gave me a shot of confidence. No need to grab the first thing that came my way. I'd sit tight, wait for the right offer—

—and wait . . .

6

. . . The Love Boat meets the Soul Train . . .

And the days got longer. So did the list of companies where I'd sent my résumé. Only one of those made the future any brighter. Next thing I knew, time sprang forward, coincidentally during the same week I received my final unemployment check, the one with the tactful reminder "YOUR BENEFITS HAVE EXPIRED." I, on the other hand, was scrambling not to fall back. I got seriously involved in my own game of bill-pay Sudoku, adding the amounts due and subtracting from my dwindling funds, moving the numbers around to keep my checkbook balanced and get the payments in before the due date. Did I say I hate puzzles?

By the time I saw that stupid news story they drag out twice a year—you know, the one about some big jewelry store and how long it takes to adjust all their timepieces to daylight savings time—even that looked like a career opportunity; maybe I had a future as a watch-winding technician. And there's nothing like having extra time on your hands to make you aware of how much of your mail contains payment envelopes. The rest of it—catalogs, tempting you to add to your outstanding balance.

In the meantime I became a pro at assuring my family I was fine, just being selective. Right. That would presume I had something to select. It's amazing how many ways companies can tell you to get lost. Some of them don't respond at all—like it's our little secret that you bothered to think you could work for us, and we won't tell if you don't. Then there are the ones who try to make it seem like you're overqualified. You feel good until you realize your butt is still planted on the sofa and nobody is sending you a check.

After a while Mom said something snappy about beggars not being choosers. I acted highly indignant, but she had a point. Fortunately, Amber took me at my word. She had grown up with me telling her things were fine when in reality I didn't have a pot and I wasn't sure how much longer I could keep from pissing, but she always bought my game face. Besides, she and J.J. were busy looking at houses. Baby Son-in-Law and my Amber with a lawn and a mortgage? That was as crazy as . . . as my being out of a job.

But I was trying to maintain my cool. I hit a speed bump when out of the blue my auto insurance switched me from a six-month policy to a full-year one. Now I had been with them ten years, and I sure as hell didn't ask them to change anything. When I called all they would say was that it was now their policy for accounts like mine. Nobody would say exactly what that meant either. But there I was with a whopping bill that was due in no more than two installments. It didn't fit neatly in any of my payment puzzle squares, and it wasn't exactly the best time for me to shop around for another company either. They would want to know where I worked, like that had anything to do with how I drive, which, by the way, is excellent—OK, a little fast, but slowpokes cause accidents.

I was still picking at the problem one evening while I was watching Gerald chow down on a plate of the shrimp and grits I cooked, when it dawned on me I could ask him for a loan to cover the insurance. I mean, it wasn't *that* much, and in all the time I'd known him I had never asked for fifty cents 'cause I was not interested in mixing a man and my money. But this was an extenuating circumstance. I could pay him back in installments and I figured he wouldn't charge me interest.

It took me until the apple pie à la mode to ask him, and do you know what he had the nerve to wipe his lips and say? "Don't you have any savings?" I wanted to dump his plate in his lap and put him out in his sock feet, which he could clearly see 'cause he tried to play it off, say he was kidding, but I was some hot. I didn't ask him about my savings. Yes, I had a little money in an IRA, and I do mean a little. I wasn't even *thinking* about retirement yet. I was too busy paying for living. I couldn't take money out without a penalty anyway. Besides, I wasn't asking him to *give* me anything. He hemmed and hawed and finally said he could come up with half of what I asked for. I had a good mind to refuse, except I needed it to keep me on course. Later on I'd find some way to make him feel as bad as he should, so he could make it up to me.

And I deliberately avoided all things having to do with Ron. If Amber or J.J. happened to mention something—like his trip to Sun Valley—well, OK. Me personally, I'm still trying to wrap my brain around a black man in Idaho skiing, but more power to him. But I did not mention his name. I thought it more than a few times. It was kinda like me throwing out all catalogs as soon as they came in the mail. No point in looking if I don't intend to shop. I couldn't afford to be tempted.

In my wildest dreams I could not imagine that spring would have officially arrived and that we'd be approaching Memorial Day, the unofficial beginning of summer, and I would still be jobless. I mean, I was managing. I cut back and only got my hair done once a month, which had my hairdresser looking at me funny, like I was cheating on her. Same with manicures. I thought about switching to the salon with the raggedy magazines in the waiting area and the bowls of dish detergent and water for you to soak your nails in. But if I wanted my fingertips in sudsy water, I woulda stopped using the dishwasher.

And of course the change of season also brought The Cruise. Yeah, it was already paid for, but the idea of a vacation from my layoff was ridiculous, even to me. I'd take out my document packet, check out the location of my cabin and "what if" over the cancellation dates, which were long gone, and what I coulda done with that money or, more accurately, without the charge on my card. The pitiful part is I couldn't even remember which one I had used, but now I could have used it for something else. At this point, it would cost me less to go than to stay home—at least my meals were paid for. When I mentioned it to Julie, I could see she was worried, but she tried to put a good face on it. She said maybe I'd meet some high-powered executive who would want to hire me on the spot. That's what I love about Julie—she can sincerely see the rainbow in a hurricane. But I wasn't about to mention my predicament to my traveling buddies. I mean, we had been together for years, but some things I knew better than to broadcast.

The bunch of us had met when our kids were little, at a school parents' day. We were the only ones of "us" there. I was the newest addition, the fifth, and apparently the one needed to officially form a "group" or at least break a tie. We were older, younger, married, exed, transplants, natives—all working women, except for Cecily, who was married to an anesthesiologist and at home with their five children, which definitely had longer hours than a job. About the only thing we had in common were kids in the fourth grade. The first time we got together was for coffee at my town house. Before the evening was over, someone—no one remembers who, which really means nobody will claim responsibility—said next time we should have wine. So there was a next time, and out came the Chardonnay, which was the birth of the Live Five.

Our kids grew, we moved our monthly gathering to one of those chain restaurants decorated in early attic and staffed by annoyingly cheerful teenagers. Eventually we advanced to finer dining in New Brunswick and Princeton. Over the years we arranged many outings both for the kids and for ourselves—we took in a matinee of *Black & Blue* on Broadway, lost our minds outlet shopping in Pennsylvania and indulged in a Happy Mother's Day to Us spa weekend in Connecticut—two weeks after Mother's Day of course, so we were home for our fancy bottles of too-sweet cologne and the breakfasts in bed that left our kitchens looking like the aftermath of an earthquake.

Lives, jobs, addresses and spouses changed. While our rug rats got older, we did our best to stay young. Then the kids were out of high school and off to colleges and jobs, and suddenly we were empty-nesters. Mostly through Diane's persistence—or was she just the nosiest one?—we never lost touch, even though our gatherings were no longer regularly scheduled. Recently graduations, weddings, grandbaby showers and a funeral brought us together more often, and our kids weren't the only ones changing. After twenty-two years of married indifference Joyce got divorced, meaning I finally had company. Marie and Diane were knocking on fifty, and Cecily was now a widow. It seemed like a good time to celebrate, so we signed up for the Live Five We Raised 'em Right, Let's Raise the Roof, All-Out Blowout.

Now, The Cruise was like the *Love Boat* meets the *Soul Train* on the next episode of *Lifestyles of the Negro and Middle Class*. A few thousand black folks from all over the country take to the high seas on the biggest, newest, poshest ship. It was seven days packed with big stars, big food and big foolishness, all for a good cause: college scholarships for students who need some help to achieve their dreams. We'd been itching to go for years, and guess who tracked down the particulars and made sure we were all paid up before the good cabins were gone? Wish I hadn't been so efficient, but I really wanted to go. I had given Amber the wedding she wanted and she was gone—off to her new life, not my responsibility anymore. This trip was supposed to be like the first sunrise over the finally carefree me. Ha! What I got instead was a total eclipse of my life, which was definitely not on my calendar.

And did I say it was big bucks? I could have cruised for a month for what that trip cost me, but it seemed like a great idea at the time.

For months I made myself seasick, rolling back and forth, half the time believing The Cruise was just what I needed to jump-start a new attitude. Then there were the days I felt like an imbecile for spending five thousand dollars on my solo superior deluxe ocean-view stateroom. It amounted to two-thirds of my monthly nut or my total ten-week unemployment allotment, depending on what I was feeling worse about. And that was just for the cruise. It didn't include my nonrefundable supersaver plane ticket. Definitely not my perspective when I booked that little adventure. Then there was what I'd spent hunting and gathering my resort wardrobe, because I know my people. Given half an opportunity we will put on a fashion show to rival the Ebony Fashion Fair. And with an entire week to showboat in front of a built-in audience? Puh-lease. I knew I had to be ready, called myself being thrifty by shopping last year's summer sales. Guess it depends on how you define savings.

I did manage to dodge throwing the presail soiree. Diane came up with the idea in the first place, so I played dumb to her not-so-subtle hints and let her be our B. Smith this time. Of course, that meant I had to act like her lame Bahama mamas, plastic leis—like we were headed for Maui, not Miami— and some truly forgettable pineapple and crab salad were the perfect way to launch us out to sea. While we were catching up and passing around the bean dip—not very tropical, even in a coconut shell—I had a moment when I thought about telling them what was really going on with me. Then Marie started in about her grandchildren, who were all certified geniuses. Joyce could hardly cash her real-estate commission checks fast enough. Even Cecily had sold the family homestead and moved to a high-rise with New York skyline views, moving on with life after Bill. So my sorry tale would be a downer, and we had never been the Bad News Bears. Years ago we didn't find out Marie's daughter was suspended from high school for smoking reefer in the bathroom until we saw it in the newspaper. So I talked about the newlyweds and their house hunt.

Joyce gave me her business card—like I didn't already have a deck of them.

We got a little tipsy, discussed how much we deserved this trip—hell, we *earned* it and we were out for some duty-free fun. In a moment of inebriated seriousness, we even took an oath that "What happens on the ship stays on the ship." And when you start thinking real life works like the commercial, you are heading for a test of your emergency broadcast system.

Let me tell you how clever I was. My travel mates were flying to Miami at crack of dawn the day we were sailing, which I though was insane. You know how flights are always late because two raindrops fell in Pittsburgh? Or canceled because the wing fell off and there's no spare plane closer than Hawaii? If you missed the boat, you'd really miss the boat and two days of the trip before you could catch up in St. Thomas—for the cost of another plane ticket. Way too dicey for me. The others could do what they wanted, but I was arriving the day before, spending a leisurely night at a hotel near the Port. Nothing fancy—it wasn't the hotel where the official, shake-your-bon bon bon voyage party would be, but I had too much money invested to chance blowing the whole trip. At the time I called this logic.

Well, you've heard about the best-laid plans. That May day started as gloomy as February and proceeded to get worse. By the time I arrived at Newark for my one o'clock flight, delay was the order of de-day. No worries. So what if I landed at six instead of four? I was feeling quite superior, but by five o'clock bands of thunderstorms had harnessed the East Coast, and I was still sitting at the gate watching rain slap the windows.

I was also hungry as a bear but determined not to waste money on overpriced airport food, so I feasted on a leftover bag of Gummi Worms I found at the bottom of my purse, and coffee. By the time Mother Nature and the FAA got their act together and we took off, I was wired, which was not helped by the two diet sodas I drank in flight, but at 11:17 p.m., when we touched down in a balmy seventy-degree Miami, I just knew I was ahead of the game. Until I got to baggage claim and watched all the people on my plane collect their stuff and leave me looking sorrowful as one beat-up duffel bag and a broken-off suitcase handle passed me on the conveyor belt for the umpteenth time. Then the thing shut off, meaning my bags were officially lost.

That's when I met Earl at the customer service office. His cornrows were as intricate as the path he was about to lead me down. After consulting my claim check and his computer, he typed something that seemed as long as the Old Testament, then informed me my bags were sent to Fort Lauderdale, like it was the most normal thing in the world.

Now, I had done what I was supposed to—attached my special luggage tags so I could drop my bags at the cruise office at the airport, just like it said in my documents—because unlike some people, I do read directions. And I tried to maintain my dignity, because I did not want to be one of those loud, indignant black women with her hands on her hips reading somebody in public. But then he said they would deliver my bags to the hotel tomorrow, like we were done and he could go back to doing whatever nothing I had interrupted. At that moment I didn't trust Earl to get a newspaper delivered, and there I was, wagging my finger, having a caffeine-and-sugar blowup. I demanded to speak with Earl's supervisor, Rocky, who couldn't do any more for me than Earl. He apologized for my inconvenience in that "I really don't care, but they make me say this" kind of way. And I was not satisfied, but what else could I do at one o'clock in the morning?

Worry.

I had the feeling I'd entered some kind of Murphy's Law marathon. If my luggage didn't show up, how was I going to get through a week without my brand-new seafaring wardrobe? My carry-on had overnight things, a fresh blouse to go with my black pants, all my hair stuff, even a bathing suit and coverup since I had this idea I could relax by the pool before I took the shuttle to the boat.

The closest I came to water was taking a shower the next morning. Oh, there would be lots of clothes I could buy. While you're out in the middle of the ocean, with no land in sight, there are plenty of shipboard shopping opportunities— at twice the price. I had two credit cards that weren't straining their outer limits. One I was planning to use, as sparingly as possible, for incidentals on the cruise. I'd have to pick up a couple of Live Five bar tabs and join in on at least one group spa session. But the other card I was saving for emergencies— real emergencies. Did a week with no clothes or shoes constitute an emergency? I could wash underwear by hand every night, and if I got a pair of white pants to supplement the black ones, how many tops would it take to make enough outfits to get through the week—not fashionably, just covered? Yet another puzzle.

When I didn't get an apologetic phone call from the airline announcing my luggage was on the way, and my calls to them produced nothing but aggravation, I decided to be proactive. I found a shuttle to Fort Lauderdale–Hollywood International, where they continued to look at me like I was from Mars. So back on the shuttle to Miami International, where nobody seemed to have heard of Earl or Rocky. You guessed it: the shuttle back to the hotel confirmed my luggage was not, in fact, waiting for me.

I wanted to boohoo. This south Florida airport tour was not in the budget. And while I was composing hate mail to the airline in my head, I was also deciding if I should just turn around and go home—let the money I'd already spent head down the drain it had been circling anyway.

But I could see the *Colossus* gleaming in the distance—probably how Dorothy felt about Oz. I'd been planning this for a year, and I was not going to let bureaucratic bungling get in my way. So I'd make a joke about it, or I'd be the joke, but I wasn't going home.

I'll spare you the tedious boarding details. I joined the herd, moving from station to station. We know I didn't have any luggage—which struck everyone around me as deviant. Most folks had steamer trunks, shopping bags, crates—the pioneers packed lighter. My papers were in order, I plopped down a perfectly good credit card in exchange for my Colossus Card, "for all my shipboard needs and desires." The smiling young woman didn't need to know I couldn't afford any desires.

I had planned to be on board early, in my first lounge outfit, kicked back with a fruity beverage and waiting for my girls at the Shangri-la Lounge by the pool, our appointed meeting place. Instead, I rode the elevator to the fourteenth floor and dragged down the looooong corridor to my stateroom with just an hour to spare. And when I opened the door, wonder of wonders—my bags were inside waiting for me, just like they were supposed to have been in the first place.

You wanna talk about happy? I danced around my superior

deluxe cabin, which did not cause me to break a sweat, since it was the size of my bedroom closet, but they never promised spacious. This had to be an omen, a sign that in spite of the rough start, I was in for a great trip, smooth sailing on calm seas. And that my personal tide was about to turn. At least that's what I thought it meant. Unlike the day before, the sky was blue, the sun was beaming, and I tossed the rest of my worries overboard along with my emergency wardrobe plans. I unpacked, changed into a breezy pink-and-yellow number, and headed for Shangri-la.

My crew still hadn't shown up, but the reggae band and the packed dance floor let me know the party had started. I took a seat, introduced myself to Trevor, the bartender, and told him to surprise me. I did that on a trip to Bermuda once—in five days I never had the same drink twice. Trevor had sideburns shaved into a diamond at the bottom. He looked to be about Amber's age, which reminded me that after my trial-by-baggage, I had forgotten to let Amber know I'd arrived safe and sound. She hadn't called me either, which was kinda unusual. It had been just the two of us for so long that checking in was habit. We'd been told our mobile phones wouldn't work at sea—not a problem for me, but I called my child before the ten-buck-a-minute, ship-to-shore rate kicked in.

Boy, was that a mistake. Turns out Amber and J.J. had had a fight. Those two were mad one minute and lovey dovey the next—I swear, I couldn't keep up. I was not about to let her wreck my renewed good humor, so I uh-huh-ed and tuned her right out. Sometimes I almost felt sorry for J.J., but he knew the girl could argue. Maybe she should have been a lawyer. Anyway, he was going to have to handle this solo, especially since I "suddenly" felt my cell signal fading. I hope they'll never completely fix that problem—it's a great excuse. "I'm losing you, honey. Talk to ya when I get back." I flipped that phone closed, thought for a moment about calling my parents—which I knew was a worse idea than calling Amber. They would remind me—again—that I could not afford to be where I was. So I took a huge slurp of the frosty pineapple-mango concoction Trevor slid in front of me, then there was pain ping-ponging in my eye sockets.

The woman sitting next to me said, "I just did the same thing! Brain freeze." Guess my pain was visible. I nodded since I couldn't unlock my mouth and form words yet. It reminded me that Bermuda was the first time I'd had that too. I'm not usually a frozen fruit cocktail kinda woman—I'm more a Chardonnay, champagne and martini gal, and they're not that cold.

My head thawed enough for me to squint at my advisor, who looked very chic in white linen—looked like something I would pick. She told me her name was Toni. Well, Toni must have heard my thought because she said she hadn't even tried a frozen drink until she got divorced last year. Said her husband always called them silly, nothing but trouble. His advice was to stick to the basics—Scotch, vodka, maybe a little wine. And for twenty-six years she did. I tried to imagine being married twenty-six years. That made my head hurt worse than brain freeze. Anyway, I said her husband sounded like my father. She said her husband acted like *her* father, then she raised her glass. She had pretty hands—a lot like mine, but her nails were scarlet. "Here's to making your own rules," she said. I could toast to that, so we clinked hurricane glasses on it. I guessed she'd made a lot of her own rules in the last year, like it was OK to make slurpy sounds with her straw when she drained her drink to the bottom, and to come on this cruise by herself because she always wanted to. I bet ex-hubby wasn't up for either of those.

The rest of the Live Five arrived during the PA announcement for the four o'clock life boat drill. I introduced Toni around, but the others were more interested in debating whether to see Babyface or Frankie Beverly and Maze that night. Toni waved to me and said she was headed back to her cabin for her life jacket. I liked her, hoped I'd run into her again on the floating city.

After the annoyance of the lifeboat drill—like if the boat starts sinking three thousand people are really going to proceed calmly to their muster stations and wait for instructions (and will somebody please tell me how I'm supposed to strap that stupid neon-orange vest over my built-in personal flotation devices?)—we returned to Trevor's bar. Joyce promptly ordered us two bottles of champagne. Normally I wouldn't have blinked, but I had bypassed normal some months back. And I had checked out the price of champagne. I announced I wanted a light beer. My first tropical libation and the check that went with it reminded me of the big bar tab I had rung up during my cocktail chug-a-thon in Bermuda. All of a sudden I had eight eyes staring at me like I'd ordered a mug 'a blood. The usually quiet Cecily piped up and said she had never once seen me drink a beer, like I had to clear my beverage choices with her. I said it was refreshing. Really, it was cheap—I needed something to sip on, but I don't care for beer so I wouldn't guzzle it. It wasn't going to be easy, but I had to start my cost cutting somewhere.

Besides, even without a drink I felt good for the first time in ages. Upbeat. No gloom and doom—I was enjoying the positive vibe. We acted like kids on the first day of summer vacation—even went to the rail to wave at passengers on other ocean liners and yachts as we left the harbor, full steam ahead toward a glorious adventure. I decided to keep my sorry luggage saga to myself because I wasn't sure if I could make it funny yet, and all's well that ends well. Isn't that how the saying goes?

That night we shared our assigned dinner table with newly-wed seniors from a town somewhere near Charlotte who were celebrating their six-month anniversary—kinda sappy, but we had to keep distracting Joyce because it made her weepy. The brother and sister from Phoenix who raised tarantulas and always vacationed together—they were weird, if you ask me. And the guy from Buffalo with a Michael Jackson pageboy and missing front teeth who claimed to be Rick James's cousin's best friend—I was changing my seat if he sang "Give It to Me Baby," but when he asked if I was with somebody, I said yes, long term. Which wasn't a lie. But really I wanted to ask, if he could afford this trip and have the nerve to be trying to rap, why didn't he have teeth? I know what you're thinking. But at least I had teeth.

Marie and Diane tried to outdo each other with how much they knew about wine, which meant we had to order both of the bottles they picked. I said I was fine with iced tea. They looked at me like I was the one with no teeth. Well, iced tea is refreshing—and free. This economizing was going to be a serious challenge.

We managed to see some of both Maze and Babyface—which involved fast walking, from one end of the ship to the other—and fast talking, thanks to Diane and Cecily. After that, Joyce suggested we go to the Sky Lounge for a nightcap. I'd had quite enough fun for one day, and I was ready for my nightgown and a pillow. So I became the party pooper: "You could have stayed home to go to bed at a reasonable hour. It's not like you have to go to work in the morning" is how Joyce put it. All the way back to my cabin I wondered if they knew something. But how could they?

7

. . . diamonds and rubies and pearls, oh my . . .

During our first full day at sea it was close to torture sticking to my retail moratorium. Strolling the Boulevard—the ship's shopping strip of dreams—was as much an activity as aerobics and blackjack: kind of a warm-up for the next day, when we would go ashore for round one of Caribbean Treasure Hunt. From muumuus to mules I encountered many temptations. Diane thought I was crazy not to buy the brown-and-salmon clutch that would go perfectly with the sandals I had worn the night before, but I stepped away from the purse. While the others bought mink eyelashes, St. John and La Mer, I did lots of browsing and eventually picked up some magazines and a pair of red rhinestone flip-flops—on sale. I think I snapped at Marie when she said they looked like something one of her granddaughters would wear. All that restraint made me grouchy.

After lunch the others headed for the casino. I couldn't get past the Gold Dust fast enough because I didn't need help turning nothing into minus nothing. Watching other people throw away large sums of perfectly good money when their cherries didn't line up in a row or their clubs and diamonds totaled more than twenty-one was more than I could I could bear. I could have found way too many things to do with their losings if they'd just handed me the cash, so I set off to explore the *Colossus*.

Don't ask me how, but I found the wedding chapel and watched a couple who looked too young to even eat rum-raisin ice-cream giggle and sniff through "I do." He wiped his tears with his pocket square. She pumped the bouquet like Rocky after the final knockout as they walked back up the aisle. Whatever floats your boat. After that I checked out the lunatics on the rock-climbing wall—there was actually a line of folks waiting to make fools of themselves. I heard the bowling alley before I saw it—I coulda stayed in Jersey for that. And I didn't even pause at Hang Ten, the surfing beach, 'cause Gidget I'm not.

I actually ran into somebody I knew, a musician friend of my ex's from back in the day. He was playing bass with one of the bands. Everybody but Marie had seen at least one familiar somebody. Joyce had bumped into four or five people, but she belongs to every organization you can think of—anyplace she might meet somebody looking to buy a house, sell one or know someone who was. I was hoping I'd find Toni. Maybe she was out shopping too, for stuff that pleased her, not hubby.

After a refreshing siesta—something I never did unless I was sick—I headed up to see Trevor and meet the girls for cocktails and our color commentary on the poolside fashion extravaganza. The profiling and promenading started around three. Hardly anybody was actually in the water—too early in the trip to get those fresh hairdos doused. Now, I understand self-confidence. And I know that nobody has a supermodel body—not even supermodels and certainly not me. That's OK. But I have never seen such an assortment of bellies, butts and boobs spilling out of tank tops, thongs and way too teeny string bikinis that coulda used some rope. Come on, stretchy fabrics are forgiving, but some of the stuff people squeezed into was a sin. There were women strutting their neon-iridescent-sequined-see-through ensembles like showgirls. And don't get me started on the Speedos—talk about Lycra abuse. We knew it was wrong to enjoy it so much, but we couldn't help it.

Anyway, I was in the glass scenic elevator, heading for my fashion fix, when I spotted this man—just his profile, really—his jaw, shoulders, the way he stood. For a second it looked like Ron, and then this tingly, twinkly feeling washed over me. Now, I knew it couldn't be him. Amber and J.J. weren't speaking to each other, but somebody would have let me know Ron would be on board. But before I reached my floor I was in the middle of our near-miss kiss in the parking lot, and I swear I could almost smell him.

Now, it wasn't like I couldn't get him out of my mind. Actually, I resented going through all this just because I *thought* I had seen the man. So I made myself think about Gerald, which canceled the little flutters in my belly. Then I felt bad for using him as a cold shower. So I applied a couple of Trevor's lemon limbos and tried to convince myself Gerald wasn't a fire extinguisher. He was more like my favorite bathrobe—not flashy or sexy, but cozy, comfortable, reliable—that only made it worse, since I'd been using him as a shield too. I'd been hit on more than a few times already, including by my tablemate Gums. When I told him I was seeing someone, he had the nerve to smile at me and say, "Sometimes you don't realize you like steak if you only been eating hamburger." The way his tongue darted through that gap where there should have been teeth, made me lose my appetite.

So I redirected my attention to my travel mates and floated the idea that I wouldn't debark with them the next day in Charlotte Amalie—said I just wanted quiet time to relax. Right. That went over as well as Gums's rap. So right after breakfast the next morning I was strolling past the harbor and into town with my quintet, talking about diamonds and rubies and pearls, oh my, because this was not a straw-bags-and-T-shirts crowd. I admit I'd been fantasizing about a pair of diamond hoop earrings—very versatile. You can dress them up or down, which makes them sound almost practical, but they were going to have to stay just my 'magination. We were all experienced, extreme shoppers, and from the time we'd booked the trip we'd been anticipating the jewelry-buying opportunities in St. Thomas like mountain climbers lust after Mount Everest. This expedition was not for the faint of heart or wallet, which meant I was at a distinct disadvantage.

We moved from store to store like a wolf pack on the hunt. Marie came with a list, like she was going to the grocery store, and magazine cutouts of what she wanted. Charm bracelets for her grands—cute ones with ladybugs, clowns, sneakers, hearts— crafted in enamel, gold and precious stones and not priced for kiddies. For her daughter and daughter-in-law she checked out stud earrings in their birth stones—ruby and emerald. She was shopping for diamond studs for herself—two carats each ear, minimum. I told you, they were not playing.

The day grew hotter, and the pursuit grew more intense. We went from store to store, eyeing the offerings, assessing the opportunities. Joyce focused on watches—eighteen carat gold, with diamonds, the better to show how successful she was. She settled on a tank watch that draped casually and expensively on her wrist, then negotiated like a champ, because it was no fun unless she got a deal. I actually think it's a sport with her. Once they settled on a price, the old watch went in the burgundy leather box, and she spent the rest of the afternoon flopping her hand around so everybody could see it sparkling. And she wouldn't shut up about what a bargain it was.

At first Cecily looked lost and sad—said she had mostly shopped for jewelry with Bill. I kept having to nudge her away from the wedding bands, but eventually she lightened up and started trying on ankle bracelets—said she always wanted one. I never would have guessed that. Marie was all over the place: tanzanite pendant here, fire opal ring there—she liked it flashy. And Diane liked quantity. She bought lots of little bracelets, necklaces, things that required lots of boxes and she could wear in multiples.

I tried on a few things so as not to be conspicuously unconsuming, but clearly my lack of small, shiny shopping bags did not go unnoticed. Truth is, I was usually up there with the heavy hitters. My buddies started pointing out pieces that "looked like me," like I needed coaxing. They were actually pretty good at it. I was having a hard time finding something wrong with the pieces to avoid buying them.

After a while their teasing and prodding got a little pointy, like I wasn't holding up my end of the deal. I got fed up, so I came up with a plan to shut them up. A number of shops sold unstrung pearls, which they would make into a necklace for you or you could take them home to add to a piece you already owned. They had all seen my pearl choker. I said I had always wanted to make it a three-strand necklace, which is true. I always thought that looked classy. So it became a game of finding the right size and color pearls to match.

Creamy, pink, silvery, iridescent—I never realized pearls came in so many shades and overtones. Seven millimeters or eight—it was so hard to tell. So we came to a consensus and I finally bought a strand—they called it a hank, on one of my emergency cards. I had to make it convincing, right?

So I finally had a bag to carry that seemed to satisfy everybody enough so that we could go to lunch—where I could launch into part two of the plan. Over conch fritters and plantains I pulled out my purchase and started fretting over whether these pearls would really match my pearl choker. The debate continued through crème caramel and off and on as we wound our way through narrow streets, making sure we hadn't overlooked any opportunities. I hemmed and hawed and before it was time to go back to the ship I decided to return them. They all looked so disappointed—especially Joyce who said that at fourteen hundred dollars they were a steal. Diane piped in that they were duty free so it would save me even more. Which I myself would have said at another time, but at the moment I needed wiggle room on my revolving charge.

I did my best depressed pout but said I'd take the pearls back now—which was the plan all along—and bring the necklace with me next time to match them. Genius, right? Except for one small detail: the store did not do cash returns. I almost had a stroke when the demure-looking woman in the elegant chemise and chignon pointed out the sign that read, "Returns for Store Credit Only." I had missed it during all the color comparisons and consultations. I started sweating while I tried every way I could to convince this woman that she had to give me credit. After all I was getting back on a ship, so store credit was absolutely no good to me. She informed me I could use it the next time—which was a part of my act I had no interest in hearing repeated back to me, but my sales lady was unmoved. I kept talking and Joyce looked at her watch about forty-two times—I wanted to tie her hand behind her back—but finally the others said we really had to leave, which at least saved me my dignity because I was ready to beg.

I could have kicked myself all the way back to the harbor and up the gang plank. Cecily assured me the pearls were really beautiful. She said, "Too bad you can't wear them right now. You'd feel better about them." Wear them? I couldn't even look at them, and I couldn't believe I had been so stupid, but the deed was done. I ended up giving them to Amber because I knew I'd never be able to put them around my neck without feeling like they were choking me. She and I had a longstanding "no snow globes, no sombreros" rule, but this was not a tacky mug or a stupid souvenir spoon, so she happily granted me an exception.

I was pretty quiet during dinner. Gums asked me what was wrong. I might have said something like he should concentrate on chewing his stuffed pork loin with his no-teeth self and leave me alone—which was really wrong—but he left me alone for the rest of the cruise.

Next day, in honor of Diane's and Marie's birthdays, we planned an afternoon of pampering at the ship's Nirvana spa. I had been planning to splurge on a facial, but after my jewelry fiasco I nixed that. So the girls scheduled sesame-seaweed wraps, Peruvian mud dips and volcanic-ash scrubs to go with the usual nails, facials and massages. No deluxe services for me. I told them I was fighting dermatitis on my back and stomach. It was just starting to heal and I thought it was best not to irritate it. So I had a mani and pedi—which I'd have done at home anyway.

I wasn't lying about the breakout either, except the blotchy red patches came and went at random and still itched and burned like fire. My mother said it was nerves. I didn't believe her. It was just a coincidence the itching started sometime between not getting that job and the end of my unemployment checks and flared up as soon as I read the "no cash returns" sign. Right.

Naturally I was done first, so I went looking for the others to say I'd meet them later at Prima. Dinner was at the ship's fine-dining restaurant—which of course was not covered on our meal plan, another expense I'd planned for—three of us would split the bill with the birthday girls as our guests. Except my budget was blown. I was going to have to resort to the real emergency card and hope nothing else went wrong.

I stepped behind the waterfall that led to the lounge near the treatment rooms but stopped dead in my pink foam toe separators before I turned the corner. "Does she think she's fooling anybody?" I'd know Diane's croak anywhere. "And who was she trying to impress, buying those pearls? . . . should have kept her broke self at home." Then Marie chimed in, " . . . threw that big wedding. Who was she tryin' to impress?" I got cold, freezing cold, and I couldn't move any closer, but I couldn't walk away. I steadied myself against the shelves of fluffy white towels. "I know they had layoffs at her company. You think she even has a job?" It was Joyce. That's when I heard cackling, and Cecily added, "You mean she doesn't *own* the place," in that sweet-as-syrup voice she has. I think I jumped when one of the attendants came up behind me and asked if I needed help. I was embarrassed, like she knew I was the topic of conversation. I came out of my trance enough to mutter something, then left but not before I heard, "She doesn't think we're supposed to pay for her tonight, does she?"

They were not ragging on some no-name stranger—which we did regularly—they were bad-mouthing me, and I knew it. I felt sick and sorry and mad and sad. Part of me wanted to let them know, but I went with the part that just wanted to escape.

A blaze of itchy redness blossomed across my chest as I made my way toward the elevator bank. Except with those comments repeating in my head I got on one that didn't go to my floor. I pushed some button or other and ended up in a corner of the *Colossus* that I'd never seen. I ducked into La Bibliothèque, where passengers escaped to read, play Scrabble and chess and chill. I plopped in a wingback chair in a quiet corner and stared out the window at the endless ocean until I could breathe again. How was I supposed to laugh and talk and sing "Happy Birthday" that night like nothing had happened?

You know how sometimes you can feel somebody looking at you? I don't know how long I'd been sitting there, itching and burning and feeling lost at sea when I finally looked across the room. And there sat Toni, curled up on a sofa, book open in her lap. Not to be dramatic, but at that moment it felt like I got a life preserver. She came over and told me she'd been trying to figure out if it was me or not. We talked about our activities thus far and she asked what I was doing for the evening. She'd been craving a burger and was going to the joint on the Boulevard around eight and then to see Earth, Wind and Fire, and she invited me to join her. Right then I said yes—

—and spent the next few hours debating how I was going to handle my defection. I'd have to face them eventually—either bring it up or swallow it—but that night I needed to idle in neutral a while longer. So I called Joyce, said I felt like I was coming down with something. That would give them plenty to chew on over dinner.

So Toni and I played Getting to Know You while waiting for our Swiss burger specials with grilled mushrooms and onions. I went first, and I don't know why—guess I just felt connected to her from the beginning—but while we sipped our Merlot, I told her why I was there and not dining high on the hog with my posse. Then I did the *Reader's Digest* version of my last eight months, which was more to the point than the Fractured Fairy-Tale I had told my family.

"Not to worry," she said. "The burgers are on me!" I laughed and accepted, because I felt she was being gracious and kind, not condescending. By the time we'd finished our salads, I'd found out Toni was also a Jersey Girl—living in Hoboken, but originally from Trenton. She worked in Manhattan, headed up the accounting department for a big fashion house. Yes, you would know who they are. And in that small-world category, when she was married she had lived in Princeton—whodathunkit?—right down the way from me. Toni said even after twenty years the town never suited her, too buttoned-up for her taste. So she let her ex buy her out of the house and headed north.

Naturally, the road to and from our hometowns led us directly to the Ex Vortex—not a place I visited often. I mean, with the exception of our game of Can You Top This at Amber's wedding, he was ancient history—a relic from the past, long since chalked up to being young and dumb—oh yeah, and in love.

Then Toni said, "My friends told me I was crazy to let Gerald have the house, but—"

I didn't hear what she said after that because "Gerald" was

clanging in my head like a fire alarm. My grip tightened on the burger that was halfway to my mouth. *Gerald?* My throat started to close and my heart revved up to NASCAR speed. She couldn't have said Gerald. I mean, it wasn't like Horatio, but it wasn't the most common name either. And if she did actually say it, she couldn't mean *my* Gerald. Yes, he lived in Princeton, but his wife was named Annie. I didn't know Toni's last name; she didn't know mine. They hadn't come up.

This had to be some freaky coincidence, but the sweat mustache grew on my upper lip and wet rings circled my armpits. All I could do was dig my fingers deeper into the bun. There were lots of black families in Princeton—well, maybe not lots, but there was definitely more than one black man named Gerald in the whole damn town. Wasn't there? Besides, who said her husband was black? Since Toni didn't seem to have noticed my state of paralysis and perspiration, I eased myself back from the ledge. I wanted to pick up my glass in the worst way, but I was afraid my hand wasn't steady enough to make it to my lips without spillage, so I settled for unhanding my burger.

And she kept talking—said when she was younger she saw life as an adventure, full of possibilities. "And I let him suck the life right outta me," she said. Her ex saw caution lights and police tape: safe was the ultimate goal. Once their kids—all *three* of them—were grown and gone, she wanted to shake things up. He still wanted meatloaf every Tuesday. She took a trip to the Galapagos and Machu Picchu without him, came down from the mountain, found a lawyer and left him with his ground beef.

But *my* Gerald was not divorced. So this was some other Gerald.

It had to be.

Then this couple who was being shown to a table stopped by us, grinning. She clamped Toni's arm and said, "Annie?! It's been ages!!" *Annie.* The minute I heard it, I knew I was headed over the cliff. Our visitors started into their sympathy speech about how they had heard about "the divorce"—the woman actually whispered the word and lowered her eyes when she said it. But they must not have seen me free-falling, because they kept talking like everything was fine. Toni introduced me, they nodded and went right back to their condolences, which was swell with me 'cause I was dizzy and felt like I was going to toss my dinner.

After her friends were gone, Toni explained that only people from the old Trenton neighborhood and Gerald called her Annie—said she always hated it. When she reclaimed herself she decided Antoinette, her name, was a mouthful, but thought Toni might be a fit.

She poked fun at her friends, "Acting like getting divorced is something to be ashamed of—like going to jail."

Something to be ashamed of? What, like laying up with somebody else's husband? I was terrified of what might come out of my mouth, so I still hadn't done much more than nod. I thought hearing what my backbiting friends had to say about me made for a bad day. But there I was with this woman I liked—she was smart and funny and had rescued me from my frienmies. The only rub—I'd been having an affair with her husband for the last twelve years. I wanted to run, but you can't get far in the middle of the ocean. Did she suspect Gerald had a side dish? I had always wondered. If she did, it wasn't part of the story she told, and she didn't seem to have a whiff it was me.

But for the first time in those dozen years I truly became the other woman, and I felt guilty—and ashamed. There were lots of other things I'd felt during that time—annoyed, disappointed and inconvenienced among them—but I had been a pro at sidestepping the guilt thing. His wife was his life, not mine.

Now, I hadn't lost my whole mind, so I was not about to fess up, but somehow it didn't seem right for her to be treating me to dinner.

Then Toni noticed I hadn't said anything, or moved, or that I was green, or that my uneaten burger had puncture wounds—I don't know what finally got her attention, but she asked if I was alright. I mumbled something about not feeling well; it seemed to be my theme song for the day. I managed to get myself through the meal, bowed out of the main event and wobbled back to my cabin.

Well, just damn. That changed about everything. I was completely disgusted with myself—for about an hour I took the beating my conscience dished out, because I deserved it. I replayed everything Toni had said, what I had said, looking for—I don't know, absolution, forgiveness? *It's OK, Tee, you're still a good person.* But I didn't find any. Then I had an epiphany.

Gerald was divorced and he never said one mumbling word.

The son of a bitch had been in my face, in my house, lying to me for the last two years—not directly, but by default. I was outraged—thinking about his clothes in my drawer and how I folded them just so. And I fixed him meatloaf. This is not how I expected to be bonding with Toni . . . Annie . . . whatever her name was. I wanted to pick up that ship-to-shore phone and tell him what a lowdown, miserable slug he was—something he'd clearly already made peace with. It wasn't worth my ten dollars a minute to tell him. Besides, I needed to look him in his face and say . . . I don't know what, but something that would peel paint off the walls would come out.

And since somebody needed a piece of my mind, I decided to vent on my so-called friends. Every night had ended at Sky Bar, so it was a pretty good guess that whatever show they'd seen, they would turn up there sooner or later. All I had to do was wait. And maybe it was because I wanted them to see I wasn't quite on the bread line, or maybe I was just feeling contrary, but I ordered a bottle of champagne and five glasses. I was on my second when they showed up, singing, "Evil, running through my veins . . ." Could it be more perfect?

They actually acted happy to see me, all concerned about how I was feeling. I filled their glasses and played it off like whatever had been ailing me left as mysteriously as it had arrived. The more they yakked, critiquing the show, what people had on, the more I could see that was all we had ever done— talk about stuff that didn't matter and each other. We trashed Diane's "just add a can of cream of mushroom soup" culinary efforts and her plastic-flower arrangements. We had plenty to say about why Joyce's husband had headed for the exit. And we had gone to town on Marie and her gag-me grandkids. So why was I pissed off because they did the same thing to me? Because hearing it hurt my feelings, like when Mary Marshall told the whole fifth-grade class that I was the only girl who didn't wear a bra yet. That sounded lame. You know what? It hurt, but Mary was right. Given a little time, I more than made up for that shortfall, just like I would this time.

So I didn't bust them, because I got the message. And as far as I was concerned, the Live Five had run its course. Maybe the Fake Four would survive, but I was through. We finished the bottle. We finished The Cruise. And I was finished with them.

Gerald, however, was another story. I wasn't done with him yet.

8

*That's before my head was forcibly removed
from the hole in the sand.*

Every Gerald thought made me madder. Not just angry—
mad-dog mad—crazy and foaming at the mouth. Or like
mad cow disease—disoriented and unable to walk or think
straight. The closer I got to home, the more I could feel myself
swell up, like one of those big, butt-ugly lizards with the bumpy
skin and the neck that puffs out like a balloon. I don't know if
they're really mad, but I'd stay the hell away. And I'm sure the
man squeezed in the plane seat next to me knew better than to
even dream of challenging me for space on the armrest.

It's just that in all the time we were . . . I don't even know
what to call it—dating? Hardly. In a relationship? Clearly not.
That implies you tell the other person what's going on in your
life, and somewhere along the line I lost my priority status.
How could he not tell me?! That zipped me right between
the eyes, and I think I hip-checked a woman for space at the
ladies'-room sink.

I never realized how much of whatever Gerald and I did involved what he could or couldn't do—with me or for me—because we had to keep his little secret. OK, big secret. So I never even considered asking him to pick me up from the airport. It would have been nice for the man in my life to help put my luggage in the car, tell me he missed me and take me home. But he couldn't because how would he explain his Saturday-night absence to Annie? Except that for quite some time now Toni—whom I missed already because we were absolutely not going to get to explore our friendship options—didn't give a rat's rump what he did on Saturday or any other day, or night. Except he should have said something to me. Gerald owed me that much.

Which left me with steam coming out of my ears while I scraped together enough money to take the train to the bus, because I did not have $100 for a cab. I didn't want to know if Amber and J.J. were still mad at each other, so I wasn't asking them to pick me up. Really, I had planned to catch a ride with one of my so-called friends, but since the demise of the Live Five, I was on my own. I had a mind to call him while I was waiting on the decidedly nontropical train platform. And I cussed under my breath while dragging a ton of suitcase on and off a bus and down the road to my house in the dark. But I knew I'd need more energy and more wits than I had at the time to speak to him.

Welcome home.

Next day I snatched dirty clothes out of my bag, stuffed them in the washer, threw myself in the shower, yanked on some clothes, raked a comb through my hair—sense any hostility? I stayed out of the car because I wanted to hear the engine growl, burn some rubber—bad ideas when the speed limit is thirty-five.

I let the machine pick up Gerald's calls because I was not ready to deal with him yet and I was doing this on my time. Everything he said, including "the" and "it," lit my fire. It was like one of Amber's fifth-grade science projects. If you focus sunlight through a magnifying glass on a pile of dry leaves, at first you think nothing is happening. Then there's smoke. If you keep it there long enough, the whole forest is going up in flames.

Or maybe it's what he didn't say that burned me. Stuff like, "I can't wait to see you." Or, "I'm finally free. Now it's just you and me, babe." News flash—he never said those things, but somehow I heard them, especially the last one. And I couldn't even tell you if that's what I wanted, but I deserved the courtesy of being consulted.

Besides, this was not a phone conversation. And the more I threw, slapped and dragged things around, the more I felt we should have this out at his house for a change. I was feeling the need to come out of the shadows.

Monday was never one of *our* days, but it could be now, and the sooner we resolved this some kinda way, the better, because the more I stewed, the more distracted I'd be from really important matters, like finding work. There had been plenty of on-deck networking, but nobody was sending the Gulfstream to whisk me to corporate HQ, and I'd already checked my inbox—nothing promising on the horizon.

And I wasn't calling Gerald to make an appointment either. He would just have to deal with me when I got there. So I spent all day prepping because I had to look like the best me I could be—sassy, sun-kissed, full of "I can handle it" spirit, like the first day I walked into that dealership and met him. And I wore the high heels. I had to stand tall.

Problem was, I wasn't sure about the climax of this long-running drama. Was I telling Gerald to take a hike? Was I the one making an exit? If that was the case, why hadn't I done it before? Even his wife had reached the point where she said, "So long, sappy. I have run away." Why should I stick around for seconds?

Or was I after a chorus of, "Baby, please don't go," complete with the falling-out and the cape? The man was a salesman, but what kind of terms could he offer that would make this deal acceptable?

So I waited 'til evening. I got the car washed on the way down; it had to look good too. And I made my way to his house for the very first time. Seriously, I'd never sat outside, desperate to see into his life without me. Or even driven past so I could check out his digs from an architectural standpoint. I didn't need to know if the azaleas were pink or coral, or if it looked like I imagined. His day-to-day hadn't been real to me, and I'd liked it like that, thank you very much. That's before my head was forcibly removed from the hole in the sand.

I circled his block a few times. In my mind, Gerald's house was bigger, with more land around it. Really, it was rather bland, but that's neither here nor there. I didn't see his car, but I pulled right up in the driveway, banged the door closed and marched up the walk. I saw the blinds at the bay window move, imagined what kinda crazy he must have been thinking I was. The door opened before I took my finger off the bell.

A youngish woman wearing cargo capris and a cap-sleeved tee shirt answered. She had copious amounts of hair that did not start out on her own head, and she flipped it out of her eyes to look at me. I never anticipated his daughter might be there. Hadn't seen her in ages, maybe since the aluminum bats in the sporting-goods store. That took some of the starch out of my delivery, so I said, "Hey. You don't know me, but I'm a friend of your father—"

And she said, "My father lives in Florida."

Oh. OK. I was startled but still on my feet. I said I was a friend of Gerald's. Her expression shifted. It was subtle, just enough to make her look evil, and she said, "You mean my fiancé."

That's when I experienced a flash of blinding clarity. Right then I understood that my ignorance of his divorce was in no way an oversight. It was part of the plan—the way you get a new car but keep the old one around 'cause it's reliable and it gives you something to knock around in. In an instant I was transported beyond the ugly, uncontrollable outburst into a strange calm, where I could float above the part of myself that wanted to hurt people, Gerald specifically, and focus on what was happening now without burning the house down. So I told Tressy, yes, I did mean Gerald, and I also meant I was more than his friend. She had a right to know what was in the small print.

Now, in hindsight I realize this could have gotten roll-in-the-mud, hair-pulling, knives-and-guns ugly, just like the stories on the news where you think, *Nobody is worth all that.* But there wasn't any hollering, at least not at me. She folded her arms across her chest. This time I saw the ring—punier than I would have expected too. Then she asked me to step inside, fill in the rest of the blanks.

Even though I never got further than the foyer, it was quite civilized—not tea and crumpets, but she heard me out. You're supposed to feel better after you confess, but it wasn't a relief. *Stupid* and *humiliating* are words that come to mind, but at this point I was beyond looking for absolution. This was damage control. My shield had turned into a dagger, and it was aimed at me.

I didn't drag her through the details, but it was clear that Gerald, with his safe, practical, organized self, had arranged us exactly to his liking. Guess you have to be detail oriented to keep your fiancée from your mistress, and your longtime mistress from your former wife, but now we had all collided.

Tressy didn't say much. When I was done, she asked, "Why should I believe you?"

Good question. I didn't have a snappy answer. I guess I could have been obsessed with Gerald and created this fantasy where the two of us were meant to be together and I would do anything to make that come true. Or a vindictive, spurned girlfriend who was hellbent on destroying his happiness.

Yeah, she wasn't feeling those explanations either.

To be honest, my lips were moving, but I was in some kind of trance until she opened the door again. As I walked out, she looked at me and said, "You're pathetic." That was real.

9

Guilt is nothing without someone to share it with?

My visit with Tressy was a wake-up call, and I was done pushing the snooze button.

That night I drove home in the slow lane 'cause I felt shaky and dumbstruck, like I'd been hit upside my head which, come to think of it, I had.

Twelve years and it took less than two hours to de-Gerald my house. Nothing dramatic—no bonfires or power saws. There wasn't any teary sorting through his sweaters either. I didn't hold on to the reading glasses he kept in the table on "his" side of *my* bed. I didn't take a last whiff of the Grey Flannel aftershave in the medicine cabinet. I just bagged up my dozen years of Gerald trace evidence and dumped it in the trash.

But it still felt unreal. Maybe because I didn't have any feedback. When a relationship is over—from divorce, death, defection or mutual decision—don't you talk about it? Or at least claim you don't want to talk about it? Aren't people supposed to bring you cake and comfort, or a bottle of bourbon and join the bitchfest—whatever's your pleasure? It's the perfect misery-loves-company opportunity—the more the merrier. When my ex hit the road, I had Olivia and even my parents who were happy to say, "I told you so." For better or worse, talking about it made it real. But how do you tell somebody your honey is gone when they didn't know anybody was buzzing around your hive? Which is pretty remarkable if you think about it. All those years and no one knew—except Amber, and she wasn't about to commiserate.

Julie and I only shared workplace misery. I hadn't divulged any mess from the home front, but I thought about calling her. I was pretty sure she would offer a serving of tea and sympathy without judging me—not because what I did wasn't wrong, but because she didn't appear to have a sanctimonious bone in her body. Except I always felt like she looked up to me and I didn't want to risk that, so I kept my business to myself.

Guilt is nothing without someone to share it with?

But nothing I did or didn't do stopped me from being mightily pissed at Gerald, and at myself. Or helped me come to grips with why it hurt so much—hadn't planned on that. Pathetic.

I was under the impression I could take Gerald or leave him—like prunes. He wasn't supposed to be ice cream, something I'd have a hard time giving up. Guess that idea made it palatable for me to spend all those years on a man who obviously viewed me as the *other* one, not *the* one. No, at the very beginning he didn't mention there was a Mrs. behind door number one. That should have been a hint. Then maybe I wouldn't have been surprised to find a Mrs.-in-Waiting behind door number two at the very end.

He also didn't sing the "She Doesn't Understand Me" blues about his miserable married life to a bitchy wife. Didn't keep me dangling, waiting for him to run away from home and into my chubby but loving arms. Gerald made no promises, and I made no demands. He didn't curl my toes, give me butterflies or rock my world, which was fine. I'd been there. As far as I could tell, everlasting love was as much a fairy tale as the seven dwarfs—hi ho. For most of our association I had a job, a good one, so I wasn't looking for a man to take care of me or my daughter. It was clear from the giddyup that our activity was extracurricular. I never expected to move up to the wife position.

I didn't. Really.

But the idea I wasn't even in the running when the time and the opportunity came—not that I would have said yes—talk about more than you can chew. It was an awful lot to swallow. I couldn't wallow in it, though. I had made my bed—with another woman's husband. Was that why there were no messages on my answering machine offering me the job of my dreams? Believe me, guilt spreads easier than warm butter.

So you can imagine my reaction when I picked up the phone two days later, all perky and professional in case it was a prospective employer, and heard Tressy on the line. "May I speak to Ms. Hodges?" I'd only talked to her once, but it was a memorable occasion, so I recognized her voice. How did she get my number? What did she want? I was done with her man. Finished. I might have been pathetic, but I wasn't f'ing Effie, groveling and belting, "You're gonna love me."

I dug deep, found my most high-toned voice. "This is she speaking." I sounded dignified and calm—not at all like I was worried she was some *Fatal Attraction* nut job out to eliminate the competition.

And she said, "I just wanted to thank you." What the hell? "You saved me from a terrible mistake." Seems she went to the dealership right after I left and told Gerald and a showroom full of coworkers and car buyers exactly what she thought of his secret, then hurled the ring into the woods past the body shop on her way out. Last time she saw him he was crawling through the grass trying to find it. That's Gerald—utterly romantic. It sounded scrumptious, but this treat didn't sit too well. I stood there in my kitchen, waiting to feel some satisfaction—just a little. I deserved that, didn't I? But it just added another layer of sad and sorry. And he still did not have the decency or guts or whatever it took to say two words to me. The funny thing: I really had nothing to say to him.

Clearly, it was time to redirect my attentions. I convinced myself that if I did the right thing, changed my ways, I could get back on the sunny side of the street. First thing every morning I was at the computer on some site or other, uploading my résumé, or trekking to the post office with my list of qualifications wrapped in one more cleverly worded cover letter, for the few potential employers who were retro enough to still believe in mail—

—and speaking of, it took me the rest of the week to get up the nerve and the energy to tackle the pile that accumulated while I had been away. Please note I did not say "on vacation," and you know why. And since, thanks to Markson, I'd found out the hard way that not knowing what was lurking under the flap could actually be worse than opening the damn things, I decided I would open five envelopes a day until I caught up. It felt responsible, which I was trying to be, and seemed like a perfectly reasonable amount of bad news to manage at a time.

Don't you know the first envelope I sliced open proved me right—and it wasn't even a bill, just a friendly Dear Valued Customer reminder. My car lease was expiring and I needed to make plans to 1) "Come in and select a new vehicle to lease or purchase"—excellent idea. Why didn't I think of that? 2) "Purchase my current vehicle"—what, that old thing? or 3) "Turn in my current vehicle"—and drive the Rolls that's been collecting dust in my garage instead? More to the point, this had always been Gerald territory, and I was not ready to wade in those waters yet, so that notice went in the Don't Bother Me Now file.

Next came a cruel lesson in credit management. After spending months stretching a little bit of money to pay goo-gobs of bills, I became very familiar with the "minimum payment" box, which at that point was the only thing that pertained to me. I figured if everybody got a little bit, we could all be happy. So I was shocked when I found it had doubled on the plastic-cash bill I opened next. There had to be a mistake, so I examined it in detail. That's when I discovered the interest rate had tripled. I was outraged. That was flat-out robbery. They had no right, except my inquiry very quickly uncovered the fact that they did. It says so in the extra-fine print on the Terms and Conditions sheet nobody ever reads, because who can understand it anyway, and what does it have to do with me? And once one of them hikes the rate, some silent alarm goes off signaling it's open season and they all do. Envelopes three, four and five confirmed that. I didn't need the calculator to tell me I was officially in deep doodoo and it was coming in faster than I could shovel. We don't have debtors' prison anymore, but they've got new ways to lock you up, and I was beginning to feel the chains.

Not exactly the best frame of mind for a dinner out with the kids—their treat, but I had put them off as long as I could. They wanted to hear the cruise report. So I gave them the abbreviated version, told them about the singer who cussed out her manager in front of an SRO crowd. She didn't come out for an encore. And there was the comedian who got wasted and passed out backstage before his show, which provided lots of material for the comedian who went on instead—way funnier than his last HBO special. Toni and the Live Five did not make the highlight reel.

Really, I think both Amber and J.J. wanted to make their cases that night for what kind of house they should buy. She was leaning toward something in the McMiniMansion area—cathedral ceiling–ed and master suited. Wonder where she got her taste from? My son-in-law, on the other hand, was proving to be quite the pragmatist. He was looking at multifamily fixer-uppers, because of the income and investment potential. In the short time they'd been married I had learned one cardinal rule: don't get in it. So I nodded and kept my opinions to myself, although I must admit J.J.'s argument had a lot more going for it than I would have thought before.

Fortunately, Amber's job really kept her busy and out of my hair. She'd call me on her way home from work. We'd talk for about ten minutes or until she saw a fender bender or some speed demon passed her too close. Then she'd go refocus her attention on the road, like she was supposed to. I missed seeing her all the time, but it was better than having her notice that the lawn needed mowing because I'd cut the service to once a month, or trying to explain why I didn't have the usual stash of regular, diet and caffeine-free soda to choose from, and there were no reserves in the basement.

Scaling back, way back, was part of my plan, and I was sticking to it—like I had some choice? Therefore, the Tee Hodges who formerly looked down her nose at those annoying people in the supermarket holding up the line while they rifled their wad of coupons to get ten cents off became a convert. Love those double-coupon days, and if it wasn't on sale, I didn't buy it. I discovered store-brand baby peas taste the same as the big-name ones. Who knew?

In my economizing zeal I switched to the basic cable package, because I certainly wasn't watching all those music, movie and sports channels since Amber moved out and Gerald dropped dead—oops, I mean moved on. I stayed out of the mall, put away the takeout menus—

—unfortunately Mother Nature was not with the program. We had the hottest June on record. I had not budgeted for heat or air-conditioning from April until at least the Fourth of July, like usual. But nothing had been usual, so why should the weather be any different? During summers utility bills were like another mortgage payment, so to cut down I dragged two old box fans up from the basement. I don't think they'd been used since we got central air. One went in my bedroom, the other between the kitchen and family room, aka my Reemployment Office, which is where I spent most of my time anyway. OK, some nights I cheated. How did I survive childhood without air-conditioning?

By the end of July, I'd sent out sixty-seven résumés, got eight responses, which led to three interviews—nothing worth mentioning. Hell, they weren't even worth going to. I even signed up with a couple of temp agencies. They warned me up front that since I had minimal computer skills I was difficult to place. I'd have a better shot in the fall when the college kids were back in school. Undergrads had more options than I did. That did wonders for my morale.

So did the brutal heat that continued all summer. To survive I ran the AC for a little while each morning and night, then kept the vents, doors and drapes closed—a lot like being vacuum packed—doing my best to keep the hot out and the chill in. And not feel sorry for myself, or go stir crazy, because something had to give.

Oh, and I was down to six weeks left to decide what to do about my car. I had never let it get that close to the deadline, but I was trying not to think about it. We all know how well that works.

Julie checked in regularly and we met for lunch every couple of weeks. On her. She was celebrating her promotion to manager of the Markson department, and she was in a training program to become a brand supervisor with four Nordstrom's stores in her territory. Woo hoo. I was happy for her—I was. But Markson was still stuck in my craw—

—Like Gerald. I still intellectualized, rationalized and wondered about him. Hell, I missed him, which I hate to admit, but it's the truth. It's not like my heart was broken or that I couldn't live if living is without him, like it says in that cheesy song, but there were a lot of Thursdays under the bridge and you have to miss something that's been a part of your life that long. Even if it wasn't good for you. And you know you're better off without it. Ask any junkie.

When I talked to Amber, I made it sound like my days were busy, but what do you do when everything you do costs money? How much daytime TV was I supposed to watch? All those talk shows with celebs hawking their latest movie-clothing-perfume-CD, in between new-you makeovers, the twelve-minute gourmet, the budget bathroom face-lift, and how to live a sugar/hormone/wheat/meat–free life and find health, happiness, and great sex. After a while my eyes glazed over. The soaps? I'd sooner eat a bar of Ivory than watch *As the Crap Turns* or *No Life to Live*. And when did judges start doing stand-up? Or was it sit-down?

I was as interested in cyberspace as outer space, so that wasn't an outlet. My computer was a tool, a fancy typewriter with a TV screen. It was not my friend. I didn't want it to make friends with other computers or the fruit loops who spent day and night surfing the net or the web—which both sound like traps to me, and I was looking to escape the matrix I was caught in. My little laptop was the means to an end that I spelled j-o-b, not f-u-n. Amber and J.J. tried to show me how to chat and instant message. That balloon popping up in the middle of what I was doing annoyed me. If you needed to reach me, what's wrong with the damn phone?

Which is how I felt, until I got the call that changed my mind.

In August our heat wave finally took a hiatus—go figure. It helped because I needed to feel productive to distract myself from worrying about how I was gonna pay for my life of leisure. And all I'd been able to do was lay low and try to survive the sauna that was my house. So once the day started with a temperature-humidity index of less than 100, I took advantage of the cold front to do a little reorganizing. Sounds painful, but I've always found it relaxing. When the rest of life is in disarray, my kitchen shelves can be shipshape.

I had already attacked the china cabinet, washed and repositioned the dishes I never used anyway, and rearranged the spice drawer sweet to savory, in alphabetical order. Time to move on to a bigger challenge, an inventory of my survival-shelter supply of canned goods and pasta.

So there I was in the pantry, on the step stool, elbow deep in the tomato products. I had restacked them according to type—whole, crushed, pureed, diced or stewed. It looked better than the supermarket. When the phone rang I was holding the Mason jar of home-canned tomatoes from one of Diane's domestic experiments and debating whether to classify it with the cans or with the jars of sauce and salsa, but I got down and grabbed the phone.

When I heard "May I speak to Mr. or Mrs. Hodges," my antennae went up. Everybody who had reason to call me knew there was no Mr. Hodges—not in my house. I identified myself, and he proceeded to scold me about one of my overdue credit-card accounts and when they could expect payment. Overdue? I was only a few days late. What happened to the grace period? At the moment I was experiencing a temporary economic downturn, but didn't my years of spotless credit count for something? Yes, my bank balance was anemic, but that was not his business. Neither was the fact that I'd been saved from a crash landing only by the timely arrival of my tax refund. I'd like to tell you I filed late because I *planned* for that to happen, but you know better. So while it was in the nick of time, it was chewing gum in the dam—not a long-term fix.

Don't get me wrong. I did the happy dance and took that baby right to the bank. But the damn thing was going to take a few days to clear, which somehow seems wrong. Doesn't the government have good credit? I timed my check mailing so it would arrive just as the funds cleared. Seemed an effective use of delivery lag. Otherwise the payment would have been later, but there was no point explaining that to the pimply-faced pipsqueak—that's how I imagined him. He lectured me about penalties and about how I was ruining my credit rating—like this was a startling revelation? And I definitely didn't want him telling me anything, not about *my* business.

I hadn't played More Month Than Money since I was a senseless, centless newlywed. And it was *not* like riding a bicycle. I had forgotten how humiliating the game is. So now I'm standing in my own kitchen, trembling, sweating, ashamed and embarrassed—like my secret was about to be revealed. I growled at him that the check was in the mail and slammed down the phone instead of throwing it across the room, but the tomato jar slipped out of the other hand and exploded on the tile floor—solving the issue of where to put it.

Then I was tiptoeing around, cleaning up glass and red slop and calling collection boy all the names I usually reserved for my occasional case of road rage. How do you get up every day and go to work harassing hardworking people—or formerly hardworking people—who formerly paid their bills on time but can't since whatever hard times hit them? It actually sounded like he got his jollies off telling me that if they didn't receive at least the minimum in seven days the whole balance would be immediately due and payable. Right. I was having a hard enough time coming up with the new maximum minimum, so they expect me to pay more? What kind of logic is that?

But the damage was done. Bits and pieces of me were being chopped away. I was fighting to stay positive, but it was getting harder by the day. What's a few droplets of dignity here? You won't miss another slice of pride. Oops. There goes a hunk of confidence. What was I supposed to do if I didn't find a job—raid my retirement money? That's all I had left. I already had a second on the house, refinanced when Amber was in college, to pay my share of her tuition. Unlike me, she was a good student, and I owed her that. And if her father could pay, so could I.

So after I got up the glass I got on my hands and knees and focused on cleaning tomato out of the grout, because whatever was looming ahead was too overwhelming, and at that moment I couldn't handle it. Which brought on a missing-Gerald relapse. He was the only one who had any idea how things really were—mostly. At least I had somewhere to vent. Even if he had been a horse's ass when I asked for the loan, his platitudes were better than nothing, which at that moment was what I had.

I was still on all fours when Amber walked in. Just what I needed, a surprise visit. And I can only imagine what a horror show I looked like on the kitchen floor, smeared in red sauce. It took a full five minutes to convince her I hadn't been attacked in a home invasion. I played it off as just a silly accident—not the result of a body blow from a sadistic creditor.

I cleaned myself and we sat down for a glass of wine. Cocktails with my child is still an odd concept, yet another reminder she's past the milk-and-cookies years. Then she told me she had great news, and that J.J. already knew and was meeting her there, but she had to tell me second.

Somewhere between the pink nursery and the blue one, and wondering if I still remembered how to crochet, my sky-is-falling panic was replaced by hot-cold, happy sadness. I wanted to laugh and cry at the same time. Was she ready? Was J.J.? Me Grandma Tee? How could life move so fast? My baby having a baby, and there I was worrying about sharing a glass of Pinot Grigio—which I realized she was still sipping. So of course I asked, "Should you be drinking that?" Amber looked at me, then at her glass and said, "Why not?" And I'm about to say, "But what about the baby?" when she says, "I haven't told you my news!" Which is when I realized I was acting like I'd already heard. Naturally she wanted to take it from the top, and I'd already read the last page. So I obliged her, abandoned grandmahood and returned to mamahood, ready to let her tell it her way. At least I didn't have flowers and doughnuts to deal with this time.

So I smiled at my child, eyes front, ears on, ready to listen. I hadn't really "looked at her" looked at her in a while. She sat across from me in her just-so suit—still crisp at the end of the day—her hair sharp but simple, like her makeup and nails: short, neat, neutral polish. When did she stop the fancy art and tips? Anyway, Amber sits up real straight, and I lean back, preparing myself, and she says, "I got a new job!" She kept talking about how it was in the same company but especially created for her, blady blady blah. It was so not what I was expecting that I felt like I needed a translator. Where were the bassinets and snugglies? The mother-daughter conversations about breast-feeding versus bottles? Like I could afford two booties and a box of Pampers, which depressed the hell out of me.

Then I started to catch more snatches of what she was saying. Lots of travel. At least two weeks a month? The Netherlands, Mexico, China? It was all more than I was expecting, and less. I couldn't catch up, I couldn't hold on. What did I feel? Relief and disappointment side by side? Next thing I knew, a tear was sliding down my cheek.

Amber was so wrapped up with filling me in that she never saw it. I got up, went to the sink, wet a paper towel to wipe my face and hands and complained about the heat. Wherein she said, "It's not hot in here. Have you started having power surges?" I looked at her like she'd lost her mind. And she told me that's what the older women on her job called hot flashes. Excuse me? Older women? I'd had enough information for one day, so I was really relieved when J.J. showed up and they left so I could be alone with my confusion.

Three days later Amber left on her first business trip—to Reykjavik, which I had to look up because I'm sure I hadn't thought about Iceland since fourth-grade geography. I mean, I knew it was north, but I had no idea where it was in relation to, say, New Jersey. But a few clicks on the computer I didn't much like, and there it was, a nickel-sized island in the North Atlantic. Seriously, the middle of the nowhere. OK, technically between Greenland and Norway, but if anything happened, who would know?

J.J. took Amber's trip in stride—like working on top of the world was no biggie. Now, before you go getting too excited about my baby's job—the locations might be exotic, but Amber was a company watchdog, something you can already guess she was pretty good at. Internal corporate compliance they called it, which didn't spell fun in any language, and she was a rising star. But in spite of her emails telling me how well it was going, I got a little obsessive about it. I stayed online, checking the weather in Iceland. Could it really be 62 degrees in a place named for frozen water? I had to make sure there were no fires, floods or man-made disasters—I mean, really, how much Icelandic coverage do we get on the evening news? She was up there with glaciers and volcanoes and nobody to protect her. Not to be dramatic, but anything could go wrong, and she was so far away, and what could I do about it? What could I do about anything, except worry it to death and blame her wanderlust on my ex, who used to take her with him on those gigs in Bangkok and Istanbul and who knows where. I was rereading one of Amber's emails, assuring me she was warm enough, when the phone rang.

Needless to say, after that first collection call, the answering machine had become my receptionist. I actually paid attention to the caller ID box—which Amber bought years ago after a blowup with J.J. so she wouldn't talk to him by mistake. They made up about ten minutes after it was hooked up, and I ignored the whole business until hostile parties started phoning on a regular basis.

I squinted at the number in the tiny green rectangle, didn't recognize it and let my receptionist take the call. With the volume up I could pick up if it was somebody I wanted to talk to. I'd mastered the art of sounding out of breath, like I'd just run in the door. When I heard "This message is for Thomasina Hodges," I pushed mute. I did not need to be reminded that the phone bill or my gas card were past due. I was painfully aware of every bill I had, when it was due, how much of the full balance I needed to pay to keep them from bothering me for another month. I learned how far past the due day I could be before they tacked on a late fee. And how much time I had between the day the payment posted and when the money disappeared from my checking account. My car payments took two or three days in the mail. Once the payment showed up, it took another three days for the funds to disappear. But the light and gas payments were deducted the moment they received the check. They must have some kickback arrangement with the bank. I wasn't proud about knowing these things, but they were survival skills, and it is a jungle out here.

I got my notebook, ready to write down whatever made-up name they had left—Ms. Smith or Mr. Rich: would you use your real one?—and the 800 number I should call back weekdays between the hours of 7 a.m. and 9 p.m. Central Time. Then I pressed play. "This is Leandra Moretti, from Derma-

Teq." I didn't know or owe anybody from there. "We saw your résumé posted on WireHire.com and would love to have you come in for an interview."

A job? Really? I was not prepared for good news, not that it was good news yet. I was doing my best not to put all my eggs in one basket, with the chickens that hadn't hatched, on the cart before the horse. I knew hoping wouldn't make it so, but you can understand why I couldn't help it.

10

I arrived at Derma-Teq at nine-forty-five the next morning for my ten o'clock interview. The trip took just under thirty minutes door to door, which meant it would be a manageable drive at rush hour. I was getting ahead of myself again, but I had to keep hope alive.

The complex was typical Jersey office park—clusters of single-story buildings, eight offices apiece with private entrances, nice landscaping it is the Garden State, after all. I parked in front of Derma-Teq, checked my hair in the mirror. It was a cosmetics company looking for an operations person, and it had to be me.

Leandra met me at the door, pumping my hand and talking. "You must be Ms. Hodges. I'm so glad you're here." Me too. She was tall, like basketball tall, but slight, like a dancer, and I swear she didn't look much older than Amber. Great, now I was being interviewed by children. She seemed smart, and in ways that had nothing to do with her blue eyes and mass of brunette hair she reminded me of Amber. She seemed dedicated, driven and ready to succeed. I bet she would have gone to Iceland too.

The conference room was modern—clinical, if you ask me. Huge Derma-Teq posters covered the walls with models who had been up the street a time or two, but they were fresh-faced and dewy, like they stepped right out of a rain forest. Leandra settled herself across from me and launched into her spiel. "Derma-Teq products are a revolutionary evolution in the cosmeceutical industry." Cosma-what? Boy, I got a flashback of Olivia and her Almond Ginger Body Crème, only this seemed a little more science-y. She informed me that pharmaceutical-grade botanical cosmetics actually healed, repaired and rejuvenated skin, and that the company had been in Switzerland and Italy for some time. Maybe she wasn't that young—maybe she'd just been rejuvenated. She clasped her hands on the desk, told me how excited they were to be in the States. They could have been from Secaucus and Iselin and I would have been excited.

Leandra continued to lay out why Derma-Teq was the place for me, like she had to convince me that I wanted the position. I had been unemployed for almost a year. This was not a tough sell. Then she said, "Based on your experience at Markson & Daughter, we recognize the value you would bring to our company." I wanted to know who "we" were. But I liked the value part.

Leandra had a ton of questions—mostly about the early days at Markson, but they were already light-years ahead of Olivia's kitchen. About fifteen minutes in we were joined by "Phill—two *l*s—Hilton—one *l*, no relation," head of sales. I would like to know who did his manicures. His nails were buffed to an impressive sheen. He had his own set of questions, which I handled as easily as I had Leandra's, if I must say so myself. I was getting good at the interview stuff. I just needed to walk away with the prize.

The position was new. They hadn't even come up with a title for it yet, but it would answer to Leandra, who was director of U.S. operations. And the salary was more than I had hoped for—only two grand shy of what I had been making at Markson—and, hallelujah, they offered benefits upon employment. Most places made you wait six months, like they wanted to make sure they liked you enough to pay if you got sick. It would mean I could kiss my COBRA good-bye; the payments were killing me.

I didn't try to be coy or play hard to get. I said I was available to start right away. The interview lasted a little over an hour, which I thought was a good sign. And it had all gone so well that by the end I was waiting for them to show me my desk. Instead they gave me a bag of samples and said, "We'll be in touch." Which I thought was a bad sign. They felt like parting gifts for the losing contestant.

Derma-Teq would be a perfect fit, and I wanted that job. So what went wrong? Did I act like I knew too much, or not enough? Should I have talked more about Olivia or less? I might not know beans about cosmeceuticals, but I knew the cosmetics business. I spent the entire drive home trying to figure out how I could possibly have blown it.

But before the end of the day, I got the "welcome aboard" call. It was like I'd been trapped in a mine and those words were fresh air. I would be their first manager of business development—U.S. Wow, the whole country. Maybe I could rack up some frequent-flyer miles like Amber. And you know how much I like being first. I couldn't wait to introduce myself that way. I got this flash of being a kid in college. This was the kind of job I imagined I'd have after I graduated with my associates degree in business administration. Only took me twenty-five years or so, but finally I was not anybody's assistant. Not that I'm complaining about *that* gig—it made this one possible.

And it was about time for my life to get out of the dungeon. Landing a job had been so hard, and the time it took felt like dog years. Then my fairy jobmother finally woke up from the very deep sleep she must have been in, found her magic wand and, poof, the perfect position appeared. It was so easy. I decided that when it's right you don't have to force, it just fits, like Cinderella's slipper—like with Olivia. Boy, did I fantasize about Didier coming across the industry-updates section in the trades and seeing my smiling face next to the article announcing my new position. I hoped it made him choke on his latte when he realized what a valuable resource he pissed away, not that I have lingering hostility or anything.

I called Mom and Dad, sounding like I did when I found my first job. They were a few hundred miles away, but I could hear their relief. "'Cause we were about to come get you and bring you down here to live with us," is what Daddy said. I appreciated the sentiment, but the idea of my retired parents coming to my rescue—it would be like if they had come to my high school and delivered my galoshes in front of the whole class so my feet wouldn't get cold in the snow. Having snow in my shoes and cold, wet feet would be less embarrassing. Mom added, "Next time don't keep everything a secret." Next time? Was she kidding? There wasn't gonna be a next time.

Amber was in Mexico City, but I spoke to J.J., who said, "Way to go, Mama Tee." Later he even sent me a link to Derma-Teq's website. They had branches in Zurich, Paris, Milan, Buenos Aires, Johannesburg and Shanghai. Who would have thought such an international enterprise had offices in an industrial park in New Jersey?

And I called Julie. We went out to celebrate that night. She'd read about Derma-Teq in one of the European trade magazines. But she said Nordstrom's didn't carry it and she didn't know who did. I reminded her that once upon a time, before her tenure, Markson & Daughter didn't have prime department store real estate either. And that Olivia's first counter was in the back of Macy's—the last stop in cosmetics land, just before you got to men's socks.

Eventually she let on how worried she'd been, and how she prayed every night for me to find a job—a whole lot different from the response from my Live Five crew, who basically saw my misfortune as gossip material. Well, I had prayed every night too, and lots of times during the day. I had been through some hard stuff in my life, but losing my job? I wouldn't wish that on another soul—with the possible exception of Didier of course, and Gerald. But now it was my turn to get up off my knees and strut my stuff.

The morning I started at Derma-Teq felt like the first day at a new school. I made my lunch; of course, if Leandra wanted to eat out to encourage our bonding, I could work with that. And if I had an expense account . . .

Anyway, I had already memorized the Derma-Teq product line and tried all the samples I'd gotten after my interview. Maybe I was overly eager, but my complexion did seem particularly radiant.

I had picked out my outfit the night before: black suit, chocolate silk sweater, tiger pumps—simple and chic because in the cosmetics industry appearances matter. I even splurged on a manicure. I considered red because I was celebrating, but neutral seemed more in keeping with the Derma-Teq aesthetic. My old manicurist looked at me like I had come back from the grave, and dipping my fingertips in that warm cream again sure felt good.

I hadn't realized how much I'd missed the rhythm of going to work. Seriously. I liked having a good excuse to look nice five days a week, having people depend on me and having something important to contribute.

By eight-forty that Monday morning I was sitting in the parking lot, clutching my steering wheel, petrified—didn't see that coming, but all of a sudden it dawned on me that this was only the second job I'd had in my whole life. Then I was serenaded by a selection from the What-If chorus—they stood behind me, next to me, in front of me or hovered over me like the Mighty Clouds of Doubt. They had become such a regular accompaniment to my life's symphony—I had gotten used to them showing up uninvited, unannounced and definitely unwelcome. And there they were, right on time. What if I couldn't do the job? What if I didn't fit in? What if I hated it? I couldn't turn off the song and my teeth were almost chattering, which was not in keeping with the confident impression I wanted to make. That's when my cell phone rang. It was Julie, calling to say break a leg. It couldn't have been more on time. Then she told me how nice I had been on her first day and how much it had meant. I never knew that. I barely even remember, but I'm glad it made a difference. And hearing Julie's voice sure helped me calm down, so I checked for sesame seeds between my teeth, gave myself a confident look in the mirror and in I went.

Pilar, the receptionist/customer-service rep/office manager/ sometimes translator looked effortlessly stylish in that understated, unadorned kind of way. She wasn't tall, but she sure was tan and young and lovely, and she spoke with a sophisticated accent that reminded me of someplace exotic, exclusive and expensive. Even the supporting players were classy. There was no rudeness and gum chewing. She welcomed me, introduced me around to the folks who were already in their cubicles, some of them already on the phone. I figured they must be dealing with contacts in Europe or South America. It was an intimate office, meaning the staff wasn't big. There were still a few empty desks so it looked like they were planning for growth, which was a good sign. Even though I swore I'd never do it again, it was exciting to be in on the ground floor.

When we got to the kitchenette, I wished I hadn't eaten breakfast. There were fresh bagels, fruit, yogurt, granola bars, tea, hot chocolate, juice, water and, for later, cookies, snack packs and soda. Great for employee moral. I did get coffee. And Phill breezed in to get samples and some papers before heading out to make calls up in Westchester and the Stamford–New Haven area. "Hey Tee! You're our edge. Maybe I should just call you Ms. Sharp," is what he said to me, whatever that was supposed to mean. Then Pilar showed me to my office, said Leandra would be in shortly.

When I was alone I twirled in my chair like it was the teacup ride. I could have kissed my shiny flatscreen monitor. The room was hardly sprawling, but my desk, bookshelf and credenza were pretty spiffy—some kind of mocha laminate with brushed aluminum accents and frosted glass-door panels. There was no window, but I did have an attractive framed Derma-Teq poster of a black woman with silky skin. Coincidence? I didn't know or care. It looked like a first-rate operation, and I was thrilled to be there.

Leandra looked excited to see me. We spent a lot of the morning in her office, which, in addition to Derma-Teq décor, had trophies and medals from her days as an elite collegiate basketball player. She'd even played some pro ball in Australia, hoping to make it to the WNBA, except her eggshell knees, as she called them, gave out. But it seems Steven Wu, founder of Derma-Teq, was a big fan of women's basketball, especially number 15. When she retired, he contacted her, offered her a job—she was, after all, a business-administration major, like myself. She worked a few years at the company headquarters in Shanghai, then relocated to New Jersey to start American operations. Shanghai to central Jersey—that's gotta give you whiplash.

Anyway, we took care of routine paperwork, like my medical insurance forms. I sure was looking forward to having coverage again, even if it was just to get a PAP smear and a flu shot.

Lunch turned out to be a pleasant surprise. It was catered daily by the company—soup, salad, assorted sandwiches. I heard Fridays were wild—you order what you want and they pick up the tab. Depending on the day people would gather around the conference table for conversation and a group meal or go back to their desks to finish what they were working on. That was two sponsored meals a day. What a perk. I'd hardly need the supermarket.

That afternoon I huddled with Leandra and she filled me in on my mission. Derma-Teq had found acceptance in other countries, but they didn't have a niche in the U.S. market. Their crèmes and preparations weren't prescription-strength drugs, so they had run into problems with the FDA about what they could claim on their packaging. They were definitely too expensive to be a drugstore brand, but they didn't have their footing in department or specialty stores yet either.

It gave me a lot to think about and brought me squarely back to Olivia's loft, that first newspaper article and the jars with my handwritten labels. A little before five, Leandra asked if I would stay late. On the first day? But she had a video-conference scheduled with Steven Wu for six-fifteen—p.m. our time, a.m. his time—and she wanted to introduce me. I couldn't turn that down. Who knows, maybe there'd be a trip to Shanghai or someplace else exotic in my future.

First off, he didn't look like any PhD chemist I ever imagined. Mr. Wu was definitely not the lab-coat and pocket-protector variety. It was before dawn, but he was already seriously styling with a black suit and silk T-shirt that fit him flawlessly and set off his silver-streaked hair. He looked like a rock star, an actor or a spy—merely a professional observation. And I couldn't help thinking of Olivia, who looked like a flying mess the first time I saw her. It takes all kinds. We spoke briefly. He told me how much he had admired Olivia and the Markson brand and that he looked forward to my input. I truly wasn't expecting the English accent, but something about him inspired confidence. I wanted to be a part of the team and I was so fired up that before I went to bed that night I started making notes in my laptop— on my laptop—however you say it.

Olivia had established herself as a small, exclusive brand and moved out from there. Was this a strategy that could apply to Derma-Teq? Was there confusion about who would benefit from the product? Who was their target customer? I was so excited I had to force myself to go to bed, but I had come up with a lengthy to-do list.

And the next morning, before I went to the office, I stopped and found myself a new philodendron. Rapunzel II was more developed than her predecessor had been when I brought her to the office in that little white plastic pot. I already had a spot picked out for her on my credenza. It would make me feel at home in my new surroundings, and hopeful. My departure from Markson had been so sudden and I had been so angry that I didn't have time to be sad too—but this wasn't the day for looking backward. I didn't have any sunlight, but the fluorescents in my office would be enough to keep a plant happy, and I could look forward to watching it grow to twenty feet again.

The job was all that *and* a paycheck. I was in love. On our next video conference, this one from Moscow, Steven—he said he preferred the informality of first names—was impressed with the highlights I presented from the notes I had made about resistance to the brand, and with my initial suggestions for how to reposition the products. He was particularly interested in my Markson experience and asked me to prepare a report, expanding on my findings. I hadn't done one of those since the Markson corporate history that I turned into confetti, but I was up to the challenge. Steven wasn't looking for a slick marketing package with graphs, charts and whirligigs—whatever they were. He wanted to know what I thought they could do better or differently, based on my experience. *My experience.* Clearly he understood you don't work for twenty-plus years as the right hand to the founder of a hugely successful company without knowing a thing or two. Even a sockless idiot could see that. Oops, guess not. Anyway, based on my findings we would commission an in-depth analysis of the areas I identified, then formulate a budget and a detailed plan of action to increase our U.S. market share. I was impressed with my own expertise.

Well, every day, five o'clock rolled around and I wasn't ready to go home, not because I was playing the eager-beaver suck-up. I was just into my project, which entailed buying scads of magazines to check out competitors ads, then shopping the cosmetics aisles of high-end department stores. I got sales pitches, samples and scored shopping bags full of wrinkle creams, masks, peels, eye gels, exfoliating washes, serums, epi-vitamins, day protection, night repair, anti-age, youth restore—I bought enough stuff to beautify my entire town. In between my snooping trips, Leandra picked my brain, and I compiled pages and pages of notes. Let me tell you, time flies when you're having fun—and making money spending someone else's.

I also had consultations at three of the most luxurious spas in New Jersey, and several in Manhattan—all in the name of sniffing out the competition, and fully expensed on my company credit card. I sure enjoyed signing on the dotted line to pay for my purchases—I mean the company's purchases. I hadn't had a viable credit card of my own in a while, but I felt those days were about to be over. Yep, I was counting my blessings. I didn't think I would ever say it, but whatever I had been through was worth it.

11

. . . nothing left but mint wrappers and lint.

I saw the great big chain around the door handles at Derma-Teq and could read the "WARNING" notice pasted on the door before I got out of my car—figured there must be a gas leak or something. Great. That morning I was looking forward to my new favorite healthy breakfast—fruit salad topped with plain yogurt and a drizzle of honey. Seriously, I still wasn't ready to sign on for veggie burgers, but I was taking care of myself on the inside, like my Derma-Teq regimen pampered my complexion on the outside. And I had some observations to add to my report, which was coming along nicely. I was still debating whether to show it to Leandra before our usual Monday video conference or save it to wow Wu.

My next thought was about whether I'd get paid for the day if we weren't allowed in the building. Not to be petty but it wasn't my fault. They were certainly generous with the groceries, but I was thinking about my check and you never know when you're the newbie. I was truly gleeful to be able to resume paying my bills. And eliminating COBRA put more than a little change back in my pocket, but I had a deep hole to climb out of. I sure didn't want to be short a day for the week. That money was already spoken for.

It had taken three weeks to get my first check—I had to catch up with the payroll cycle—but cashing it felt as good as going to the bank with the first check I ever earned. Maybe better. I was eager to hear Steven's feedback on what I had written. And I admit I was already thinking ahead to trying my hand at sales once we'd repositioned Derma-Teq. I'd seen Phill's thousand-dollar suits and his snazzy Jag. I mean, look at Gerald—one *g*, one *l*. He was no genius—and he wasn't exactly overstocked in the dazzle-and-charisma department, but he did very nicely. Julie had carved out a prime spot for herself too. I used to watch Olivia and think I could never convince strangers to buy even things they needed, but over the years she made me see that selling was less about the product—no matter how good it was—and more about making the customer feel smart, like they made the best decision. For the right-sized payday I could do that, and take advantage of my naturally chatty nature—like you hadn't noticed. I wanted to have the kind of relaxed, as-sured attitude that comes from knowing you've got options—and money in the bank. And I had become a real Derma-Teq believer. Of course who knew what I could grow my position into. VP Tee had a nice ring.

I got out to see if there was a phone number on the notice, or if we were supposed to report someplace else temporarily. I did wonder, though I admit only in passing, why there were no barricades, orange cones or official-looking people telling us what to do. And when I finally got close enough to read the rest of the sign, I wished for a gas leak, or a flood or nuclear fallout. It was a notice from the marshal that said, "This property seized for nonpayment of federal taxes," signed the IRS. I stared at the words, trying to make them say something else, but I've been reading since *Green Eggs and Ham*; I knew what they meant. This had to be a misunderstanding. Some kind of computer glitch that would be fixed with a phone call, and then Marshal Dillon would come back with the key and open up in time for me to get my check on Friday. But I was cool, working really hard not to dwell on how all my phone calls to Unemployment didn't straighten out squat. They merely clarified my screwed-up situation.

This wasn't like way back in the day, when the packaging vendor would call Markson & Daughter and say he didn't get the check, and I would go to Olivia's desk, unearth the bill, hand her the checkbook and say, "Here, sign this." I didn't have anybody's home phone. I didn't even know what country Steven was in this week. So I tried to breathe and waited for somebody else to show up.

Phill was first. He stormed up and down the sidewalk, cussing like a rapper—I didn't know he had it in him. Leandra just stood there like she had fallen under a spell. Next thing I knew her knees buckled and Phill caught her just before she hit the pavement. I would never have taken her for a fainter, although truthfully I was feeling a little lightheaded myself.

We sat in my car until Leandra pulled herself together and phoned Mr. Wu—at that point I wasn't feeling informal. His voicemail was full. I wondered what else had a padlock on it that day. She said she'd get in touch with me if she heard something. I said, "What do you mean, *if*?" But really, she was in the same canoe I was, and it looked like nobody had a paddle. By then other coworkers had started to show up, but I wasn't interested in commiserating or conjecture, so I went home to wait for the call. Somebody had to have answers because you don't do business like that.

Despite my attempts at CPR, hope was fading—fast. But I did write checks for the bills I was going to pay. They were in their envelopes, signed, sealed and ready to drop in the mail as soon as I left the bank from depositing the check I was going to have by the end of the week. Except days passed with no news, and I got the uneasy feeling that Steven was in Zurich, making withdrawals from his Swiss bank accounts before deciding whether to head for the Caymans or Mumbai.

After a week and a half with no word and no check, I knew I was back in the pit, covered with grit, wondering what is this shit? And when was it going to end?

Well, I had kept my joblessness secret the first time, but I guess I learned some kind of lesson, so I came clean—mostly— and told my family that I was out of work, again. But not how broke I really was or that I didn't have health insurance. Mom and Daddy wanted to send me money. Right, like I was going to take a cut of their Social Security checks—uh-uh, I was not that desperate—yet. But worse than that, Amber and J.J. came by on a Saturday morning and perched on my couch again, all serious, like the day he proposed. This time they each took one of my hands, told me they were there if I needed help—money help—just let them know. And I was done. Yes, it was touching, and I was supposed to be proud that they had become such mature, responsible people, but truthfully I was crushed. Here were my children, because I'd known J.J. long enough to think of him that way, offering to bail out dear old Mom. It made me feel small and I hated that. So I assured them I'd be fine and sent them on their way as soon as I could so I could sit in the middle of my sofa and bawl.

That's when the light went out—my own personal little light, you know, the one I'm supposed to let shine—it drowned in the flood I let loose, because I'd already robbed Peter and Paul and borrowed from Jack before I knew there was a Jill, and I was thinking about all those envelopes I couldn't mail, because my available balance was forty-seven cents. That's not even two quarters, not two hours at a parking meter, not a newspaper or bus fare around the corner. I was a grown woman, worked all my life, raised my child, and that's what I had in my bank account? That was beyond pitiful. By that time I had already been through my coat pockets and purses, found all the loose change and "oh happy day" dollars. There was nothing left but mint wrappers and lint.

And seeing the kids sitting on my couch had reminded me they were closing in on their first anniversary. How had I gone from one of the most beautiful days in my life—not to mention the single most expensive—straight down the chute into my own little ring of Hades in just a year?

It also reminded me I too was approaching an anniversary. It was about to be one year since my previously manageable life unraveled, thread by thread, and nothing I had or hadn't done made that better. Paper is the one-year gift, right? And I was trying my best to get a little piece that said "Pay to the Order of . . ." but it was becoming harder to figure out my next move, and I needed to do something quick.

So, since I'd already done the cash-advance dance on my last useable credit card, I broke the emergency glass. There wasn't a whole lot in my retirement accounts, but I figured it was enough to take the heat off and get me through the next round of Wheel of Employment. And to quiet the phone calls, because the reminders that I'd "forgotten" about my phone, electric or MasterVisAmexicard payment were coming hot and heavy. I wasn't sure which I despised more—the real people with the snarky attitudes, like it was their money, or the automated calls: "This message is important. Your account is seriously overdue . . ." If they couldn't afford a real person to talk to me, I didn't have to put up with tape-recorded harassment.

Now, you know I was desperate. I swore I'd never walk through Markson's doors again, but there I was in the waiting room of human resources, trying to casually flip through the latest issue of *Global Cosmetics Industry* and ignore Didier's assistant as hard as she ignored me, pretending her eyes were glued to that folder she was reading until she escaped out the door, I'm sure to tell that no-sock-wearing crook I was in the building.

Do you know the benefits manager had the nerve to tell me I couldn't withdraw 401(k) money because my situation did not qualify as a "hardship emergency"? I needed to have medical bills, tuition bills, be buying a house or on the verge of eviction. And it still involved paying a penalty—I had to be even more pitiful to avoid that. No salary for almost a year? You talk to a hundred people and ninety-nine of them will call it a hardship. The hundredth has Oprah money.

My only other option was to raid my little bit of IRA—first stock I ever bought. I opened the account in a fit of flushness, probably after I'd watched some TV financial guru pontificate about what it costs to retire and how if you manage your funds, and expect an average return of 10 percent, you too can live in a beachfront house and drive a sports car in your golden years, like my parents. Sounded good at the time. And I got 10 percent alright—a 10 percent charge to get my money now, plus I had to pay federal and state tax off the top. That amounted to almost half the balance, so I got barely enough for a seashell and a spinning rim, which just didn't seem fair. But it allowed me to deal with the immediate payments due and have a little room to maneuver.

On my way back from the post office, bills mostly paid and a little bit of money left in my account, I felt a sense of accomplishment—until I stopped for a fill-up. My credit card was denied. Normally I would have argued with the man, told him he needed to get his machine fixed, 'cause it must be broken, but I knew I had just mailed that check. I didn't want to make a fuss. I know how I looked at people when their card was denied, so I snatched it back, dug in my purse and came up with a five. The nozzle was out before I put my pocketbook down. I was shocked to realize that five dollars' worth of premium wasn't enough to move the needle. I never actually looked at the total before—I'd just make sure the tank was full, stuff the receipt in the glove box and keep on driving. So I did not pass go or stop at the mini-mart for the bag of chips I had a hankering for. I went directly home, fully aware it was crunch time, time to address my car-lease situation post-Gerald.

Now, you must understand, my car was sexy, sleek, stylish, sumptuous—a lot like me. When Gerald leased me my first luxury wheels, I couldn't believe I could afford something so beautiful, something that turned heads, made people who were stopped next to me in traffic smile and tell me, "You are *drivin'* that car." I felt what they meant, and I'd smile back, then take off fast and smooth, imagining them admiring my bumper. I was proud of that car, and proud of me for having it. So what would it mean if I didn't anymore?

I had leased a new car every other year for the past twelve, but I was afraid the streak was about to be broken. And I couldn't see how I was supposed to walk in, turn over the keys to *my* car and walk away with nothing. After all I'd paid? It wasn't right, which, come to think of it, sounded a lot like my situation with Gerald.

Well, talking to myself wouldn't solve anything, and talking to him was out of the question, so I called the dealership to find out when he *wasn't* there. The answer? Not that day, or the next—or ever. "He's no longer with the company" is what the cheery woman on the phone said. Huh? That got my tongue.

So the break was complete, which was some kind of milestone. I hadn't realized how often I imagined him with his feet propped up on the open bottom drawer of his desk, so I could be specifically angry at him. Now I didn't have a spot to aim the mad at. Gone. It was like he had never been there, which is how it should have always been. But I wasn't done being upset, which meant absolutely nothing to customer representative Tricia, who was eager to make an appointment to discuss my vehicular needs. I said I'd just drop in. I left out the part about as soon as I got the nerve. Sounds stupid, but without Gerald I didn't feel like I belonged in that posh, shiny showroom that smelled like leather and success, and that they'd all know.

But I still had to manage my auto issues. So I got dressed up one morning and went in. Maybe it was hearing my options from somebody I'd never seen before, but no matter how Tricia, in her quietly quality silk shirt, black skirt and pearls, broke it down, there was no deal. I asked about re-leasing the car I already had, but that didn't change the monthly payment by enough to pay my already reduced cable bill. Then I asked about buying the car I'd been leasing—that was more per month than

I already paid unless I spread the payments out over six years. I wasn't asking for a mortgage. What had they been doing with all that money I sent every month? It was supposed to count for something, wasn't it? Then I took a stroll through the Certified Pre-Owned lot. Somebody came up with that term because they figured out nobody in their right mind would pay that much for a used car.

I spent two hours acting like I was giving the sales spiel serious consideration. When I left I said I needed to weigh my decision, check out some other options. Really, I needed to catch my breath, because in a hot hurry I was going to have an empty garage, and in order to work anywhere, I had to have transportation.

Which is what I thought about in the middle of the night when I wasn't sleeping. Oh, I'd go to bed, drift off with the TV on and wake up in the middle of some freaky cop-squad autopsy drama and shut it off before they figured out where the arm came from. Ever notice how quiet it is at 2 a.m.? And how there are no distractions to keep your mind from feeding on itself? Chomp. Chomp. After a few nights of that, I decided I had to screw up my nerve and go car shopping.

Realistically, what I had to do was reduce my monthly nut, which at the moment was like a Brazil nut—big, ugly and hard to crack. I needed something more in the peanut area. I hadn't actually shopped for a car in years—I just picked out the color and the trim package, signed some papers and switched keys—still hadn't ditched that silver *T* key ring. The whole process was a shock. I started my research watching car commercials—more convenient middle-of-the-night viewing. Even found some with cash-back offers and zero-percent financing—sounded practical.

First off, Amber'd had toy cars the size of some of the little things I looked at—and they felt about as sturdy as a Forever Barbie convertible. Then the salesperson would ask what I was driving now. When I told them, I could see this, "Then why are you here?" look flash across their faces. They'd find out after we put together a deal, which was extra hard for me because I didn't want those little toys anyway. Then they'd go for that chat with their manager. Turns out that zero-percent stuff is reserved for their "highest qualified" customers. And I was no longer one of those. So they'd come back and get jiggy with the figures. No sale.

So I lowered my sights from new and began my tour of used-car lots. I quickly discovered the perfect balance between age and mileage was unattainable. How do you drive 87,000 miles in three years, by making round trips from Miami to Seattle? At first, three years old was my limit. I was not interested in anybody's worn-out wheels. Then I went to four years, then five. I really wanted something I could pay for with my IRA money—one less bill I had to worry about.

J.J. tried to get me to call Ron to go shopping with me, but I was embarrassed all by myself. I didn't need company, certainly not Ron's. Besides, this wasn't going to be my last car, just a tide-me-over until I got my situation right.

So I began what I called my classic-car period, because, really, ten years is not so old, right? I mean, I remembered when new cars looked like my not-hot wheels—it was a very popular model. There were tons of them still on the road, which I took as a good sign. And the sturdy battleship gray made it look dependable. And my car insurance was lower; not as much lower as I hoped, but lower. And it had a CD player. And it took regular gas. And I felt awful driving past *my* car, which I parked in front of the house, and inching that one into the garage, where nobody could see it. Tricia arranged to have my sassy ride picked up on a flatbed because I couldn't bear to drive that last mile and leave it. I told her I'd made other arrangements. She said she was sorry. So was I.

I didn't go anywhere for a week, and when I finally had to leave the house for groceries I snuck out at night, parked way in the back of the lot, so in case I ran into anybody they wouldn't see me get in. But it was good for me, a move in the right direction, being a responsible grown-up, taking my medicine. Pick one, they're all annoying.

And I found another job, the old-fashioned way—I answered a newspaper ad. The job was pretty low-tech too. It was with a car-insurance broker, Neighborhood Auto Brokerage. If you measured by distance, offpeak, the office was an hour, each way, which had absolutely nothing to do with the prime-time drive jive I'd have to dance twice a day. My monthly income wouldn't come close to covering my monthly outgo, especially since I was going to spend almost as much on gas and tolls as I had been on my car lease, and benefits wouldn't kick in until I'd been there three months. But they were well established— a member of the Chamber of Commerce in good standing, sponsored a Little League team, had billboards along the highway. This time I checked. So even though it paid way less than Derma-Teq, it seemed pretty likely that I would get paid. NAB—not the best acronym—was a small, old-fashioned setup. Believe it or not, in addition to computers they still had typewriters and adding machines, and there wasn't a taupe half-wall cubicle anywhere—just one big open room. And the owner of the company was not some international man of mystery. Julius was there every day, in the trenches, with his old-country work ethic and his short-sleeved shirts that never quite stayed tucked into his pants, like he had been for thirty-seven years.

My job was painfully dull. I followed up on claims. No expertise or reports required. And my coworkers were . . . nice. If you put all seven of them together you wouldn't come up with six ounces of pizzazz, or any parts of a dress-for-success wardrobe—this was strictly a dress-down crowd. So I got with the program as best I could. They made room for me, sort of. And I tried to be friendly, sort of. I wasn't kidding myself. It was a job, not a career move. I didn't expect to climb up the NAB ladder. From what I could see, everybody had their rung and was holding on for dear life.

But I needed a payday in the worst way, and since the fairy jobmother hadn't waved her magic wand and filled my email box with offers I couldn't refuse, choosy was no longer an option. So I gave Julius forty hours of phone calls and paperwork, and in exchange he gave me a check. I even tossed in a little office organization, gratis—the kind of thing I used to do for Olivia, mostly because it made things easier for me to get my job done. I still sent out résumés, hoping to find a slipper that fit a bit better. But I smiled and squeezed myself into the shoe I had. I chipped in for birthday cake, put five dollars that should have gone in my gas tank in the football pool, laughed at Julius's corny jokes. At seven every morning, I got in my considerably less than sassy carriage, trying to be grateful it hadn't turned into a pumpkin. But I did not buy a plant for my desk.

12

Some things are worth forgetting.

The kids spent their first wedding anniversary in London. Amber went for work. J.J. joined her later for a week of romance. They say the first year is the hardest and I hoped that was true because they made it through and I was proud of them.

I too had passed a milestone. I began the commemoration of my first post-Markson year with Julius plopping a pile of forms on my desk. They had been returned by one of our insurers because I forgot to add the time-date stamp. "You screw up," is how he put it. And honestly, I didn't know if he meant I had or if he was calling me names, but the bottom line was that it didn't matter. What else is there to say? It meant I had to get out my phone log and retrace the chronology of every one of those accident reports. Makes for a spellbinding day.

I didn't usually break for lunch until one—it made the afternoon shorter—but by noon I was cross-eyed, so I stopped for my cuppa soup and the other half of my breakfast bagel. Yep, the former Takeout Queen had become a brown bagger, because that's what she needed to do if she was going to eat. Not that I hadn't occasionally brought lunch from home in the old days—leftover lasagna or mac and cheese was yummy enough to have twice in a row. But truth was, at Markson, everybody came to me for the lunch 411 because I knew what was good where, how long it took for delivery, whose specials were worthy and, most important, which menus to circular file. So much for the good old days. Not that there's anything wrong with BYOL—Bring Your Own Lunch—'cause I found out there's really no such thing as a free one at Derma-Teq. And it's healthier for me too. OK. That's just a little too perky. I didn't even like lunch boxes when I was in third grade, so hauling homemade cuisine was a good habit that would take some getting used to. But by this episode of *Tee Tightens Her Belt*, our heroine was hyper-aware that she could have two weeks' worth of instant ramen noodles for less than the cost of one Monte Cristo deluxe platter. Besides, I had vowed not to go back to my wild spending ways—job or no job.

See—I really was trying.

So one second I'm gnawing on my bagel and pretending to listen to one of my coworkers give me an hour-by-hour recap of her weekend. The next I'm crunching something hard and gritty, which I knew was not a pumpernickel. What is a pumpernickel?

A trip to the ladies' room confirmed it was a tooth or, more accurately, a chunk of dental filling. Oh joy. It was one that had been root canaled back when I could afford such luxurious indulgences, so at least it didn't hurt. Of course, the health insurance that hadn't kicked in yet wouldn't include dental anyway, so whatever it took to fix my miserable molar was on me.

What's one more hole when you're trying to extricate yourself from a crater? Let's see, a trip to the dentist, or electricity? Decisions, decisions.

By quitting time I wasn't even halfway through my do-over stack—gave me something to look forward to the next day. In my formerly employed life, if I made the mistake, I'd have stayed to correct it, but NAB wasn't the kind of place where you worked late to show your diligence and ambition. The hours were eight to five, lunch was not paid. Everybody, including Julius, was out the door by five fifteen, tops.

I stopped at the drugstore to pick up a temporary tooth-filling kit. I remembered seeing them advertised in the back of magazines and wondering what kind of idiot practiced do-it-yourself dentistry. Now I knew. I had no idea if it would do the job, but for $4.99 it was worth a try.

The stuff looked like ABC gum. You remember from second grade—Already Been Chewed. And it smelled like Silly Putty. The directions said to pinch off a piece slightly smaller than the cavity you're filling and roll it between your fingers. Using a hand mirror and the tip of my tongue as a guide and handy measuring tool, I determined the hole was about the size of the Grand Canyon, so I thought my piece was just right. It's not easy working in your own mouth. Your hands block the view. They also didn't tell me—or did I skip that part?—the *Insta* in InstaDent is no joke. Before I could get it in place, half of it was crumbly, like old plaster. The rest coated the wrong tooth like cement. It took twenty minutes and sixteen toothpicks to chip my first attempt from between my teeth. A half hour, two tries and an aching jaw later I had plugged the hole that started the whole adventure. The result was lumpy, but it would do until I could do better.

I was in the kitchen, on the final countdown to the all clear to eat and drink—my patchwork had to set. My glass of Chardonnay was ready and waiting when the doorbell rang. Mine was not the kind of neighborhood where folks popped in to borrow a cup of sugar or hang out over a pot of coffee, so I assumed my visitor was a soccer or band kid selling candy or magazine subscriptions to raise money for uniforms. I considered pretending I wasn't home, but with all the money I'd just saved on dental bills, even I could spare a dollar or two. Before I opened the door, I peeked out the window, because I was a woman who lived alone. It could just as easily have been Freddy Krueger. Now that I think about it, I don't think he rang doorbells.

And it wasn't Freddy—it was worse. Hands jammed in the pockets of his khaki pants, rocking back on his heels like he always did, stood Gerald, regular as you please, like he belonged there. I was stupefied. Not only that he had the gall to show up at my house, but the man was at the *front door*. For twelve years the lying sneak had parked his car of the week with its dealer plates in the driveway, come through the garage and knocked on the side door—three raps. "It's our signal." What, so I wouldn't confuse him with my other boyfriend who might drop by on Thursday night? Gerald said he was being discreet, protecting my reputation. Like I was the one who had something to hide. But little ol' me was so flattered by his trifling chivalry that I forgot to remember he made a living telling people what they wanted to hear.

Now, I got hot and my heart started to pound like a war drum while I debated whether to open the door or ignore him. But as much as I wanted to make him wait and watch him skulk away, I was also dying to know what could possibly make him think it was OK to show up at my house after almost six months, like he might be welcome.

Before I opened the door, I dabbed at the sweat on my forehead and upper lip and checked the mirror. Any self-respecting woman about to come face to face with the man who done her wrong would want to look her best. Besides, I needed to make sure there were no stray flecks of tooth goop still sticking to my chin. As luck would have it, I had been so intent on my dental duties that I hadn't changed out of my work clothes yet. And no matter how dressed down my colleagues were, I was not showing up at the office in jeans or a warmup suit. I had kicked off my shoes upstairs, but I had just done my toes a few nights before so my feet looked cute. It would have to do. When I opened the door, I looked pretty good, if I do say so myself.

But Gerald said it for me.

"You look great, Tee." He started out grinning, like that was supposed to make me melt. But I stood in the doorway, with my arms folded across my chest, a lot like Tressy had greeted me. It was as chummy as I intended to get. So he tried a more serious expression, said he would have called, but he figured I'd hang up, which showed he hadn't completely taken leave of his senses. He was dressed more casually than he would have been on a work night. Then I noticed the name of his new employer embroidered on his polo shirt—definitely a step down in motor status, but who was I to judge?

I kept my voice real low when I spoke, so he'd have to lean in to hear me. It was also a way to keep myself from yelling my head off, which I had no intention of doing on my front steps. I told him I had half a mind to slam the door. He sort of laughed until he saw I wasn't laughing with him. Then he started rubbing his hands together, and I realized the ever confident and suave one was uncomfortable. Which was a state I'd never seen—and I liked it. A lot.

Gerald said something about it being a chilly night, but I wasn't giving him an inch—or a foot—across my threshold. So I ignored him and told him if he was looking for his stuff, he was way late—I'd thrown it out ages ago. I tried my best to sound cool and detached, even though Nervous and Mad were having a fight to the finish on my insides. I thought Excited to See Him might have shown up, but clearly it was defeated in the last round. He said that wasn't why he'd come. And then the fool said he wanted to apologize.

I snapped right back, told him to go right ahead. He looked stunned, like he thought *wanting* to apologize was the same as *doing* it, and wasn't that good enough? I just waited. Then he cleared his throat, hunched his shoulders and mumbled about being sorry, said I deserved better, that he should have told me. Guess he thought he hadn't stepped in it quite enough, so he had the nerve to add, "I miss you." That was all I needed. Pissed Off got a stranglehold on Nervous. Gerald had jumped in the deep end, and instead of tossing him a life preserver, I was ready, willing and able to hold him under and watch him flail a while.

I cannot tell a lie. I had fantasized about seeing Gerald as a broken man—on the street penniless and homeless—maybe sharing a ratty old refrigerator box with Didier. My fantasy life is on the dramatic side. And I had only thought a million or so times about what I would say to him if I had the chance. Of course, nothing I actually said that night was part of my well-rehearsed dream speech. But those "what goes around" moments are only perfect in the movies. I was content to see him squirm.

I was stone-faced when I said I agreed with him—he was about as sorry a man as I ever hope to know, and I've known a few. I was really getting warmed up and he was rocking again. That's when I asked if he meant he should have told me he was getting divorced, actually divorced or getting married again. By then I needed to take a breath because I did not want to run out of steam before the end. That's when I wondered out loud whether missing me had anything to do with being dismissed by his fiancée, who, by the way, called to thank me. The look on his face made me smile for the first time since I opened the door.

Gerald tried to defend himself, said I wasn't being fair. Maybe I wasn't, but I hadn't gone looking for him or written some ranting letter hoping to have the last word and hurt his feelings like he hurt mine. I was done. Through. Remember, he rang *my* bell, so I felt justified in having my say.

Then I had a question for him. Did he think he could drop by, say "my bad" and I'd forgive him and pencil him in for Thursday nights again? Or that I'd invite him in for a roll in the hay because poor ol' lonely Tee must be needing a little somethin' somethin' by then?

I could tell he was gathering his words. After all, Gerald had spent the last twelve years giving me advice, telling me how things should be, what I needed to do. And I had let him. So that part was as much my fault as his.

He jammed his hands back in his pockets, stared down at my feet—I was wearing red polish, his favorite color—tough. He cleared his throat and said, "I . . . I was wondering, uh, about the money you borrowed." What the—?

I honestly didn't know whether the loan was an afterthought or the real reason for the drive-by, but in that moment I completely understood how perfectly normal people can lose it. "I don't know how the knife got in my hand, Your Honor. I just snapped." But as much as I wanted to do him physical harm right then, I had presence of mind enough to know Gerald was not worth jail. He had taken up enough of my time. So I held on to the door to keep my hands from accidentally ending up around his throat, and I said, "Get out of my face. And don't you ever come back."

He stared at me—eyes all squenched up like I was speaking Gaelic. I stared back, and it didn't take him more than a couple of heartbeats to do the translation. He shook his head like I had just blown my chance at supreme happiness and I didn't want to reconsider. Then he walked away. I don't know what got into me—yes, I do—but when he got close to the driveway I called after him, "Nice minivan," and slammed the door so hard the bell rang.

That's when I realized I was trembling, which only upset me more. How dare he make me angry enough to shake? It was only then I remembered I didn't tell him I'd met Annie too. So he'd know all his secrets were out. I started to yank the door open, but I could feel tears threatening, and I would rather water my lawn naked at noon on a Saturday than let Gerald see me cry.

I wanted to explode. Scream. Throw things. I stood in my foyer a minute getting a hold of myself before I decided I needed assistance, which needed to be stronger than Chardonnay. So seeing red and propelled by a high-octane blend of outrage and indignation I marched toward the liquor cabinet in the family room—and slammed my bare foot full force into the wrought-iron magazine rack—perhaps more proof that God really don't like ugly.

First came the flash of white light. Then, before I felt the pain I heard what sounded like Velcro when you rip the pieces apart. Hint—nothing on your body should make that sound. Ever. My foot had gone one way, my baby toe went the other, and I was scared to look down because I wasn't sure if it was still attached or stuck in the rack. I can't say which I thought was worse, but the possibilities made me woozy.

How to adequately describe the pain? Imagine your foot being slammed in a car door over and over again, while someone holds a blow torch to it. I have yelled really loud for far less hurt. Part of me thought I *was* hollering. My mouth may have actually been open. But I was too stunned to make a sound, like there was somebody around to hear me anyway.

Breath came in short, shallow gasps. Instinctively I knew I had to get a grip, so I held on to the back of my lounge chair and forced myself to look down. I was horrified at the melon-sized blood splotch—water not cantaloupe—that had already seeped into the fibers of my oatmeal-colored carpet. I kept telling myself that passing out was not an option, but I was so cold, which I was sure wasn't a good sign. I finally locked on my foot and could see my toe was still attached, not by much. Then I got light-headed again.

The phone was on the counter between the kitchen and the family room, maybe twelve feet away. On another day, only a few steps. Just the thought of putting weight on my foot made me want to throw up, but I knew I had to get across that room. I'll never be fully able to explain how I did it. Honestly, that's OK. Some things are worth forgetting. But I ended up with the phone in my hand. Now, what was I supposed to do?

Calling 911 seemed crazy. I wasn't dying, right?

Then I considered taking myself to the emergency room.

My driving foot was OK, and the hospital was only fifteen minutes away. But the room was melting like grilled cheese—not a good way to drive. So I dialed. What was the nature of my injury? Woman versus magazine rack. Yes, it was more than a stubbed toe.

By the time they showed up I remember fussing about getting my purse—like there was money or a health insurance card inside. And I insisted they lock my house.

I remember the ER nurse asked me my name. Then a doctor examined my foot. He said, "Man! That looks really bad. Hey, come look at this . . ." Which would have been funny on TV, but I was not amused.

And then, mercifully, I got an IV drip that put me out of my misery.

13

Welcome to my daymare.

The good news—I was finally pitiful enough to get money from my 401(k). That was also the bad news. Do you have any idea how much you can spend on a toe? Not even a big toe. My baby toe was a stumpy thing. There was barely enough nail to polish, but it required X-rays, orthopedic consults, surgical reconstruction. That toe had more medical intervention than I have had on my whole body, in my whole life, which is all well and good when you only have to worry about the copay. But that little episode ushered in a whole new round of bills to add to my collection—wads of them. I couldn't believe they charged for every gauze pad and tissue. How do they keep track? Average per patient by injury, illness or surgery per day, then round it up to the nearest hundred bucks? I got bills for tests I don't know if I passed or failed, from doctors I don't even remember, not that I remember a lot—but I'd have let them take off my whole foot if that would have made my toe stop hurting. What the hell are telemetry, a tilt-table test and transcranial

Doppler? And why do they all begin with the letter *T*? Was it random, or would I have had a whole other set of exams and probing if my name was Mary? Paranoid? Maybe. Maybe not. But thank heaven for modern medicine. They kept me well anesthetized—I will save you from the gory specifics of the ankle block, let's just say it involved lots of very long needles. I am not a big fan of pain. And I don't buy into the Honor in Suffering school of thought. Giving birth to Amber was my last experiment in grin and bear it, and if I had it to do over, I would take the epidural.

Anyway, somewhere along the line, after about the nineteenth person walked past my gurney and examined my tootsie like, "Gee, they don't have one of these in the textbook," a woman from emergency admitting came to get my particulars. She asked if there was somebody I wanted to call who could meet me there. With Amber and J.J. gone, the first and only person I thought of was Julie. It was a quarter to the late-night news and I hated to bother her, even asked if they could just call me a taxi, but they wouldn't release me by myself. So I dialed and apologized profusely for bothering her so late. She was already in bed, but she arrived in half an hour, wearing jeans and an inside-out blouse, and she installed herself as my own private nurse. I kept apologizing and she kept saying she was glad I called.

It was three-thirty in the morning by the time I was discharged, with bandages that made it look like I had a football attached to my ankle instead of a foot. On the way home we stopped at the twenty-four-hour pharmacy and picked up the pain pills my doctor had prescribed. Honestly, I can't tell you if they took the pain away or if they made me not care if it hurt, because I was floating in my own wonderland and Alice and the Cheshire Cat were welcome to join me. The warning on the bottle tells you not to operate heavy equipment. They needn't have worried. Under the influence, I couldn't have managed anything more complicated than my toothbrush and the remote control anyway. The stove was out of the question. At the rate I was going, I'd set myself on fire and burn the house down, so if I couldn't toast it or nuke it, I wouldn't eat it.

I took up residence in the family room because my bedroom involved stairs. I wasn't ready for those. Julie got me settled on the couch, propped my foot on a stack of pillows, as instructed. I don't know what I would have done without her because I could barely remember my name, much less how-tos for a nearly detached body part. She made sure I had groceries, figured out what I might need or want before her next visit and made sure it was handy. Then she blotted as much blood off the carpet as she could and brought a throw rug from the spare bedroom to cover the stains that remained, because looking at remnants of my own bloody footprints was a little too *CSI* for me. And the last thing I needed were flashbacks, or a reason to what-if myself into a worse state of mind than I was already in. Like, what if I had passed out from the sight of my own blood and bled to death on my living-room floor? Or what if I had tried to take myself to the hospital, lost control, gone over the double yellow line and right into the path of an on coming truck? Or . . . well, you get the idea. Definitely not where I needed to be using my imagination.

Somehow I didn't mind Julie rambling around in my house. It felt perfectly normal, which is a long way from the Brooklyn girl whose first rule was trust no one. She had certainly seen me through the good, the bad and the loathsome. Guess my problem had been trusting the wrong folks. So I gave her my spare set of house keys to hold on to because I realized that with Amber and J.J. out of the country there was nobody in a two-hundred-mile radius who had keys to my house—in case I got locked out or something worse. Funny how all those years as "friends" with the Live Five I'd never once thought of doing that—and none of them had either. Maybe it was because we didn't really get to know each other. I mean, what did we really have in common besides whining or bragging about our kids, wining, dining, shopping and bitching? You know, come to think of it, I don't think any of us ever got together unless it was all of us. We were a group—all or nothing.

Julie offered to stay with me. I almost said yes, which gives you some idea how close I'd gotten to her and how wigged out I was, but I decided to be a big girl and made her leave just before dawn. I knew Mom and Daddy would have driven up in a heartbeat if I asked them, but having my parents play nursemaid was more helpless than I was prepared to feel.

For the first few days I dozed on and off, round the clock—days, nights, afternoons, it didn't matter. When I was awake I stared at the tube—programs I'd never ever seen. Before then I had no use for the all-cartoon channel, but suddenly I saw the humor in a talking sea sponge who wears orange knickers. Truthfully, the drugs made the Skycam traffic report just as hilarious.

I also got hooked on design TV. I'd get sucked into the beautiful, serene places with rambling gardens, remote-controlled window treatments and marble palace bathrooms connected to custom closets the size of my garage. Those fantasy décors were miles from the chaos of my life. But really my favorites were the organizing shows. The befores boggled my already clouded mind, because I could not believe the mounds of crap people ignore. The spare bedrooms and basements piled floor to ceiling with wrapping paper, beat-up toys, three decades of fashion don'ts, stereo equipment, high school sports trophies, hand-me-down furniture, unopened Chia Pets, a FryDaddy and various other gizmos and dodads—they were bad. But the piles of junk people stepped over and moved aside every day in their bedrooms and kitchens—that was even worse. How could they live like that? The afters almost made me cry, because usually the home owners were close to tears too. In the span of sixty minutes it was like they'd been rescued, saved from drowning in their own debris and given another chance at life—sort of *Queen for a Day* with room dividers and modular shelving. And if you're too young to remember that TV show, look it up.

Julie called at least twice a day to make sure I hadn't OD'd or accidentally almost amputated anything else and she came by regularly with provisions—stayed long enough to get me upstairs to take a shower, which was a trick in itself since I had to put on a stylish plastic boot with an adjustable elastic band around the top, because I had been instructed to keep my stitches dry and to change my bandages twice a day—talk about yuck. I don't exactly faint at the sight of blood, but if you remember I did get just a little queasy. I wasn't even good at playing Dr. Mom with Amber's assorted cuts and scrapes but I mommed up 'cause I had to. But dealing with my own toe ooze made me woozy. So Julie would wait patiently outside the bathroom door until I was clean and my wound was redressed. She called Amber in London and assured her I would be well taken care of, and that she didn't need to cut her assignment short and come home. I kept thanking Julie and saying I didn't know how I could ever repay her, and she said, "Don't be silly, Tee. That's what friends are for." Which also almost made me cry—something that was happening with alarming frequency, so I blamed it on the drugs.

In my lucid, nonteary moments—those little windows between painkiller doses wearing off and kicking in where I almost felt normal—I pacified my parents enough to keep them in Maryland so I could worry about my job in peace. Julius was a good guy. NAB even sent me a fruit basket, which was extremely decent. I'd have traded it for a check, but I wasn't getting one of those. The sad and sorry truth was I had no sick time. And even though I assured them I'd be back at my desk in two weeks tops, I didn't want them to decide they couldn't hold my job, because believe me, I was all too aware I was expendable. Then my foot would start throbbing and I'd take another pill and drift back into my purple haze.

J.J. came by directly from the airport—Amber had given him his marching orders—not that she needed to. I know he would have come on his own. But thank goodness, he called to see if he could bring me anything, because it gave me time to stash the mail I was sorting between the sofa cushions, comb my hair and slap on some lipstick so I wouldn't scare the boy to death. I mean, he'd caught me with my hair in rollers once or twice over the years, but around about then, personal grooming was at the bottom of my to-do list. He came bearing flowers, and since Amber obviously hadn't schooled him on the no sombreros rule, he also brought me a replica of the Tower of London—how appropriate (of course, I think they only did beheading there, no betoeing). I acted happy for my souvenir and, thanks to my medication, I was jolly enough to send him on his way with a satisfactory report for my daughter.

I was glad I hadn't already tackled the mail before J.J.'s arrival, and grateful for my chemically induced cushion, when I opened the letter from my mortgage bank—the one that upped the rate on my adjustable-rate mortgage. The envelope didn't look any more important than junk mail, but as soon as I saw my loan number on the letter I knew exactly what it was. In the back of my overtaxed mind, I also knew it was time, but I had no place to put that information, so I let it surprise me. And it did. Right into as near hysteria as I could come while taking a controlled substance. Three percent sounds insignificant. I remember thinking that back when I was signing my name next to the yellow arrow on all those refi papers. They wouldn't lend me the money if I couldn't afford it. Right? But even in my impaired state I knew there was no place in my budget to add another $937.54 a month.

So instead of freaking out, I laughed like I didn't have good sense as it dawned on me that it was completely inconceivable for me to come up with enough money each month to stay in my house—not possible, not in the cards, the bad joke was on me. From the time Markson showed me the door, I'd been playing Duck, Duck, Goose with my finances, so it was almost a relief to be officially busted, game over, uncle, I surrender. I would have waved a white flag if I had one. Anything to make it stop.

Then I fell asleep with the letter still in my lap. I dreamed about driving, not in the jalopy. I was in my old car, the snazzy one, and I was so happy. The day was sunny and lovely, and I was traveling smooth and fast on a winding mountain road. With no warning the car cut off, but it kept rolling downhill, faster and faster, and there was no guardrail, just a steep drop with no bottom. I stomped on the brakes, but they didn't work, and the wheel was so tight I could barely steer, and the sun was in my eyes, but it started to rain, and it was harder and harder for me to keep from going over the edge. Just as I felt the front tire leave the road, I screamed. And I woke up screaming, sweaty, heart pounding. That's when sleep ceased to be a refuge. From then on my dreams were plagued by giant rats chewing on the roof shingles, derailed trains tumbling from bridges, ferocious bears banging on my patio doors, mazes of staircases with no exits leading to nowhere—and that wasn't because of the drugs. Where could I go if I wanted to? My world had shrunk to one room, the kitchen and the guest bathroom.

Being awake was no picnic either. I obsessed over whether the lights would stay on. I'd pick up the phone to make sure I still had a dial tone but jump when it rang, shudder when the mail dropped through the slot. I might have continued doing the backstroke through the doom lagoon, but Amber came over after she got back, and she was appalled at the condition of my place. She had some choice words for me too, like, "You look scuzzy, Ma." Yes, she is my mother's grandchild. "J.J. said you looked bad, but not like this." And here I thought lipstick had fooled him. So I let her cheer me up while she changed my sofa sheets, did laundry and picked out more outfits for me to wear, because I'd pretty much settled into two pairs of sweatpants and a baggy blue hoodie—I don't even know why I owned it. And she searched my shoe racks until she found sandals I could buckle around the bandages. It was a pair I didn't remember. When did I buy sensible footwear?

I at least made an effort to appear chipper, which was hard to do while we went cane shopping. I wanted the smart black one with the mother-of-pearl handle. I bought the standard issue, adjustable gray metal jobby, which really perked me up. I caught a glimpse of myself in the store window—right between a portable commode and a truss. I looked like kin to

Miss Jane Pittman. But I also knew the next stop on our lovely little mother-daughter afternoon was a follow-up at the orthopedist—ka-ching.

All the while Amber chattered—about the elegant hotel on Park Lane where her company put her up, and the swell boutiques and the clothes she bought because she was moving in a different circle at work and she needed to look the part. She wanted J.J. to buy a suit in London too, because the tailoring was so sharp, but he wouldn't spend the money. And she couldn't wait to go again. I mean, I had a great time when I went to London with Olivia, but was I ever that perky? And what was wrong with J.J.'s American suits?

I decided to send up a trial balloon, as much to see how it floated as to hear myself say, "I've been thinking about downsizing—selling the house and getting . . ."

And she was off. Talking about the great new high-rises in downtown New Brunswick, with penthouses and spas and panoramic views. Well, at least she was not going to break down because I wanted to unload the old homestead, but I wanted to say, "Earth to Amber, there will be no penthouse. You see what I'm driving, don't you?" I let it slide, though—didn't have the heart or the energy to burst her bubble. I would be in the market for something less grand, bigger than a tent by the side of the road, and indoor plumbing would be good.

When she left, I was worn out. Before that year I was generally a happy person, but at that point cheery was as exhausting as, say, trying to keep up with a cheetah, and it seemed just as pointless. I also knew it was time to wean myself off the heavy-duty drugs so I could get back to work. I had to at least tread muddy water until I could unload the house and get back on my feet—both of them.

Whatever notions I had about how much better I felt went straight down the toilet on day one without my meds. The throbbing of my foot kept time with the beat of my heart. It was a duet I could have done without. I took the over-the-counter stuff, as recommended, which helped a little. It was the difference between a jackhammer and a kettle drum—one is more out of control, but you can't exactly ignore either of them.

So ready or not, in two weeks I was back in the bucket seat, strapped in, ready to hit I-287, the Middlesex Freeway, except it wasn't really free. All the stopping and going, merging and maneuvering took a great big toll out of my hide. I was grateful I hadn't mangled my driving foot, but exhausted by the time I parked. I hobbled to my desk—

—to meet a two-foot stack of files and 612 emails. Obviously they missed me. My office mates even rigged up a copier-paper box and a chair cushion as a makeshift footrest. And I didn't want to tell the story again, especially since I couldn't say what really precipitated my tumble. Except they all wanted to hear it—the part about it sounding like Velcro was a crowd pleaser. And other than occasionally limping to the ladies' room or for coffee, and twenty minutes to down my tuna-salad sandwich, I kept my nose in my work and did my best to ignore the SOS coming from below my desk. And by 5:04 I was inching back to the car to reverse the rush-hour follies.

The routine boredom kept me occupied enough not to have time to think about my problems. By night I didn't have the energy for more than a bowl of soup and curling up on the couch. I was still skittish about the steps. The more I spread out, the more things could go wrong. So I kept my world small and close, hoping trouble wouldn't find me. Besides, I didn't need reminders of how my life used to look, all that mattered was the present.

And on weekends I pretty much stayed in my temple of gloom. I didn't bother opening the drapes. I liked the dreariness; it matched my mood. I knew I had to figure out how to get my house sold. It was either that or lose it. I figured I'd come out of it 2,200 square feet lighter and with a little money to sock away. Under other circumstances I would have phoned up my good old buddy Joyce to have her list the place. When I got overwhelmed by all those ads in the Sunday paper I still toyed with the idea. It would have been so easy because there were so many brokers, but who was good and what if I made a mistake—and at least I knew her. Which is exactly why I had to run the other way. Even I knew easy wasn't the answer, but did everything have to be so damn hard? All at the same time? One thing after another in a never-ending stream of the worst-case scenario meets crappy timing, thus creating a perfectly awful storm in my life. I mean, how much was I supposed to take? And did I have to lose everything? It wasn't fair.

Now, I could get my whine on and not come up for hours. But I really just wanted to know when it was going to stop raining on me.

Not yet.

It was a particularly snarly Tuesday morning. My traffic-radio station told me there was a five-mile backup ahead because of an overturned tractor trailer carrying live chickens in the right lane, and the Department of Transportation didn't seem to have a poultry protocol. Par for the course, there was something toppled over, fender-bent or otherwise disabled pretty much daily, going and coming, and I hadn't had time to figure out the alternate route. I was starving, I had to pee, and with nothing to do but think, I sank into the money pit, running a tab of how much this tie-up would cost me. I know I'm always harping on money. No matter where it looks like the story is going, it comes back to dollars or the lack of them. That's because no matter where I was, or what I was doing, money was on my mind—from first foot out of bed in the morning until my head hit the pillow. If I woke up in the middle of the night, sleep was over. You want to talk about the little engine that could? Once that baby got started, there was no stopping her. Who could I pay? How long before I got the collection call? Would the car get me through the winter? Money was a constant in a way I never could have anticipated—that and occasionally hoping Didier would cut himself shaving and contract flesh-eating bacteria. Bitter wasn't a taste I usually craved, but with him, I savored the flavor.

So there I was trapped on the highway, stomach growling, praying for bladder control. The traffic report repeated every ten minutes on the ones, and for the last 184 minutes I'd heard, "Cleanup from the incident on 287 is ongoing. It's quite a fowl-up." Ha ha. The van in front of me had exhaust that smelled worse than cat pee and rotten eggs, so I did my best to keep my distance. But if I didn't roll forward as soon as the van crept two inches, the idiot behind me laid on his horn, like that was gonna get anybody anywhere faster. Oh, and my foot hurt, but that's a given. I was obviously late, which I hate. Julius isn't crazy about it either. That's when I noticed the needle on the temperature gauge was two clicks from the big red *H*. What the hell! I knew there was coolant in the radiator, and it wasn't that hot outside, but that needle kept waggling upward. I still had a ways to go before I reached the truck, but the radio said the road would clear after that. If I could just drive at normal speed, the engine would cool enough for me to get to work, and one of the guys at the office could tell me what to do. I worked with those kinds of guys, the ones who know a little something about what goes on under the hood. So I turned on the blower full blast to get some of the heat away from the engine—learned that from driving my ex's hunk of junk. Hot air spewed out of the vents, which is exactly what I needed on a sixty-five-degree fall day. I rolled down the windows I could reach—yes, I said roll—feeling very much like an Oven Stuffer in need of basting, or turning, or how about getting me out of the oven. My manual ventilation system worked for a while, even though I could feel sweat coating my scalp and my hair rising like bread dough, and let me tell you, in case you never have the pleasure, there's nothing like the smell of steamed cat pee and rotten eggs on an empty stomach.

But deliverance was in sight. I was about thirty yards from the truck carcass, dinking and dunking with merging traffic and looking forward to my liberation, when steam erupted from under my hood. This could not be happening. The nightmares were bad enough, but I was wide awake. If I could just get to the shoulder, I'd be out of the way, but my windshield was steamed so bad I couldn't see, poking my head out the window made my eyes water, and my fellow drivers were not feeling charitable enough to let me over, so I had to stop. Which meant there were now two lanes of blocked traffic, creating an almost total standstill. That sent the idiot behind me into orbit, and he was now joined by a whole bleating chorus of frustrated motorists. Welcome to my daymare.

I wanted to tear up the registration and walk away, off the road, into the woods, someplace quiet where nothing was wrong and nobody was looking for me. Except walking was not my strong suit right about then. Cars peeled off around me, fighting to get to the one open lane, and the honking fool behind me stopped right by my passenger side and leaned out of his car, so I could fully experience the force of the finger he was giving me and let loose a tirade the likes of which I hope never to hear again. Good morning to you too, you moron. By now my whole body is shaking, I can hear the traffic helicopter hovering overhead, and I'm sure I have elevated this route to the top of the "highway headaches" list, and I know I have to get myself out of this somehow, but my roadside-assistance plan had gone early in my economizing. I had never used it, which didn't mean diddly at the moment.

So I got out, used my car umbrella to pop the latch on the hood and avoid scalding myself and stared at the engine, because I'd seen people do that when their cars overheat. I'm sure I looked as helpless as they did, but it gave me time to clear my head. And in that moment of heightened awareness I determined that what I needed immediately was a tow truck. And the only possible connection I had to one was Ron.

Boy, I did not want to make that call, but I was squarely in a period of my life when what I wanted had zip to do with how things went down. So I dug in my purse, praying I'd been careless and distracted enough to leave his card—which I had no intention of ever using—stashed somewhere in the creases or recesses. I knew J.J. would have happily given me his number, but why make two awkward calls when one will do?

With the contents of my pocketbook splayed on the seat next to me, I shuffled, for the third time, through the pack of discount club cards in my wallet, and there it was, with his cell number on the back. It was too noisy for me to think about how embarrassing this was, so I just dialed—after I'd gotten my glasses off the floor so I could tell the difference between the 3s and the 8s.

He sounded worried when I identified myself, asked if everybody was alright. Guess he wasn't exactly expecting to hear from me so bright and early—or anytime. Then I wondered if I'd woken him up, and maybe I should have called the business number, because this was really work related and maybe this wasn't a good idea. Then I remembered to say yes, the kids were fine, and I apologized for bothering him and blathered on about being stranded in the middle of I-287. And he said oh, and asked if I was the disabled car they just reported on the radio. The backup had grown to seven miles. Great. But he said he'd send a truck for me. I don't know how many times I thanked him before we hung up. I'd figure out later how to pay for it. Then there was the problem of what was wrong with my steaming sack of sedan, and how much would it cost to fix it, and how would I get to work in the meantime—that's when the state policeman showed up beside me, looking somewhat weary of cars breaking down and cluttering his roadway. I told him a tow was on the way. He used the patrol car to nudge me to the shoulder. What a relief ! I was stranded by the side of the road, not in the middle of it, which makes a huge difference. After that I spaced out for a while, watched them get the tractor trailer back on its wheels and round up the last of the birds. What a production. It made pulling my car onto the flatbed Ron sent seem like a snap.

The driver helped me and my cane climb into the cab, and even though I was thankful for the rescue, I realized I was disappointed it wasn't Ron who had come. I wondered what it would be like to see him. I hadn't since our hibachi outing. Or if he'd even be at the shop. I didn't ask. But the driver let me off in front of the building, and Ron met me at the door. He even looked good in his crisp blue coveralls, but everything in the place was sharp, which I should have expected. The tow truck was shiny black with purple and fuchsia lettering—definitely not half-steppin'. And this wasn't some grease-monkey garage. It was like the Mayo Clinic of classic-car restoration. The place was spotless, with checkerboard floors that looked like the winner's flag, and the technicians—because I couldn't exactly call them mechanics—looked like they were about to scrub in for surgery. There was an aqua Continental convertible with suicide doors being prepped for work. A yellow Karmann Ghia, like the ones I used to think were so cute when I was little, was being lowered from one of the repair bays. Then there were his specialties—the muscle cars: a Shelby Mustang, a Pontiac Grand Prix having an engine-ectomy. I was embarrassed I had them tow mine in. Ron said, "Haven't had one of these in a while." Right. How about ever? No wonder the tow driver took it around back.

We stopped in the waiting room for coffee, then Ron led the way to his office. I followed, convincing myself I wasn't disappointed he hadn't kissed me on the cheek. The walls around his desk were covered with photos, some of cars he'd restored, some from his racing days, posed next to his Demon Dodge. Yeah, he looked fast. We made small talk—about the weather, the kids. He told me he'd gone with J.J. on some of his house-hunting expeditions to help him check out the systems—plumbing, heating and electrical—and give him advice on what would make a sound investment. Hadn't heard about that from Amber's end, but I was glad J.J. had reached out for advice, which I clearly should have done with my automobile choice.

After a while one of the guys came back, said he'd had a look at my car. He lost me after radiator, thermostat, water pump. I must have looked dazed because Ron took over, asked about parts, how long it would take. I heard the guy say a couple of days and Ron said go ahead. I'm sure I looked kinda green around the gills when I asked him how much this would cost. He said to let him worry about that. I was sure he'd let me arrange some payment plan that didn't involve midnight phone calls from collection agencies. The truth was, I didn't have space for another worry at the moment, aside from how I was going to get to work for the next few days. He must have heard me think it, because he said, "I can loan you something to get around in until your car is done." Well, then I didn't know how to thank him, but he said, "Come on, let me get you the keys, so you can get on your way."

Ron didn't really have loaners. His customers were multivehicle owners, and some of his restorations took months, so he lent me his SUV. Fortunately, it wasn't one of those gi-normous ones. I stood on the running board (much easier than getting in the truck), thanked him again, gave him a kiss on the cheek— because what he was doing was genuinely nice, and I sure did appreciate it, from the bottom of my heart. I turned on the CD player when I got on the road. He had some nice tunes, jazzy sax, real good driving music. And I know I had a smile on my face. I had almost forgotten that sometimes a crappy day can get better.

When I went back to pick up my car a few days later, I was feeling kinda down about turning in my coach and going back to the pumpkin. But when I stopped in the office for the bill, I was completely outdone. The clerk handed me my keys and a receipt with a total due of $00.00. I said there must be a mistake, but Ron wasn't in. Fine. I'd settle it with him later. Then I walked past the car three times before I recognized my license plate, because my ug-mobile was mouse gray no more.

I'd call it titanium, with metallic sparkles that flickered in the sun. The interior had been shampooed, the seats gleamed, and the bent antenna was ramrod straight. And the engine purred like a happy kitty.

I didn't catch up with him until that night. He said he hoped I didn't mind that he took the liberty of doing a paint job—said it was a new color he wanted to try out and he thought I'd like it. Right. He also said the repair was on the house. I said he couldn't do that. He said, "Yes, I can. Sometimes it's good to be boss."

14

*There's no room for the right thing
if you don't let go of the wrong one*

That night I kept checking the garage to make sure I hadn't dreamed the whole thing because it didn't make sense. Neither did a lot of what I'd been through in the last twelve months, but at least this gave me a smile and made me feel special. That hadn't happened in a while. And when I drove to work the next day you couldn't tell me my ride wasn't the cutest thing on the road. The guys at the office thought it looked pretty nifty too. Julius even said I should let him know if I ever wanted to get rid of it. That's quite a turnaround. Granted, he'd never seen my coupe, and I started to say something about what I used to drive, but for once I put my hand over my own mouth and accepted the compliment.

When I checked in with Julie to say hey and tell her what Ron had done, I mentioned I wanted to do something for him, to say thanks, but I didn't know what because it would involve a trip to the store, which I couldn't afford. Before I got any farther with my rendition of the "No Luck, Life Sucks" blues, Julie said, "If you really want to do it, you'll find a way. There's a reason they call it a *token* of appreciation." Well, that snapped the rest of the words back in my mouth before I got to the chorus. Julie wasn't usually so blunt, but she got my attention. We didn't talk much longer. It's hard to say much with your lips poked out. But once I got past the sting, I realized she had a point. It's the thought that counts, right?

It took me a while to sell myself on the concept. I had always been a fan of the flashy statement—the more impressive, the better. But when I came home and went in the kitchen to scramble some eggs, because that's what I wanted for dinner, I took stock of my cookbook collection. Yes, a lot of it was decorative, but when Amber was growing up I really used to cook from the recipes, especially the cookies. There were always bake sales and classmates' birthday parties, but no matter the season or the occasion, Amber requested my Yummers. That's what she said the first time she tasted my double chocolate cherry nut cookies. "Yummers, Mom." After she got to the age when the size of her jeans took precedence over dessert, I had pretty much hung up my baking pans. If I wanted to give somebody goodies, I'd buy a gift basket, so I was reluctant to fire up the oven. What if they didn't look professional? I had to throw that one out—a whole lot of store-bought cookies try for that "homemade" look. Suppose they didn't taste that good? Mind you, I never had a leftover. If J.J. was in the house they barely made it to the plate. Suppose Ron didn't like cookies. At that point I knew I was stalling. When you come right down to it, who doesn't like a cookie? And since I was bestowing tokens, I added Julie to my list since I appreciated all she had done, including kick me in the butt to get me moving on this. So far the best thing about losing my job—and believe me, it took a whole lot to put that sentence together—was getting to know her outside of work. And while I was at it I'd make Amber and J.J. a batch—not the anniversary gift I envisioned, but I was sure they'd get a kick out of them, even if Amber only ate a couple.

So baking became my project for the week. One night I got out the recipe—the cookbook automatically fell open to the page. It was creased and stained with butter, batter, vanilla and little fingerprints—lots of memories. I checked for ingredients I already had and made a grocery list. Next day I stopped on the way home and did my shopping—which didn't cost much at all—and that night I found my trusty cookie sheets. While I was at work I remembered I had a stash of decorative tins in the pantry, the ones that are too pretty to throw away and you never figure out what to do with them. I managed to find three I liked and some paper doilies for the insides without needing the step stool. I also checked my usual hiding spots around the house and found a frame I had bought because it was pretty and on sale. I had come across a snapshot of Amber and J.J. from back in the day, huddled over their homework. I thought they'd like to have it.

Friday night I prepped walnuts and dried cherries and measured out my dry ingredients, which lets you know the state of my social life. Hermits go out more often. But by the weekend I was ready to rock. I must admit I was in a good mood that whole week. My project gave me something to look forward to. Standing at the counter like I used to was not going to work, so I made myself a workstation at the kitchen table, put on some tunes—there hadn't been music in my house in I don't know when. And the smell—you cannot be grouchy in the presence of cookie aromas. And while I tried to keep my sampling to a minimum, I am happy to say I hadn't lost my touch.

I had just taken a batch out of the oven when the jingling of keys meant Amber was coming in. I thought she'd be pretty surprised to find me doing my Shaniqua Stewart thang, but she came in fuming. "I'm sick of him acting like we have to save every penny. My father already gave us money toward the down payment."

Uh-oh. Another wrinkle in wedded bliss. Seems Amber had found her dream house and J.J. did the math and for him it did not compute. Brand-new, four bedrooms, five baths, a three-car garage, granite, stainless-steel appliances—all it was missing was a moat and a throne room. I liked London too, but the Queen's house has been in the family a long time. She couldn't afford to buy it now either. I asked how much it cost. It was amazing how easily the number slid off her tongue. It sure made me choke. Amber fumed that it would be tight for a while, but they would both get promoted and make more money.

I might have said the same thing—last year. Then she talked about how I had taught her to buy the best because people will always recognize quality. Sounds like me, doesn't it? She proceeded to quote chapter and verse from Tee's Economics 101: "Buy it now, it'll cost more later." "Sometimes you have to spend money to save money." "What's the point of having good credit if you don't use it." And the ever popular "Isn't that why I go to work every day? So I can afford the nicer things in life?"

I had no idea my child was such a devoted disciple. But I was living through the flaws in my theory, and however painful it had been for me, I was apparently a little too good at keeping the downside hidden from my daughter. Yes, she also got the hard-work message, and I never wanted to burden her with my worries, certainly not as a little one, and definitely not now.

But I guess I had done her a major disservice by not letting her see the whole picture. Truth was, I didn't start to see the whole picture until it was right up in my face and I couldn't look anywhere else. Man, I couldn't even get through baking without a major life crisis.

So I gave Amber a cookie and told her to sit down. This was going to be harder than the sex talk. I didn't think anything was more embarrassing than explaining why he sticks *that* in *there,* but admitting I was going, going, gone broke? It was difficult to make myself look her in the eyes.

I didn't know where to begin, so I jumped in before I could chicken out—'fessed up that I wasn't thinking about selling the house for convenience. I couldn't afford the mortgage anymore. It felt like when I'd told her there was no Santa Claus. I could see her lip start to quiver, and I had to keep talking or we'd both be red-eyed and snotty. I did my best not to sugarcoat the story. I had to let her know I had made mistakes with my money— big ones. I had to do whatever was necessary to keep her from following in my heavily indebted footsteps.

First thing out of her mouth was how she and J.J. would fix it. I had to stop her right there—told her thank you very much, but no. Nothing would make me happier than to see them in their own house, one they could afford. What her daddy gave them was nice—very nice—I admit it, but unless they added more they would be saddled with a mortgage that would put a hurtin' on their cash flow. I assured her I'd get myself straightened out and no, I wasn't sure how, but she had to let me handle that. Then she fretted about how much I'd spent on the wedding. I had to admit that if I'd known then what I know now, I'd have done things a little different. OK, a lot different, but I loved every minute of it. I didn't regret it, and neither should she. And that was the honest-to-God truth.

By then I was exhausted, so I fixed their tin of cookies, gave her the photo, told her to stop, get some milk and go home to her husband and work it out. Oh, and I made her promise not to tell her father about my money problems. They talked, he and I didn't and he just didn't need to know that much of my business.

And after we hugged and she kissed me good night, I mentioned, as nonchalantly as I could, that my Thursday nights were now free. Well, Amber's smile would have lit up the Milky Way.

Julie was easy. I invited her over for dinner after work one night. Nothing fancy—burgers with onion rolls, my fresh-cut seasoned fries and a salad. After that I presented her token of my appreciation. She was tickled. I made coffee and we had the TV on in the background while we nibbled some of the baker's batch and talked about nothing in particular, like how happy I was to finally be back in my bedroom, and how I'd found a pair of flat slides in my closet that fit over the taping I still had to do to my toe so I wouldn't have to go through the winter in sandals and socks.

Julie told me she hadn't been home in a while, so she planned to visit her family in Toronto over our Thanksgiving, then she looked up at the TV screen and said, "Will you look at that mess." It was one of my organizing shows and they were tackling a home office with papers, cartons, shopping bags, files and the samples for their T-shirt business thrown all over the place. Julie wrinkled up her nose and wondered how anybody could run a business like that. "They can hardly find the computer." I told her how I had to tame Olivia's clutter bug back at the beginning in the loft. She couldn't believe it. "Everything was always so nice at Markson." I was happy to inform her I was the reason and told her what I was doing at NAB. I had found stuff in that office that had been there since low-rise pants were around the first time. They were called hip-huggers then, and why anybody needs a new generation of butt cracks to look at I'll never know. Anyway, organizing the stuff at the office had made my day and everybody else's go smoother, not to mention the break it gave me from yet another disgruntled claimant.

We kept an eye on the progress while we talked. The moldy turkey sandwich they found buried in a long-lost box of office supplies was nasty, and why a grown man would become un-hinged over parting with his Mighty Morphin' Power Rangers lunchbox was beyond me, but we stopped to watch the "reveal." The room looked three times bigger, and there was a whole wall of good-looking storage for inventory and supplies, papers had a filing system to call home, the new L-shaped desk had sleek accessories and a place for everything. I always wondered how long the rooms stayed in their pristine state, but hey, at least they had a good start—the rest was on them. Julie said it was a miracle. I said, "I can do that." It was just logic, common sense and a dollar's worth of style. And she said, "Well, you should charge for it." I told her I had always made it part of my work-day, so I was getting paid, and she said, "No, like a business."

A business. Yeah. Right.

But Julie was serious. And I said I was hardly in a position to start a business. Money was tight, I was tired when I got home, I had never taken a design course . . .

And she said, "If you really want to do it, you'll find a way." It was becoming her theme song already, but when I thought about it, Julie had pretty much reinvented herself after Markson let her go. She had started as a receptionist and was on her way to sales executive. I'm not even sure she saw that coming, but somewhere along the line she decided to go for it.

So I promised I'd think about it. Which I did while I cleaned up the kitchen. Yes, I was good at organizing things, but who was going to hire me? And how was I going to advertise, and what would I charge, and I needed a job, not an adventure. Then I saw Ron's tin on the dining room table, which gave me something else to worry about. How was I going to get him his cookies?

I mean, this whole episode started with him, but his was the only box left and they were best while fresh, so the clock was ticking. And what was my problem? I don't know, it just seemed so fourth grade for me to go marching into his business to give him my goodies, so to speak. I didn't want to draw attention to myself and have his employees whispering about this woman whose car he painted, because I was sure it wasn't something he did every day, and there was no reason for him to have to explain it to anybody, not on my account.

And I didn't know his home address, which meant I'd have to ask Amber or J.J., and I didn't want them to wonder what was going on, because it was nothing more than a simple thank-you. Or I could call him at the shop, disguise my voice and ask him to meet me behind the tree on a dark corner, so I could get him "the stuff." I hadn't worked it out by the time I went to bed. But when I laid back down after a middle-of-the-night, "get-up-and-pee-'cause-there's-no-point-holding-it" bathroom run, I told myself to just call the man. He was a friend of the family who had done an exceptionally nice thing for me—that's all. Whatever might have been, wasn't—I had seen to that. Surely he had not been sitting home waiting for me to come around. I chose not to get specific about what he might have been doing and with whom. There are things even I don't need to know.

So next day I got up, looked in the mirror while I brushed my teeth and gave myself the lecture about being a grown woman who was perfectly capable of a simple thank-you. Is that why I dialed the shop four times before I stayed on the line long enough for anybody to answer? When Ron came on the line I temporarily lost control of my tongue, and before I regained it I had asked him if he could come by my house that evening because I had something for him—probably a lot like what I'd said to Julie, but when I'd hung up from her I hadn't spent the rest of the day beating myself up for sounding juvenile or wondering how I got myself into this in the first place. Come by the house? What was I thinking?

When I got home Ron was waiting out front in a vintage acid-green Charger. It saved me from changing my clothes forty-two times and wondering if I looked OK. He walked up the drive, opened my car door for me and said, "Nice ride." I said, "Yeah, it's a classic—like me." That part slipped out.

As I put my key in the lock it dawned on me that Ron was about to step over the threshold and into my house. Guess part of me thought he'd ring the bell, I'd hand him the box and say thank you and good night, like this was a UPS pickup. So I'm trying not to panic as I give the place a mental once-over. Did I fluff the sofa cushions? Had I cleaned under the seat in the powder room? There are some places you don't look as often when there's no man in the house on a regular basis. I knew my bed was made—not that that had anything to do with that night, I just like for things to be in order, in case somebody should happen to see them.

Anyway, now we were inside, and I realized he had no idea

what this visit was about, so I cut to the chase, mostly because I was too antsy to do anything else. I had sorta rehearsed my thank-you speech—how I couldn't begin to tell him how much I appreciated his help, and that I didn't know what I would have done without him. I did try to keep it under forty-five seconds—like at the Academy Awards—but the music might have come on. When I gave him the box he said I didn't have to do that. I said I wanted to, and I did. It had been rather humbling to be at the mercy of not exactly strangers but people who had plenty of their own stuff to take care of without having to tend to mine.

And I was right. Of course, he liked cookies, but after he'd had a couple I realized I hadn't planned how the rest of the evening would go. You should have dinner before dessert, right? So I asked if he'd eaten, I could rustle something up. He said he hadn't and suggested we go to the diner not far from my house—if that wouldn't cause any problems. Perfect opening. I said it was no problem for me and these days I didn't have anybody else to consult. He kinda nodded, but I was sure happy to have that on the record—not for any particular reason. And the diner was an excellent idea. Thanksgiving was coming soon, but I wasn't sure I was prepared to cook with Ron again yet—or have him watch—but I was starting to relax enough to have a real conversation, which would be a first.

We had a nice dinner. I ordered the roast beef, because I never cook it for myself. He had flounder. We talked about the kids and their house-hunting dilemma; he had heard the story from J.J.'s side. Bottom line: he thought they'd work it out too.

We talked about some of everything in no particular order. He made me laugh—that had been missing from my repertoire for quite some time. I told him about the wacky world of auto-insurance claims and how it was an industry I didn't care to explore any further. And I'm not sure what made me say it—maybe because he was the only bona fide entrepreneur I knew—but I mentioned the organizing idea I had kicked around with Julie. I explained how it wasn't some crazy notion I had because I'd seen a TV show. I had really done it.

He said I should go for it. His business had started with a rented bay at a local gas station, flyers at classic-car shows and word of mouth. That was amazing seeing what it grew into. Ron told me how the shows about customizing your ride had increased his business; he was trying to get the shop featured on one. "Make a plan and get out there. You don't know if the water is hot or cold unless you stick your toe in." And he said if he could be of assistance, to let him know.

While he was talking I kept thinking how I had blown this—for Gerald? What had I been thinking? And I realized I hadn't been—I had just been doing what I was used to doing, whether I liked it anymore or not. OK. Lesson learned. There's no room for the right thing if you don't let go of the wrong one.

Ron held my hand as he walked me to the door—good thing my foot was still on the mend or I might have been tempted to skip. While I looked for my keys he told me how much he was going to enjoy his cookies, and that he wasn't usually like this, but he didn't plan on sharing them with anybody. Uh-huh. I'd been unlocking that door for years, but suddenly I had trouble getting the key in the hole, so to speak, but I finally got it open. And he kissed me good night. This time I stood there and took it like a woman, no bobbing and weaving. Definitely more than a peck, we had full lip-to-lip contact, but no dueling tongues. Mercy, it made me dizzy. He said he'd be in touch, made sure I had his cell digits, said I could call him any time.

I came in putting on water to boil for tea—herbal because I needed no caffeine; I was having my own wave of delayed tremors. There hadn't been any activity in that sector for quite a while. Yeah, I closed my eyes and did the instant replay until I started feeling giddy, but I reined myself back from a gallop to a trot. We had at least gotten back to the starting line, where Ron and I could be friends. Whatever happened after that, well, I'd have to wait and see. I had an awful lot to sort through.

So I got ready for bed and let my mind wander to the conversation Ron and I had had about my business—whoa, that's a phrase I had never used before. I thought of what Julie had said, about making it happen if I wanted it to, but it seemed a little crazy. Yes, my little bit of degree was in business administration, and I sure had the advanced tutorial for all those years with Olivia. I remembered the first time I saw her with those pigtails and the pots in her kitchen. She didn't even remember she needed labels for her first order until it was almost ready for delivery. And she survived. There were definitely mistakes—like the soap that didn't fit in the boxes she'd ordered for it—but somehow the slipups and close calls never kept her from venturing out further the next time. I'd be scared for her, but she moved right ahead, like failure never crossed her mind.

Then, because I had to, I eased back into the day-to-day—made myself a turkey sandwich for lunch, laid out my clothes for in the morning. It became clear to me that before I could even think about wrangling the chaos in somebody else's life, I had to tame my own. My first order of business? The house had to go—before they came and got it.

15

"Somebody scream!"

As you may have figured out, some choices I weigh a long time. I shuffle the possibilities in my head until it hurts, and even after I make the informed decision for miney instead of mo, I worry it's a mistake. Then there are the situations where I get my mind set and jump in, consequences be damned. But more often than not, I'm guilty of decision by default: I deny, delay and dillydally until I'm out of options and the choice makes itself. Yes, I was sad and petrified, but I was determined not to procrastinate about selling the house until I found myself trapped in the corner wondering why I was holding that wet paintbrush. I'd heard winter was a bad time to put your house on the market, but I needed to get a move on.

So there I was in the supermarket after work. Christmas was two weeks away, and the aisles overflowed with Yule fuel—inflatable snowmen, candied green and red cherries for that fruitcake recipe you've been aching to try—and where exactly do green cherries come from? There was eggnog for spiking, ham for baking and cardboard fireplaces complete with stockings for stuffing. All that was missing was the figgy pudding and Tiny Tim. Bah, humbug. I was definitely feeling more than a little Scroogey.

I'm sure some of it was acute mall withdrawal. It was my first year away from the retail races. I had always been a first stringer, but this year I was on the sidelines, without so much as a shopping bag, but the jingle bells of my phone and the chorus of collection calls reminded me why.

Amber and J.J. would be in Dallas—again—and my parents were headed for a dude ranch in Arizona with another couple from Shoreline. Who made them Roy and Dale, and where was Trigger? Even Ron would be out of Dodge, headed for NASCAR preseason in Daytona to hook up with a buddy who ran the pit crew for an up-and-coming contender. Suffice it to say, I was expecting merry and jolly about as much as Donner and Blitzen.

I was about to drop a bag of triple-washed Romaine in the cart to join my other decidedly nonholiday staples when I noticed the ad on the back of the kiddie seat—because obviously you need something to look at if you don't have a four-year-old banging the heels of their light-up sneakers against your cart and screaming for Marshmallow Froot Loops instead of multigrain O's. You know the ones: "Let us fix your aching spine. Free Consultation" chiropractor ads. Or the dial-a-lawyer ads: "Injured by a chiropractor? Free Consultation." This time the ad was right on my street and up my alley. "Buying or Selling—Let Me Take the Hassle Out of Your Real Estate Deal." There was a smiling photo of a perfectly ordinary woman—no starched and streaked hair, fake nails or Cruella DeVil makeup. Lily Gardener—no kidding, her parents were either hippies or comedians—didn't look like one of those "I eat condos for breakfast" überbrokers. I called her from the parking lot. She sounded as normal as she looked, so I made an appointment for her to appraise my house.

Ms. Gardener—"Call me Lily. Plant me early and I'll make the blooming sale"—came by at seven-thirty on Saturday morning. She was pleasant and clipboard efficient. She questioned me about the age of the roof, the furnace, and all the systems and finishes in between, scribbling notes during the whole tour. I asked if a winter offering put me at a disadvantage. She said spring was the hot season, "but when you need a house, it's always spring." She said my neighborhood and school district were pluses—glad to hear it, I always thought so. She pronounced it a good starter house. That's funny, because for me it was an ender house.

By eight-fifteen Lily assured me that even in a soft market, the house was worth more than twice what I paid for it. Except I had to keep in mind that the equity I had eaten up on the second mortgage and the ARM would reduce my net proceeds. Then she estimated the value of my chunk of the American dream—both "as is" and what she could sell it for if I painted the bedrooms, put in a hardwood or tile kitchen floor, replaced the powder-room vanity and installed a new garage door for better curb appeal. According to her, two weeks, and about six grand, give or take, would up the listing price by at least twenty thousand—maybe more. Great. I had to spend money I didn't have to realize theoretical profits. On the plus side, she said I kept a lovely home, without the usual clutter and tchotchkes, so my house wouldn't need staging. I'd seen that on DecorTV— they come in, cart away the home owner's snapshots and tacky mementos and replace them with generic showroom furnishings, because obviously buyers have no imagination and can't see how their stuff will fit in when they're looking at yours. I thought that only happened in Malibu or on Park Avenue, not in little ol' Jersey.

I was just glad for whatever I didn't have to subtract from my ever-shrinking bottom line. So minus-ing the commission and taxes, I could still come out of the sale with enough to make a serious dent in my credit-card debt and have a few bucks left over. Not enough for that diamond tiara, a month in Bora Bora or the penthouse Amber thought I should look at, but I could get a crown for my tooth, and while I might still be in a hole, I'd at least be able to see out of it again. The big, red, all-capital-letter question: Where was I going to find six thousand dollars for upgrades?

I already nixed Amber and J.J. Besides, they had finally found a house they both really liked and were closing right after the first of the year. Julie offered to lend me the money. But that was too big a strain to put on a new friendship, no matter what she said about her new salary.

Don't even think about Ron. The car was enough.

Which left my parents. I had come clean with Amber, but what was I supposed to say to Mom and Daddy? I was grown, had been on my own and getting into and out of my own trouble for a few decades now. How was I supposed to say, "I messed up and I need your help"? I hate being a disappointment. But the sad and sorry truth was I didn't have a choice.

So I had to change my tune. I was practicing, "Ain't too proud to plead, baby, baby," but I didn't really have to. When I called, they both got on the phone. I brought up everything under the sun, including Dad's friend Mr. Ferguson's golf game, until my father finally said, "Do you need some money, Tee? We've got it, and you know you can have it." Excuse me? Was that my father? The one who had had no trouble letting me know when I was too old for an allowance? My mother added, "We already told you to ask. It's about time you paid attention—acting like you don't wanna tell us nothin'. We're not dummies, you know." That's the Mom I know and love.

Somehow when you become an adult, and have children of your own, it's easy to forget you'll always be your parents' *child*—and that their radar is as tuned to you as it was when you *thought* you got away with sneaking in past curfew. That, and I suspect they had a spy—code name Grandbaby. Anyway, they overnighted the check—for twelve thousand—with a note that said, "It always costs twice as much as you think. We'll check in from the wild, wild west. Love and Merry Christmas, Mom and Daddy."

OK. I could dissolve, or I could just get it done, the faster to pay them back. So I made my list, checked it twice, then hit the home-design warehouse with my projects all mapped out. Before you can say "renovation," I had a cart full of paint and had ordered ceramic tile for the floor and a bathroom vanity—those would be delivered the following Saturday. The garage doors would take a month. To quote my friend, "If you really want to do it, you'll find a way."

Oh, before he left town, Ron came by and made me pick out a tree. I wasn't planning to put up a garland, a light or a ball, but then he showed up in his bright red pickup truck. Who needs eight tiny reindeer if you've got four hundred horses under the hood? He took me to a Christmas-tree farm where we traipsed through the snow, along the rows of pines and spruces and fir—don't ask me the difference, but they smelled good. Normally, I'm up for the biggest tree I can fit through the door, but I didn't have the heart. It reminded me this would be my last Christmas at my current address. So I picked out a cute little one; it wasn't as tall as me, but it was chubby and full. And I don't know what possessed me, but when he was carrying it back to the truck, I made a snowball and threw it at him. I missed. Probably because I'm way out of practice. He said I was lucky his hands were full.

So Ron helped me decorate. I hadn't trimmed a tree with a man since my ex—he liked to toss the tinsel too. What is it, a guy thing? But I dug out the Christmas music, and instead of coffee I made us some hot chocolate while he was out in the garage getting the last few pieces of firewood because he said all fireplaces must have fire—it's a rule. It was fun I wasn't planning to have; maybe that's what made it so good. He got me to promise to go ice skating with him later in the season, toe permitting. But skiing—I didn't commit to anything more than the lodge. Yes, my health coverage had come through—which was the best gift of all—but I wasn't breaking any more body parts any time soon. I didn't have a name for what we were doing, what we were to each other, but I wasn't convinced I wanted one. I enjoyed being with him, but at the moment my hands were full trying to save myself. Oh, and he did bring some mistletoe—but before you go there, all we did was kiss under it. He's quite the kisser. Thinking about it still makes me all melty.

While I was sitting home one evening, looking at my little ol' tree, I got inspired to dig out those Christmas cards I'd bought the year before and never mailed. I even went to the post office for Christmas stamps. And I wrote checks to two of the charities that had sent me a blizzard of mail. They weren't big. It was what I could afford, but it reminded me there were folks in worse shape than I was.

So I got through the holiday without trauma or drama. Julius, bless his heart, gave us a week's pay as a bonus. I went to candlelight service on Christmas Eve with Julie and her sister Arlene, who was visiting from Toronto. And I'm sure some of you are wondering—and have been for a while—about me and church and why, with all my trials and tribulations, it hasn't come up. I haven't mentioned it because that's kind of how I feel about it. My relationship with the Almighty, and when, where and how we communicate, is personal and private. Maybe it's from my checkered church past—Catholic school 'til fifth grade, my mother is AME, Daddy is a Baptist, Mary Marshall, my best friend from third through fifth grade, was Pentecostal, my ex was a Buddhist and Olivia was a Jewish Anglican. I had been to church or temple with all of them—sort of a potluck worship experience. So I'm not a heathen; I just have my own way of relating. And believe me, without faith I'd never have made it this far. Well, after the service they came home with me for lasagna and salad—red and green, in keeping with the season. Next day Julie fixed Christmas brunch, and after that we all went to the movies, like we used to when we were teenagers.

By the new year my life became a blur of activity. Luckily I had a long-standing relationship with Franklin, my carpenter and general handyman. He took pity on me when I first moved into the house and it became clear I didn't know a sink trap from a pilot light. Over the years he had done everything in my house, from installing replacement windows to hanging Sheetrock when Amber let the bathtub overflow and water leaked through the family-room ceiling. If he couldn't do it, he knew who could. I wouldn't have survived without him—and neither would my house. He said he'd miss me. I said I'd give his name to the new owners.

Then there was the slight detour of getting Amber and J.J. moved into their new place. It was freezing cold that day, and I thought my child was going to give herself a stroke when the movers bounced the coffee table down the front steps, but she survived. I told them they could have some of my furniture once I got myself relocated. Wherever I went, I wouldn't have the kind of space I had gotten used to. At first Amber kind of screwed up her face—our tastes are very different. Not surprised, are you? But I said it didn't have to be forever. It takes a while to furnish a whole house. It would beat empty rooms and an echo. She saw my point. So did my son-in-law.

Fortunately, getting my house in order didn't cost twice as much as estimated, so the rest I used to ease my monthly squeeze. But by mid-February the renovations were complete. The house looked spiffy enough to make me wonder why I hadn't made those changes when I could have enjoyed them. Oh yeah—I couldn't afford it.

The asking price Lily and I agreed on was less than I would have liked but more than I could have imagined when I bought the place. I was hedging my bets toward a fast sale. I didn't have time to hold out for maximum profit.

Leaving my house while Lily showed it, and letting total strangers tromp through, serving up opinions on the way I lived, was torture. "The master bath is too small." "I prefer white cabinets in the kitchen." "I wanted a fenced-in yard." Who asked you? Then you have to live like you don't really live there because you could have company at a moment's notice. Heaven forbid there's a plate in the sink. Lily said the aroma of fresh baked apple pie might be a lovely touch. I started to say, "Then you can bring one," but I kept my mouth shut. And the bath towels I was really using were in a storage bin under my bed so the ones on the towel rack looked fluffy and fresh. What, the buyer is not supposed to think you bathe?

By week three I was antsy. Forty-six pairs of feet had waltzed through the premises and kept on walking. If the last year of my life was any indication, I was sunk. There wasn't much negotiating room in the price; I couldn't afford to go much lower. But week four was the charm. We got a serious offer from a couple with two kids, four and seven, and they were preapproved for a mortgage. Glad somebody has good credit. We signed contracts, inspections went smoothly. They wanted to close within sixty days. That's when it became clear to me I wasn't going to live there any longer, which meant I had to move somewhere.

Why hadn't I been looking? Dumb, huh? But you already know my decision-making style. Maybe selling the house used up all my proactive energy. I don't know, but I had to find a new residence pronto.

For a hot minute I thought about buying a condo. Lily strongly encouraged it, but I knew most of them cost as much or more than I had paid for my whole house. Yes, that was back in the day, but come on. I wasn't prepared yet to spend that much for a two-bedroom matchbox—a thousand-square-foot, second-floor walk-up with outside parking? Give me a break. And I wasn't kidding myself. I knew my credit rating was shot to hell, so I wasn't getting the preferred-borrower mortgage rate. Would they give me one? These days, who knows. The banks aren't in such hot shape either. Truth was, I wanted a time-out—to live in a place where I wouldn't have to worry about a busted hot-water heater, leaky faucets, toilets that won't stop running, mulch, leaves, snow, repaving the driveway, replacing the roof, repairing the garage door, or what I would do if another rainstorm uprooted a tree in my front lawn. That was the owner's problem. For a while I wanted no worries—only a place where I could just be.

As soon as I mentioned my dilemma at the office, everybody had a suggestion about where I should live, so pretty soon I stopped talking about my search, because I did not want the second floor over their second cousin's store in Carteret, the garage their brother-in-law in Jamesburg turned into a one-bedroom apartment, or half of the duplex Aunt Esther rents in Spotswood.

I scoured the Sunday papers, tore out ads for places that looked like possibilities and spent my after-work evenings checking them out. There were dozens of brand-new construction "apartment home communities" like the one Amber and J.J. just left, but their walls were too thin. I wasn't used to hearing my neighbors' burps, sneezes and other personal noises. The layouts were awkward—designed to maximize space and minimize grace, the rooms were small, and the rents were astronomical because you got to be the *very first* tenant. One leasing agent repeated that about a dozen times while she showed me the apartment. Big whoop. I couldn't get that worked up about a room because no one had put a sofa in it before me.

I liked Julie's complex—it had been around since the '60s—solid brick construction, decent-sized rooms and closets, and none of the apartments shared interior walls. I have no idea how they did that, but it didn't matter because there weren't any two-bedroom units available for at least six months. I needed at least that much space. Besides, I know I could have ended up on the other side of the complex, but I wasn't sure I was ready for that much nearness. I wasn't being antisocial—really. Julie had turned out to be my bestest, dearest friend—in a way

I didn't realize I had missed since I was a kid. I mean, after I confided my no-bra status to Mary Marshall and she blabbed it to the class and all the boys started calling me No-Tit Tee: we didn't make it to best friends in the sixth grade. How do you do that to somebody you go to church with? Then, in high school, a girl I thought was like my sister iced me so she could get in with a hipper crowd. So after two strikes, I was out—kept my feelings and my business to myself. Which, come to think of it, could be why the Live Five suited my friendship requirements so well, for so long—or at least I thought they did. But with Julie I really felt she was someone I could count on in good times and sucky ones, and that when the occasion arose, I would do the same for her, but that didn't mean I was ready for us to be Lucy and Ethel.

Then, two weeks into my search and a month from closing on the house, Julie told me there was a "twin" to her complex, owned by the same company, built around the same time. She said it was about five miles from hers and they had two two-bedroom apartments available—would I be interested? Obviously, the short answer was yes.

A week later I signed the lease. So it was time to pack up my stuff and move on. I was still on my "do not put off what you can do today" kick, so once I had signed the contract to sell the house, I started consolidating and weeding out. I didn't have to make all the decisions right then. The kids said I could store things in their basement, maybe have a yard sale in the spring. That would be a hoot. I didn't grow up in a neighborhood where you spread clothes, books and household items on your lawn for other people to buy. Well, there aren't actually many lawns in Brooklyn, and nobody was interested in your *old* stuff anyway. But going to yard sales was a hobby in these parts, so I could get with the program—make back a few cents on the dollar. It all helps.

You never realize how much stuff you can accumulate in a house. I had clothes in all the closets—makes separating the seasons so much easier. There were storage bins in any and all available nooks and crannies. Some of it was stuff I had forgotten I owned. Clearly, I didn't need it if I didn't remember it was there, and some of it I was probably still paying for. It was sobering, really. Part of the reason I couldn't afford to stay in the house was because of all the things I'd bought, and now I couldn't take them all with me. Ironic, huh?

I didn't sleep my last night in the house. All the packing was done. J.J. had rounded up a bunch of his buddies to help with the move the next day—I have the best son-in-law. I was camped out on the couch again. It was closer to the door, and I'd already said my good-byes to the rooms upstairs. Periodically I'd get up, roam around taking the last lap of the old-memories tour. I have to say Amber and I had a good time there. I hoped the next family would too. I wasn't leaving them a haunted house. Truthfully, handing over the key would be a relief—and getting the check. Once it cleared, I was going to have my own private bill-paying party—and when the DJ says, "Somebody scream," that would be me, with pure relief. I was just sorry I had let it all come falling down around my ears. Maybe I needed to hear the crash to let me know it was time to move on.

I didn't hate my new apartment. I know that isn't the same as loving it, but it's a long way from miserable, which is what I bet you were expecting me to be. It didn't take me long to get settled in—thanks to my smooth move plan: less than twenty-four hours after the truck had left, clothes were in drawers and pictures were on the walls. I'm not saying it felt like home already, because I'd be lying, but there was something kind of cozy about the way my life fit into my new space.

In a way, moving was like going on a diet—and succeeding. All those excess pounds you'd been packing on little by little—the ones you chose not to notice—have vanished and you feel lighter, freer. So when I looked around my newly svelte surroundings, I liked the trimmed-down me. Two bedrooms—I made one a guest room/office—living room, dining area, kitchen, bath and a half. I even still had a fireplace and a little patio—just right and all on one floor.

Once Amber was gone, even before my world shriveled to two rooms after I'd hurt my foot, the house was well on its way to outsizing me. I hadn't realized that just one other person makes such a difference. At first her absence was an opportunity for me to spread out, fill up some of the emptiness—which I don't mean to sound like I was lonely, because I wasn't. But so much of the place was unlived in. I had a dining room I used twice a year max and a basement warehouse where I stored enough napkins and pickles to last into the next millennium among other stock-up sale items. You know me—everything had a place, and I knew where and what it all was. The problem was I ended up with too much of all of it.

And I'll tell you one thing: toe trouble or not, I did not miss the stairs.

16

. . . the only thing standing in my way is me . . .

I f you really want to do it, you'll find a way." It was like one of those songs you can't get out of your head. It's fine at first, but at some point you just want it to leave you alone—but it won't. I kept hearing Julie say it, and quiet as kept, the thought of starting a business hung around in my head more than I let on. NAB was a dead end—they might as well have posted the big yellow sign on the door, maybe next to a U-turn. And even though I kept my résumé in cyber circulation, since Derma-Teq I hadn't gotten any nibbles that led to a full-course meal, and you know who ended up hungry behind that fiasco.

Since I had peewee-sized my life, my money worries weren't erased, but they weren't eating me up all the time either. So after work and on weekends, while normal people were having a life, I consumed the "stash or trash" shows like popcorn, looking for proof I couldn't do the same thing as much as confirmation that I could. I was well aware that in untelevised "reality," it took longer than a day or two and cost more than whatever they tell you to turn a dump into a showcase. But I would look at my notes—yes, I took notes—and try to figure out how much time and money an actual makeover would take. I surfed online and found companies that did shelving units, file drawers, attractive boxes, bins, desks and file folders, ordered some catalogs, even found an organization for organizing professionals—with a code of ethics, a local chapter, a certification process. I could even qualify to join as a provisional member. How did I get anything done before the internet? I went to stores that sell nothing but storage to contain all the other stuff you bought. It was a constructive outlet for my shopping expertise. I was observing, not purchasing.

Those design shows always have a Mess Master who gets credit for the transformation, but I knew there were a pack of Mess Minions behind the scenes, sorting, stacking and arranging 'til the break of dawn. I did not have minion one. What was the timetable to do a project solo? Granted, I wasn't looking to reconstruct your playroom or design that north wing you've been thinking about adding to Southfork. My specialty—if you can call it that—is organization. But should I focus on decluttering offices, since I had done that, homes—actually I'd done that too, at least mine—or try to do both? What would I call myself, my company? It wasn't exactly the most important piece of the puzzle, but I had come up with a name. Hadn't tried it on anybody. Hell, I couldn't say "my company" out loud because it sounded, well, crazy.

Which brings me to the biggest question I kept asking myself: Who was I kidding?

It's so much easier to talk game than to shut up and play. But what did I know about starting a business? Zip. Nada. It's not what my associate's degree was about. They taught me how to work for somebody else, not for myself. And yes, I had been there with Olivia from almost the beginning—but not quite. I wasn't around when she hatched Markson & Daughter. Did it pop into her head one day, while she was folding laundry or taking Hillary to preschool or examining cucumbers in the market? It's a big leap from a hobby she started to keep from upchucking when she was pregnant to offering a product for sale. How did she arrive at the notion that she could turn her homemade potions and lotions into a bona fide, moneymaking enterprise? It never occurred to me to ask. Besides, her ex was rich, so what did she have to lose? Except she still had to muster the confidence to take herself seriously, research ingredients, standardize formulas, find jars and labels—which is where I came into the picture. So even though she was still concocting her brew at the kitchen table when I met her, Markson & Daughter was already an entity, at least to her. Where do you go for that?

Besides, what was I supposed to do for money? You need capital to start a business, and I didn't know anybody who had enough money to be called capital. Not that I needed a lot. I wouldn't have inventory or require a warehouse. Each job would be custom. I'd order supplies and furnishing to suit the client's needs. And when I realized I was thinking about clients, I had to take two giant steps back, because I had not said "May I."

And with Olivia gone, I didn't have famous or important friends who would talk up my new venture—give me an edge to quote Phill, two lls. I mean, even the village idiot knows it's all about whose ear you've got and who takes your calls, right? Just because I was sure I could organize with the best of them didn't mean anybody would actually let me try it in their house. I mean, would you? Well, maybe, but you already know a lot more about me than most folks. Anyway, I didn't have time; I had a full-time job—taking me exactly nowhere. Isn't that where this started?

Trust me, I had plenty of arguments for why I shouldn't chase this crazy idea, but I couldn't let it go. And Julie wasn't giving me any slack or letting me feel defeated before I could start. I mean, she herself was exhibit A. Two years ago she was answering phones, greeting visitors and making sure we didn't run out of coffee and bottled water. A year after that she was happy just to get a gig as Christmas help at the Markson counter—which, you will remember, appalled me. Now she was a department manager, about to be in charge of the brand for all the stores in New Jersey, New York and Pennsylvania—truly a caterpillar-to-butterfly transformation.

On an afternoon when I was being a truly doubting Thomasina, she said, "We start where we start, and some people get a head start, but it doesn't mean they always finish first." When did she get so wise? Right under my nose.

But I still wasn't convinced or willing to admit I had never contemplated a move that scared me so much. So even though we had both gotten our sack of lemons at the same time, Julie was now sipping cool, sweet lemonade and munching on luscious lemon bars, while I was still chomping on rind and seeds and complaining about the nasty taste. So I chewed—always mindful of my home-filled tooth—and I stewed.

I guess she'd had enough of my naysaying the day she told me if I was so smart, why didn't I quit coming up with questions and try some answers for a change. Alrighty then. Julie knew me well enough to be sure I'd take the dare. So I opened my mouth before I could reason myself out of answering and said, "I do have a name." We were on the phone, but I could just see her head cock to the side, waiting to hear it. There was no backing out, so I told her **"To a Tee."** It came to me during one of my daily traffic crawls, which had become my daydreaming time. I had even played with the fonts on the computer to come up with just the right look—creative, modern, sleek. I hoped I sounded confident when I said it, because it was the first time anybody—including me—was hearing it aloud.

Apparently Julie said, "It's perfect," but I never heard it because I was so busy defending my choice—it's easy to remember, it speaks to the service, it uses my name, it's part of my mission to create an environment for each customer that fits their needs to a tee. I had even gone back to my very outdated marketing and business-administration textbooks to jog my memory. When Julie could finally shut me up, she told me she agreed 100 percent, then leapfrogged to business cards and brochures, which she was already planning to distribute in the employee cafeterias and locker rooms of the stores in her territory and on the bulletin board at her church. Then I had to stop her because she was getting carried way, and it gave me a headache. I had a name for my make-believe business, and she was already advertising it. Before we hung up, she said she'd told her Markson rep I was starting my own company. Which I know was meant to really light a fire under my pot—and it did.

I was 97 percent sure Julie's sales rep wouldn't know me, and even more certain he couldn't find Didier's office without GPS, but gossip spread in that company like the flu. So the idea that word about my venture might find its way to the big corner office made the stakes instantly higher. Funny how motivating that was—the opportunity to prove, if only to myself, that I could do just fine without Markson.

And that night I dreamed about Olivia for the first time

since she died. She was in her pajamas, sitting on the porch in her rocker, like she had been that last day. But I was sitting with her and we were having our very first conversation—from the afternoon I showed up at her loft looking for a job with the listing I'd swiped from the placement-office bulletin board in my purse so no one else could apply. I was writing on a notepad and Olivia looked over my shoulder, admiring my penmanship and saying, more to herself than to me, "Definitely destiny."

Hmmm—maybe it was.

The next day at work, in between fender-bender follow-ups, I played with slogans for **To a Tee**, doodled logos, made notes on my blotter about what to include in the flyer. When I got home I turned on the computer, and instead of checking the sites where I'd posted my résumé, I started a **To a Tee** file; now that I'd said it, I couldn't stop. I transferred my notes from the office and swore off design shows until I had put some part of my so-called business plan in action. Daydreams feel good, but I had to make a move toward something real or let them go.

I knew that from my very own laptop I could create flyers, business cards, brochures and postcards—I just didn't know how. Lucky for me, my globetrotting child had it covered. Amber came by long enough to give me a crash course. When I first mentioned my plan, she teased me about becoming an entrepreNegro, but she and J.J. were all for me exploring my free-enterprise zone. He offered to do my accounting, when I had some. My graphic-design lesson lasted about an hour. No argument from me. I know where Amber inherited her recessive patience gene. But she made it look so easy. And maybe because it just feels wrong being instructed by the person you taught how to eat with a fork and to always wipe from front to back, I didn't let on that I only understood about half of what she said.

Despite numerous accidental deletions, files I forgot to save, and the cuss words that went with them, nine nights later I had printed business cards and prototypes of flyers. I played up my experience at organizing Olivia's business, which sounded a whole lot more impressive than keeping my kitchen tidy. I tacked them to my bulletin board, taped them to the kitchen cabinets, the bathroom door, left them on the coffee table. I admired them, compared them. From day to day a different one became my favorite. When I started working for her, Olivia didn't have all this.

Now what was I supposed to do?

How many did I need? Where would I distribute them? And what the hell would I do if I got any response? I don't want to say I was paralyzed—that sounds so dramatic. But forward progress screeched to a halt.

I don't know if I was waiting for Olivia to reappear in my dreams, or a genie to pop out of my computer and show me "the way" Julie kept telling me I'd find if I wanted to, but since she was in training for her new position, and Amber was in Mexico City, nobody was bugging me about my progress. So I wasn't making any.

I was catching up on the papers one Sunday afternoon and relaxing after a Satruday at the dentist, finally, when Ron called, asked if it was a good time for him to come over and take care of the scratch on my car door. What scratch? Then I remembered J.J. pointing it out to me during the move. The mark was so small, I had missed and dismissed it. And as for Ron, I hadn't seen him since he got back from Florida, not that he hadn't left messages. I wasn't exactly avoiding him, but with selling the house, packing, moving, working, inventing a business and the graphics that went with it, I hadn't fit Ron into the schedule. Guess I could have called the man back, huh?

Now, I was busy, not dead. I'd definitely thought about him from time to time—our diner dinner, the postcookie lip lock and the merry mistletoe encounter had kept me entertained when I needed a break from my fun-challenged life. And obviously Baby Son-in-Law had taken it upon himself to update good old cousin Ron—at least about the condition of my car.

Ron's call ended my lazy Sunday daze, but one of the nice things about my smaller digs was that all I had to do was tidy the newspapers, ditch the tea mug, swipe away the toast crumbs and I was ready for company.

I did put on my brand-new jeans. I had pretty much retired from denim when Amber was little. At the time I was interested in looking grown and responsible. Well, one day I was over at their house, helping Amber measure for drapes; she was going to get custom but decided they were too expensive—for now. She said she'd splurge when they moved to the next house. OK, she got at least some of my money sermon. Anyway, she pulls out some magazine—the spring fashion issue—and flips to the spread showing the dos and don'ts of denim for all ages. She points to a diva with a slick gray chin-length bob and says, "See, Ma, she's seventy-three and she looks hot. You'd look great in these. You're not *that* old." Not *that* old? Thank you very much, daughter dear.

We were going to the mall anyway, so she dragged me from store to store—exhausting, I was definitely out of practice—and made me try on about 602 pairs. Straight leg, boot cut, flairs, classics, plain, embroidered, sparkled. I had two rules. No low rise—I was not interested in spillage. And no cargo style, because there is nothing I want to put in the pockets around my knees. Finally she pronounced the winner. I thought my butt looked too big, and when did jeans get to be $100? She said they looked just right, and they were 30 percent off—an early Mother's Day present. Wonders will never cease. She said I needed a fresh look to go with my new bachelorette pad. Is that where I was living?

Anyway, I had on a cute white shirt and my big hips in my hip pants when I buzzed Ron in. Now, it's no secret that I found the man appealing. Except nothing about our association had seemed exactly kosher to me from the giddyup. I still hadn't wrapped my brain around whatever it was we were doing—how-some-ever, cute counts. So I fluffed my hair and let him in. He gave me that killer smile, a peck on the lips—said he was just letting me know he was outside working on the car, then he went back out. Was I a teensy bit disappointed the kiss wasn't more, well, you know, more. You betcha, but what did I expect? The man kept tossing the ball in my court, and I wouldn't play catch. But it did seem kinda rude to have him out there all by himself taking care of my bodywork. So I grabbed a jacket—red suede, not new, but it was cute—and joined him.

Ron had on jeans too, so I was happy with my wardrobe selection, not that it meant anything special or that he even noticed. He was busy examining the ding on the rear passenger-side door like a surgeon—ran his hand over the nick, looked at it from different angles, and finally pulled a couple of mysterious-looking tools from his bag. He assured me it would look like new when he was done and went to work. Hell, as far as I was concerned, thanks to his surprise paint job, it already did. He was bent over, with his machine whizzing and whirring, which gave me a perfect opportunity to check out some things from different angles too. I must say, looking at him definitely rekindled my fondness for denim.

Half an hour later he was packing his equipment and telling me it shouldn't get wet for a few hours. I assured him I wasn't planning to head to the car wash. He laughed, then he asked how my plans were going for the new business. One of the two informants must have snitched. He said being on his own was more than a notion, but so was a job if you're doing it right. "At least I don't have to wonder what the boss is thinking." I 'fessed up—told him I'd hit an impasse after completing my research and stationery-design phases, but I couldn't figure out what to do next, so I hadn't done anything. Then he asked if I wanted to go for coffee. I said I'd make some.

As usual, Ron's presence had me somewhere slightly left of myself. He looked around while I rummaged in the freezer for the bag of Blue Mountain I had been saving for a special occasion. When he came into the kitchen he said he liked my new place—that it suited me. My sample flyer was in his hand and he said, "This looks ready to go." And I said, "Go where?" I didn't have an ad budget or a listing in the phone book. I wasn't ready for a website yet. I kept circling the same problem. I had to have clients to get clients, but where was I supposed to find them?

"Paper cars."

What was he talking about? So he explained, without making me feel like a total airhead, that I should go to the parking lots of the places where people who might be interested in organizing spend time and money—office and home superstores for a start—and put my brochure on their cars. Oh. How many times had I come out to my car and found some flyer stuck under my windshield wiper? I said, mostly they end up in the backseat. And he said most of them will, "but you only need the right few people to answer."

He said he used to do it when he first got started, and that weekends would probably be the place to begin, but it wouldn't hurt to hit the stores midweek too. Uh-huh. Can't you picture me running from car to car with my stack of yellow and blue flyers? No? Me either. Then I heard Julie's voice in my head—about making it happen.

That's when Ron told me there was a core group of young car freaks who hung out at the shop. He encouraged them, gave them pointers—his way of letting them know they could learn to do more with cars than just drive. "They'll do anything I ask to get an up-close look at a short-block Aluminator or a twin-cam supercharger." Clearly the blank look on my face let him know I wasn't fluent in auto lingo. So I poured coffee and he translated—short answer, they make the cars go faster. He also told me that when I was ready, all I had to do was name the stores and he'd get his crew on it.

I was planning to ask if he wanted cream or sugar, but instead I blurted out what was on my mind. "Why are you always so nice to me?" As soon as the question was out of my mouth, I knew I wanted to hear his answer—and I didn't. The man took the coffee cups out of my hands—I had gotten out the good ones to go with the good coffee—and set them on the counter. It looked like he didn't have to go far for the answer and I was gonna get it, ready or not.

So he puts both hands on my shoulders and turns me around so I was facing him head-on. He was quiet, looked at me long enough to make me even more nervous than I already was. I felt pretty much like I did back in that parking lot after we did the sushi samba, and that's exactly where he took me.

He said he liked me and thought he had explained that before. He didn't know why, "'cause you really give me a hard time, woman." But he wasn't looking for a logical explanation. "Why do I like red? Because I do. Period. Which is OK with me." Then I had to lean against the counter because I could tell he wasn't finished, and if I was going to keep listening and standing, I needed some help. I could feel the heat from the coffeemaker on my back—at least I think that's where it was coming from. Ron hadn't let go of my shoulders. Then he said, "Where I come from, you do nice things for people you like. It shows them you care."

So I'm trying my best to breathe, keep my knees from knocking and desperately trying to find something to say that doesn't sound idiotic. Except he tells me he's not done yet—that last time he tried to tell me how he felt, I interrupted him with my announcement about Gerald. Well, he didn't know it was Gerald, but you know what I mean. So Ron says he knows I'm not seeing anybody now—and I got another whiff of my daughter. Then he says, "Let's get the age thing off the table." His hobby wasn't hunting cougars and I wasn't part of some leftover adolescent fantasy about his high school history teacher. He said that he wasn't serious about anyone either. Mind you, he did not say he had been sitting home watching the Discovery Channel and pining for me, which is good, because I would know the man was lying or weird.

OK. So there was nothing I could identify as really wrong— you know, like him, me, a wife and a fiancée. After all, I did know his people—at least some of them. *And*, he had asked my daughter if he could take me out. It was like he was reading my mind, because he said, "This isn't some kind of 'sneak n' meet motel' 'Me and Mrs. Jones' jones. I really want to get to know you. Out in the open." But then I couldn't get Billy Paul out of my head—I must have been eleven or twelve when that song came out, and even though I didn't *exactly* know what it meant, I kinda liked the sound of "a thing goin' on." Couldn't wait to have one too. And there it was right in front of me—live and in person. A thing I could have. The man was smart, fun, kind, good looking, very nicely self-employed, and he was standing in my kitchen saying all the right things—after he'd *done* all the right things. It wasn't like he looked or acted like some young diddy bop with no clue what it meant to be a man. He wasn't an old fogy, set in his ways with one foot in the Social Security office either. And let's not forget, he wasn't anybody else's thing. And I really liked him. So what was my problem?

That's about the time Ron started telling me he knew he was interested when he met me at the wedding rehearsal. Guess I wasn't acting as motherly as I thought. He said I was attractive, confident, funny and gracious. Me? He added headstrong—was that a nice way to say stubborn? He wouldn't be wrong. And I'm trying to listen to the man, but I was struck by a moment of personal clarity. Had my lousy and limited male history left me silently singing my very own "he done me wrong" song? Ex gave me the first verse. Gerald got credit for the second. And the chorus, "It'll never happen again," was my refrain. Was it time for a new tune? And if it was, could I carry it?

So while it's dawning on me, however slowly, that the only thing standing in my way is me, Ron is steady talking. He could see right away that I liked myself, and he found that incredibly appealing. And that he got all that *before* our first date. The first, first date. The one I don't want to remember—postwedding. He was gentleman enough to call it a date instead of what it was. He was sorry it was such an embarrassing night for me, and that it would never have happened if he'd had any inkling I was too wasted to be a consenting adult. He laughed and said that made me a dangerous woman.

Then the mood shifted—it was subtle, but I could feel it. The smiling Ron had been replaced by a serious one I'd never seen before. He finally let his hands slip from my shoulders— slid them down my arms, squeezed my hands and let me go. I was glad I still had the counter for support, because all of a sudden things didn't feel so good anymore. His hands were gone and so was the heat. I reached for my cup of cold, unsugared, unmilked coffee because I had to look somewhere other than at him for a minute. I needed to remember my name and where I was, but before I could collect myself, he said, "I won't bother you with this again, Tee." Then he said that every time we'd gotten close to starting something, I'd put up roadblocks and detour signs. So this was it. Either we were going to take a ride and see where we ended up, or we weren't. Oh, he said he'd still take good care of my car and help me get the flyers out because he believed in what I wanted to do. That it would be terrific to see me when our paths crossed at Amber and J.J.'s. But that this part, the personal pursuit, wasn't a door he was going to knock on anymore. "Believe it or not, I have found women who actually like me." He tried not to grin, but he couldn't help it, and right then, in that instant, I realized I had already been missing his smile—and his hands. That I didn't have to do without them, and that I had to tell him . . . something.

So I said, "I really, really like you, Ron." Not very original— rather junior high, in fact, but I was out of practice and my heart was pounding so loud I didn't even hear myself. So I said it again. Because it was true.

He said, "You coulda fooled me!"

We both kinda grinned behind that and I opened my arms—welcome. For real. And when I said, "Let's see where it goes," I really meant it. I told him I didn't expect him, or me, to make promises we couldn't keep. All we had to do was explore what might be possible. And, for the record, I told him I was coffee-drinking sober.

The next morning, before Ron left, he asked me if I'd ever explored the possibility of hang gliding. I hit him with a pillow and said I was consenting, not crazy. But who knows? It already felt like I had dived off a cliff and I was hoping for a soft landing. Yes, I said the next morning, and yes, I know you want details. And unlike the first time, I've got 'em, because I remember every single solitary moment of that night—and morning. When I woke up, I knew exactly where I was, who I was with, *and* what had happened. In fact, I had to make myself stop replaying—and reliving—bits of that night over and over again, so I could get some work done. But if you think about it, I've shared an awful lot of my personal business—embarrassing stuff that folks just don't talk about, like money. And being the other woman when I knew better. But there are some things even I am not giving up—and this is one of them. OK, I will tell you this: remember the morning after the last first time, when Ron told me it had been great? Well, that's like calling the Pacific Ocean big. It's technically accurate, but let me tell you it doesn't begin to paint the picture.

17

Sometimes life handles itself.

Email is still not my favorite method of communication. I prefer the telephone—I mean a real telephone, the one in your house, attached to the wall—even if it's cordless. But I have finally accepted the need for a phone that travels with me. It doesn't have to sing me a song, show me clips from my favorite TV shows, allow me to decode a message from a distant planet or get the scores from the game last night. My cell is a tool I have in case of urgency—it's always been for me to call other people, not the other way around. "Do you have another number where you can be reached?" No. Because I'm generally not happy when my purse rings. So I wasn't thrilled when I realized that if I was going to be in business, or at least look like I was, I had to have another email address and a second phone number. I suppose I could have used the ones I had, but since I was taking the shotgun approach to advertise **To a Tee**—five thousand flyers and the Ron Squad—I was keenly aware that passing out my personal contact information in parking lots was not the best idea, because after a bit more prodding and soul searching, Ron wasn't the only plunge I'd decided to take.

He suggested I get one of those prepay-as-you-go phones initially. I could change the plan but keep the number when the business took off. *When* the business took off. He never let me say if. He was right there with Julie in the "Oh Happy Day, the Sun Will Come Out Tomorrow" club for Positive Thinkers, which I guess is exactly what I needed since it's what the universe sent me. But I was still a novice.

And as for Ron, it was still early—we hadn't pledged our undying devotion, moved in together or gotten matching tattoos. Come to think of it, I never asked if J.J. has the Chinese luck symbol tattooed anywhere. On second thought, I don't want to know. But Ron is so different from Gerald—I mean, other than the fact that they're both men, there isn't anything else they have in common—well, OK, except me. There are lots of things I like about this relationship—first, that it is one. I don't think twice about calling Ron at home, seeing him on a Saturday or a Tuesday or any other day that fits our schedules. I like meeting his friends and having a robe and a toothbrush at *his* house and not having to drive two hours to go out to dinner so no one we know will see us. I like that when we talk about the future, I say we and so does he. I like that he not only makes me feel connected to him, but he helps me feel connected to myself. And then there's the sex that I'm still not going to tell you about— let's just say that it's never been better. Maybe there *is* something to that younger-man-older-woman thing. I think, and I may be going out on a limb here, but I think that Ron and I are the way it's supposed to be. I don't mean in a carving-your-initials-in-a-heart-on-a-tree or writing-a-sappy-song-about-it kind of way. But the way it is when it works. Best of all, we are having fun. I did not go hang gliding, but I watched him—with my heart in my throat. What? You think it's part of the natural order of things for a human being to be towed behind an airplane? Well, he was literally on cloud nine. And I made lots of cookies. We were taking it week by week, which is as far ahead as I cared to look.

And if Julie was a cheerleader about my business, Ron was a cattle prod. On Memorial Day we went to a cookout at Amber and J.J.'s—the first official fire-up-the-barbie in the new house. There was lots of joking about the frozen-turkey fiasco, and I think Amber was as happy to see us together as J.J. was to light the fire. Right before we sat down to eat, Ron presented me with a provisional NAPO card so I could say that I was a member of the National Association of Professional Organizers on my promotional material. The man is seriously on the ball.

After the blitz—or the first wave, as Ron called it—I was an email-checking fool, and I'd look at my cell phone every six minutes to make sure I hadn't missed a call. By week three I hadn't received so much as a wrong number or Viagra spam, and I was ready to pronounce the whole episode a colossal flop. Ron was ready to launch the second wave.

We went back and forth a few times. Ron said, "You have to give people a chance to find you." "What's the point? It was a dumb idea," was my take on the situation. But he kept at it, and I remembered that I usually gave people and situations at least two strikes. I couldn't cut back to just one on myself.

So the second wave launched right before the Fourth of July. And I waited, and worried, and was pretty much ready to give up. Then Julie stopped by after work one day with a bottle of wine. We were sitting on the patio—she'd had a particularly gnarly day at work and needed to vent—and you know me.

I always need to vent. Honestly, though, it was refreshing to hear Mary Poppins complain. I was beginning to think the girl didn't have it in her. I kept hearing this buzzing from inside— it sounded kinda far away, but I went inside to check, poked my head out in the hall to see if maybe it was coming from a neighbor's apartment. Then Julie said it was a cell phone. I had given the business line a different ringtone, but I hadn't heard it since I'd picked it, so how was I supposed to remember what it sounded like?

I scrambled to find my purse, all the while figuring it was a wrong number or a prank call from some kid who found the flyer. So for the first time, in my best professional voice I answered, **"To a—"**

She started talking before I got to the **"Tee."** Her name was Elena, and three weeks ago she had come out of the office-supply warehouse—"You know, the one in the plaza with the phone place and the TJ Mega store. I'd been there too, but I didn't find anything good that day." Elena didn't stop for a breath. She had snatched my flyer off her windshield, balled it up without looking and tossed it in the backseat with her packages because it was starting to rain and she was in a hurry. "No knock on your flyer. Great color, nice paper, really professional. You have to tell me who designed it. I'm going to need to do some kind of brochure-like thing. Did they give you a good price?" Elena talks a lot. Don't say it. But her comment about the flyer made me feel good.

Anyway, she said she was a lawyer, and for more than a year she'd been contemplating leaving the firm she was with— "because it's run by imbeciles in pinstripes"—and going out on her own. In the beginning she planned to work out of a home office to save on overhead, "but I'd look at all the crap in my spare bedroom, turn off the light and run the other way. That is so not like me. But now I've got to get out of here. I'm on the verge of desperation. How soon can you get here? Please tell me tomorrow." Clearly the trusting type. She gave me her address, which was only ten minutes away, and we made an appointment for the next evening.

Julie was ecstatic. I was terrified. When I called Ron that night, I was in a tizzy about how I was going to get the job and keep my job—the one I actually got paid for. He said, "One step at a time." Told me to just go on the appointment, and he made me promise to call him just before I went in and as soon as we were finished, because you never know about people. I hadn't actually focused on the going into strangers' houses part before. Instead of getting my back up about how well I could take care of myself, because I was, after all, born and raised in Brooklyn, I was actually touched by his concern. See, I was mellowing.

The next day I was jumpy as a cat on the Garden State Parkway when I headed up Elena's walkway, but she yanked the door open before I reached the stairs. "I had a bet you'd show up and look normal. My boyfriend said only lunatics call people from flyers on windshields. Nice outfit. Where'd you get it?" is how she greeted me. Whatever I imagined she'd look like, she didn't. I think of female attorneys wearing suits and stylish pumps, not cutoffs and barefoot, but there she was, ponytail pulled up on top of her head, looking like Who let Daisy Mae off the farm?

Elena talked the whole time she ushered me through her house, which was lovely—at least the living room, dining room and kitchen, which I later found out were the rooms she rarely used. Then we came to the scene of the mess. Think landfill— laundry baskets full of LP's, wrapping paper and promotional coffee mugs, a doctor's scale, a cello, a dress form, diving tanks, a Nirvana poster, a piñata dangling from the ceiling fan. Now imagine that this stuff looms precariously over your head, like one hearty sneeze would cause an avalanche. And there was no actual space in the room where your foot would touch the floor if you tried to step in. I couldn't even tell if she had hardwood or carpeting. You get the picture. But she had just shown me her basement, which was almost empty. Guess she saw the question on my face, because she said, "I can toss stuff in here and shut the door behind me." Uh-huh.

The good news? The room was a pit, and she definitely needed my services. I also saw nothing to suggest the hidden freak show Ron was worried about. Turns out Elena, counselor-at-law, was a whack-a-doodle but definitely not dangerous.

After the guided tour, we sat on her deck to confer. She lit a cigarette and offered me a beer—I chose the diet iced tea. Her law degree was from Rutgers. She had made junior partner in a corporate firm where she had started as an associate right after graduation. "Bores me senseless." She flicked ashes toward the rose bush. I could tell she didn't take well to boredom. Elena said she was thirty-five—"time to pony up or shut the hell up and play checkers." Well, we were both embarking on a new phase in our careers, but I'm not convinced I'd have reached that point without the grenade that had gone off in my employment sector.

Elena wanted to have all her ducks in a row, including a few clients she had just started feeling out about the hypothetical possibility of her leaving the firm and opening her own shop. And she needed her new office ready to rock before she left the nest. I came into the picture because she had been at the car wash, cleaning the month's worth of coffee cups, granola-bar wrappers, soda bottles, newspapers and other debris out of her car where she said she almost lived because her commute was so long—you know I could relate. "It gets kinda piggy in there." I sensed a trend. Anyway, the flyer fell to her feet, she saw the bright pink paper and couldn't remember what it was, so she opened it up but almost couldn't read the number because it had gotten wet and the ink had run. Then she said it. "Destiny. Definitely destiny."

I got chills.

I told her about my background—what I had done for Olivia, leaving out the eerily similar start to our relationship. I also told her about how I had cleaned up thirty years' worth of chaos and clutter at NAB. When it was time to talk terms, I got even more nervous. The minimum NAPO *hourly* rate—which is what I had decided to charge—was about equal to half a *day's* NAB pay. Talking about money was never easy for me, but that hadn't gotten me anywhere I wanted to go, so I pressed on—said my charges didn't include costs for any subcontractors I would need, like carpenters or electricians, which of course I wouldn't hire without her approval. Elena didn't flinch, said it sounded about right. Then I remembered I was talking to a lawyer, so my hourly quote probably sounded downright bargain basement. She gave me her timetable. She wanted to be open for business right after Labor Day and asked how we were going to proceed. Apparently she had made up her mind.

The project sounded simple, but I knew it wasn't. We'd have to purge the room, and I was sure Elena was more attached to her overflow than she was letting on. Then I'd have to find acceptable places for the items that made the cut. After that we could set up her office. How was I going to do all that in six weeks of nights and weekends? I could hear Ron reminding me that the truth was always simpler—fewer moving parts. So I explained that I still had a job I wasn't ready to leave yet, which limited my available time. I promised to see what I could do to accommodate her and call her back with a workable schedule in a couple of days. She got it, since basically we were doing the same thing—planning our exit strategy. So we shook on it.

And my hand was still shaking when I called Ron from the car to let him know I wasn't being held captive by some trash-worshipping loony with a vendetta against organizers. He wanted to meet me at my place to celebrate my first client, but I needed to think. Make a plan. Figure out how I was going to approach Julius. I needed to focus, and Ron understood.

The next morning I went right into Julius's office, asked if I could close the door—which I think I had seen shut only twice since I'd been there. I told him my story—starting with **To a Tee,** what it was and why I wanted to do it. Then I laid out the plan I had worked on most of the night.

I had a client. I needed at least one full day off a week, preferably two. I wanted a ten-hour workday. I'd start earlier but needed to leave at the same time so my evenings were free for my client. It would reduce the hours he had to pay me, but I would give him almost the same amount of work. In addition I would be available by cell phone during the time I wasn't in the office, to answer questions about any of my files. I finally paused for a breath, then added, "And I'd like a reference."

He sat back in his chair. It was one of those wooden swivel numbers from about 1955, and it needed 3-in-One oil in the worst way. The squealing sounded bad from my desk. Up close it was seriously annoying, but Julius didn't seem the least bit perturbed. He looked at me a long while, too long, tapping his fingertips together like he was deep in thought. Meanwhile sweat streams were running down my back. Could have been because it was eighty degrees and the air conditioner in his office was the same vintage as his chair. Or was it my nerves? Perhaps one of those power surges Amber asked me about and my nurse practitioner had warned me were just around the corner. In any case, whether he could see it or not, I was sweating like a bull.

Finally he spoke. "I like that you have thought about this, Thomasina." He told me he admired my gumption in trying to start my own business. Gumption? Who has that anymore? But Julius wasn't exactly the type to say I had big brass ones. He told me he always thought I was smart, even when I "screw up" it wasn't because I was stupid or lazy. Was that a compliment? I didn't know, but I kept listening, waiting for the answer. Come on, Julius, just say thumbs up or thumbs down. And did I have the courage to quit if his answer was no? The Elena project would last about six weeks. What would I do if I didn't get another client?

It felt like I'd sat there for hours before he said, "Your own business—this is good. And I like to help. I think this will be fine." Hallelujah! I still didn't know exactly how it would fly, but at least he'd given me the chance to try my wings.

I didn't exactly show up at Elena's looking like a farmhand, but I didn't wear the cute jeans either. I was ready for serious hefting. And I came armed with a contract. After all, I was dealing with a lawyer. It was pretty basic. I used a template I found online. Elena looked it over and signed on, which let the sorting begin.

I don't want to say I bit off more than I could chew, because, as you know, I have a pretty sizeable mouth. But Elena was a trip. The first challenge, just like it is on TV, was getting her to relinquish stuff she had stashed that she had no use for, would never have any use for and didn't have any business saving in the first, second or third place. Like the fly-fishing equipment she bought after she had seen *A River Runs Through It* in 1992. Elena went fishing once. "It looked so relaxing when Brad Pitt did it." But it bored her senseless. What a surprise. Then there was the easel, canvases, brushes and tubes of oil and acrylic paint—because she thought painting might relax her too. After two attempts she realized she was no Picasso and she was done with that. Ditto the cello. I think Elena came without a relax setting.

We worked our way from the threshold in—skis, an inflatable kayak, copies of every college and law-school application and acceptance letter, her prom dress, eleventh-grade butterfly collection—she had grown up on a farm in southern Jersey. Never would have guessed that, but I guess the wardrobe was a hint.

And don't think this process went smoothly. We debated and rebutted every ironing board—she had three. We kept the best one. Memento—"When was the last time you looked at the program from the Ice Capades when you were ten?" "But it was the last one they ever did." And appliance—"I'm really going to use that juicer again." "Sure. Right after you take up macramé."

I'd describe my style as tough love, and I kept reminding her of the goal—the first office for Elena, counselor-at-law. Over time we trashed piles of crap. And discovered the floors were oak. I think she'd forgotten too.

Then I had to find storage units to go in the basement and garage, for the now streamlined remaining items. That's when I found out making up her mind was not Elena's strong suit. We'd go through options for shelving systems and she would have weighed the pluses and minuses forever if I hadn't kept reminding her Labor Day would be here in no time. Then she'd finally make a decision. And call the next day to make another one. That girl changed her mind more times in six weeks than I've changed underwear in my whole life. After canceling the shelving order three times, my new strategy became to wait a minimum of three days before finalizing anything.

I ate, drank and slept the Elena Project. Because I knew as soon as the space was cleared, the next hard job would begin.

She showed me dozens of photographs of offices she liked, but they were all contradictory. She wanted neutrals but liked color. The space should evoke a feeling of cool but be warm and inviting, be modern but traditional. She wanted the office bright but hated overhead lighting. I wasn't a decorator. I was an organizer. I could find the proper office furniture to give her space, good flow, make sure it had the right bins and dividers to manage her supplies and files and give her sufficient workspace with room to grow. Paint chips, rug samples, fabric swatches and furniture finishes were not my territory. But I made friends with the in-store design people. They got me through and I learned a lot, but there were at least forty times a week when I was sure I'd lose my mind.

Thanks in no small part to my former handyman, Franklin— who was not exactly a minion, but he wielded a mean hammer— I maintained my sanity. He was only too happy to work with me because it had the potential to expand his own client base. And he saved my butt even when I didn't know it needed saving. Occasionally I was even thankful for the serenity of NAB.

I didn't see as much of Ron as I would have liked that summer, but we talked every day and squeezed in time whenever we could. Amber was busier than ever—in line for her boss's job, so because Paris was her company's largest foreign office, she spent most of the summer there—poor baby. My favorite son-in-law sent me an email I was thrilled to get—and you know how I feel about my inbox. It was an article from the *Financial Times* about Interpol arresting Steven Wu in Thailand on charges of international fraud and money laundering. Sometimes life handles itself. And Julie? Well, Julie had met a man. And what was it she said to me? "You know, Tee, you don't know what's around the next corner if you don't turn it." Alrighty then, Miss Julie.

Now, unfortunately, in real life it's not like the home or business owner moves into a hotel and they show up for the final reveal and ooohs! and aaahs! at the amazing, miraculous transformation. Elena was there every day, or night, with questions, comments, suggestions—because it was her house, her office, and, of course, her money. So I paid attention. Smiled. Listened. Nodded. Showed concern about her wishes and suggestions. And did I say smile and nod? She was my customer, after all, and you know, just like they do, that they're always supposed to be right. Even when they're wrong.

Elena worked my last half a nerve, but she also taught me a lot. She has a good heart and a big mouth and she was so tickled with the results—I was pretty impressed myself—that she took it upon herself to spread the word about her new find—that would be me. She knows half of the lawyers in the state—80 percent of the female ones. I think she personally sent my brochure to all of them and offered tours of her new office as proof of my skills.

When I started, I had no idea how many people work at least part time from home—and a whole heap of them watched the same before and after shows I did. And they wanted their space to look like the ones on TV—polished and professional—

but didn't have the time, patience, or frankly, the taste to create it on their own. Which is, of course, where I came in.

And I really, really love what I do. I shop all the time, but with other people's money and they pay me to do it. Heaven. Franklin likes working with me because the jobs are simple from his point of view—in, out and on his way. And he's gotten more extensive jobs as a result.

I busted my hump for the first eight or nine months, keeping up with my NAB work, consulting with prospective clients, shopping, supervising them as they made sense of their possessions. Some days I felt like a therapist—OCDD, Overwhelming Crap and Debris Disorder, goes deep. Probably back to the time mommy threw away the box of broken Crayolas, the one-legged GI Joe or the knobless Etch-A-Sketch. And ta-da! Let the hoarding begin. Now, I don't want to toot my own horn, except I sorta do. I'm good at it—always was, way before anybody paid me to do it—I just like things neat and orderly. And I have a knack for easing people through the transition from slop to sleek. Oh, I know there'll be plenty of backsliders, but that just assures me repeat customers.

I stayed up nights deciding whether it was time to leave NAB. It had taken me for-freakin'-ever to find any kind of job with health benefits. The idea of letting that go kept me up many a night. It was never really more than a bridge to the next opportunity, but knowing I'd have something to cash on a regular basis sure was comforting. It wasn't as scary for Olivia—Eliot was the safety net, no matter what. When I talked to Julie about it, she reminded me I had a safety net too. I was completely and totally, for the first time in my adult life, debt free. Now I used my plastic like cash and paid the whole bill at the end of the month. I really thought about getting a new car—something in a snappy convertible—but I got so many compliments on my Ron-mobile I decided to let it ride for a while. And I had been careful to put money aside. I don't know if it was a full cushion yet, but it was at least a pillow.

Ron reminded me he used to have a J-O-B, and that it had made him miserable. Then he said I was friskier when I was self-employed. I threatened to show him frisky. He was not a-scared.

Daddy and I had a long talk about it. He was still old school—you get a good job and you stay there until your pension kicks in. I reminded him that pensions were an endangered species. Then my mother—*my* mother—got on the line and told me how proud she was. She didn't exactly understand how the money came in, but she knew I was making it happen. "Do what you gotta do and don't look back." *My* mother.

So I let go. And the world kept on turning. I was a wreck the first few months—and I was a good bill collector for myself, like I had been for Olivia, not like those heartless bloodsuckers who used to harass me. We all deserve to get paid. But I had time to take on more clients, stir up more business. I got the idea to do presentations for sorority alumni chapters and professional organizations. I got lots of good contacts from that.

And to show how far I've come, I started a blog with organizing ideas. It doesn't cost anything, and I like it when people make comments and ask me questions—not that I'm a know-it-all, but I do have some expertise. And it was the blog that got me noticed by a community newspaper. They asked me for my top ten home-office organizing tips. Clipping the article and putting it in my brand-new scrapbook reminded me of starting one for Olivia, with that article, about the Ginger Almond

Crème, with the labels I had handwritten. Well, that pretty much brought me full circle.

So I was working hard, making plans. I had this long-range hallucination about franchise opportunities. I was enjoying my love life—hadn't used that term in a couple of decades 'cause what I had with Gerald wasn't love, and it certainly wasn't a life. I was pretty much feeling I had it all—quite a turnaround. Then this envelope arrived in my mail—a big one—from Markson & Daughter. It had been forwarded from my old address, just in the nick of time. It had been almost a year since I moved.

I treated that envelope like it was radioactive—dropped it in the middle of my dining-room table and circled it at a distance. What the hell could they want with me after all this time? I was so upset I didn't know what to do with myself. What were they starting with me now? Well, I decided I wasn't letting it drag on and torture me. So I stood there—because I wanted to take it standing up—and I ripped open the envelope.

Inside I found another envelope, from a law firm. What the hell? I ripped into that and read—and read.

My whole life had fallen apart when Markson let me go. It was damn hard to pick up the pieces. I flipped through pages of wherefores and insomuch as-es. Then I just laughed, in my apartment, by myself, and cried.

When Olivia died and Hillary was so detached, unconcerned, callous and money grubbing, I was mad. But I was hurt too. It seemed like Olivia had forgotten where we had been and how she had gotten there—because of *we*. Well, she hadn't. The estate was just a long time figuring out where all the pieces went, and they were slow letting people know which ones were theirs. It seems Olivia valued my participation more than I'd known. And she had left me quite a handsome token of her appreciation. Oh—and a permanent seat on the managing board of any corporate entity that acquired the company should that eventuality happen. Pretty cagey for a hippie girl, but she knew her daughter. So, basically, she had made me Didier's boss—at least one of them. Does it get any better than that?

Well—yes.

Amber and J.J. had another one of those hand-holding moments on my couch. I don't know how much longer I can survive these, but it's getting to be tradition. Amber started babbling about how this wasn't part of the plan and how she didn't know what she was going to do. Her voice was getting higher and tighter, and I'm starting to think she got passed over for the next promotion she'd been working so hard for. Or worse, she'd lost her job altogether, or maybe J.J. had. Or they were being transferred to Bangalore or Budapest or Baton Rouge.

J.J. squeezed her hand, rubbed her arm and said it was a surprise to both of them, but they were happy. Amber looked like she was about to have an ing bing—hadn't seen one of those in a long time. Then she blurted out, "But I don't know how to have a baby."

I felt like I'd swell up and float, like one of those birthday balloon bouquets, which surprised me. Amber had been charging so hard on the career path, I had given up the idea of her being a mom yet. Besides, that made me Grandma Tee. Me? Grandma? The name was gonna take some getting used to, but I swear in that moment my heart got bigger, ready for somebody new to love. I could even imagine how happy my ex would be when he found out. And great-grandma and -grandpa? They'd be bragging all over Shoreline as soon as they got the news.

So I got up and hugged them both. That's when Amber

started to boohoo. I told her people have been having babies for as long as—I don't know, as long as there have been people. She would survive. Of course, at that moment she had no idea how that was possible. So I admitted she was a surprise too, and that at eight weeks I didn't have a clue how I'd manage either.

"But this wasn't supposed to happen for another seven years," she told me through her sniffles. You will be proud of me because I did not laugh, since I was supremely aware that what happens, and what's *supposed* to happen, can be so far apart you can't even see it in the distance. Then she looked at me with her tear-streaked face like she just wanted me to make it better. For the first time in ages I saw my little girl, looking just like she did the day she didn't get the part of Pocahontas in the second-grade play. So I held her, let her cry. And poor J.J., Lord love him, sat there patiently waiting. I winked at him over Amber's head and let her sob until she was through.

This time I did not quote The Fool's Guide to Motherhood. I quoted John Lennon—told her life is what happens while you're making plans and that she would be a wonderful mother, my son-in-law would be the best dad, and I would be the sassiest, hippest grandmother ever. Oh, and that I could already see Ron helping J.J. build the swing set for the backyard.

Would I want to change anything that happened? You bet your sweet behind. Because what doesn't kill you can really piss you off. But the problem is if you mess with one part, how does it change the others? Would I be where I am now if I had changed what happened then? I don't know. I'm not even supposed to know, and if I could have gotten here without going through all that mess, I'd be the first to sign up. But right now, I'm glad to be where I am, and to be with the people who surround me. And I'm writing it all down—there are probably a few parts I'll need to edit out—so I can give my grandbaby a word or two of advice, not that they'll listen. Some things you just have to learn for yourself.

Tee's Double Chocolate Cherry Nut Yummers

OK. Since I didn't give you the intimate blow-by-blow—so to speak—between me and Ron—I kinda felt like I owed you something. So here's the recipe for my Yummers. I know it's not quite the same, but it's all you're gonna get. Besides, you can have these for your very own, unlike my Ron—him I'm not sharing. Or you can make them for *your* special someone.

Enjoy!

¾ cup chopped nuts—*I like walnuts or pecans—think I'll change it up and try Macadamias or hazelnuts next time.*

¾ cup dried cherries—*they're a little sweet and a little tart. Remind you of anybody?*

1½ cups bittersweet chocolate chips

2¾ cups all-purpose flour—*no need for triple sifting—it's not that complicated*

1 teaspoon baking soda—*not from the box that's been sitting in the back of the refrigerator forever*

1 teaspoon salt

1 cup (2 sticks) butter, softened

½ cup granulated sugar

½ cup brown sugar packed—*light brown, dark brown— whatever shade you like your sugar*

1 teaspoon vanilla extract

2 eggs

6 ounces semi-sweet baking chocolate

I like to get organized first, find all my ingredients so I'm not digging around for the vanilla after I've got everything else ready and waiting. You did put it on the grocery list, right? Also, dig out those cookie sheets. When was the last time you used those? Not counting supermarket slice, bake and serve cookies. Anyway, no need to grease the pans. There's enough butter in the dough to take care of it.

Start water in a double boiler. I'll tell you what it's for later. A rolling boil isn't necessary, but it should be hotter than from your tap. And preheat your oven to 375°F degrees. Now, it only needs to preheat for ten minutes, so if it's going to take you a half hour to get this together you can wait to turn the oven on, but remember to have it hot before you put your cookies in.

I give my nuts and cherries a rough chop. You want to leave them big enough so they're identifiable in your cookie. I combine them with the chocolate chips in a plastic container with a lid and give them a shake so they mix evenly. Set aside. Hint: leave the top on. It makes sneaking samples while you're working more difficult.

Combine the flour, baking soda and salt in a small bowl. Set aside. Beat the butter, granulated sugar, brown sugar and vanilla in a large bowl. I guess you could do it with a fork or whisk, but a mixer makes them a whole lot lighter and fluffier than your so-called hand whipping. Besides, you know you're out of practice. Add the eggs, one at a time and beat after each addition. Set aside.

OK, now it's time for the boiling water. Put the 6 ounces of semi-sweet chocolate in the top of the double boiler. Stir the chocolate occasionally until it's all melty and shiny—no tasting. I know it's hard. Yes, you can use the microwave if you must hurry this along—check the package of chocolate for directions. By now your kitchen is smelling like you're making something extra good (which you are). Let the chocolate cool a minute. This would be a good time to make sure the oven is on, or clean up a little. I hate to get finished and have the kitchen look like a wreck.

Add that shiny, melty chocolate to the butter and egg mixture and combine until the dough is evenly brown. Gradually blend in the flour mixture.

Get out that old wooden spoon. Stir in your nuts, cherries and chips. This requires some elbow grease, but try to distribute the pieces evenly so there will be goodies in every bite.

Drop by rounded tablespoon-full onto your ungreased cookie sheets. The size of your cookies is up to you. I like mine around 2½-3 inches, but leave plenty of space in between. They'll spread a little.

Bake in your preheated oven for 9-11 minutes. Ten minutes is perfect in my oven. They'll look a little soft on the top, but they're supposed to. Let them stay on the cookie sheet for about 2 minutes, then remove to a plate or wire rack and let them cool. It's really hard not to start sampling during this step, but they're really perfect if you give them that little extra time. So start brewing your pot of coffee, making sure your vanilla ice cream is at just the right scooping temperature, or pouring that cold glass of milk. By then the cookies have firmed up but the chips are still molten. Yummers!

You should end up with 27-30 cookies.

Hint: The next day pop them in the microwave for 10-15 seconds to regain that just-baked taste. If there are any left the next day.

Dear Readers,

Telling Tee's story was a hoot—as close as we've come to a story that tells itself. We love her voice, her attitude, her honesty, her humor, her flaws and her flair for the ironic. OK we are biased, but as a character, we think Tee is terrific. It was great getting to know her. And we look forward to hearing what you think!

When we first came up with the idea for *What Doesn't Kill You*, we weren't exactly sure how it would work. We hadn't written in first person before, but from the start Tee was in your face. We felt a narrator would be too removed. People always want to know how we work together. Now we were planning to write not just together, but solely from a single character's point of view. Hmmm . . . Could we pull it off? We love a challenge, so we had to try.

Surprise! Channeling Thomasina Hodges proved easier than we anticipated. Seems she was a part of our collective storytelling mind that was longing to talk. Without much encouragement, Tee began to speak—about the disappointments, disasters, pitfalls and perils she had to maneuver through, past and over on her road to self-discovery. Had she been waiting her turn all these years (we know patience is not Tee's strong suit)? We don't know. But she was quite obviously ready to be heard.

Sadly, we are aware that an awful lot of Tee's journey is all too common in our current economy—some portions of her experiences have touched our own lives in a personal way. *Downsizing, foreclosure, outplacement, joblessness, redundancy, recession,*

283

outsourcing, cutbacks, and the mortgage crisis are regular headlines in the daily news. And all of those numbers and percentages that get tossed around represent folks trying to figure out how they're going to keep it together. Most of us either know someone whose life has been impacted by one or more of these realities, or are managing their own personal meltdown. It's rough getting through those times—definitely no joke. But as with all hard times, humor helps get us through it. Tee found out that while the situations and struggles will piss you off mightily, mostly they won't kill you. The process may toughen us up, make us stronger, force us to face bad habits that need our attention and find solutions we wouldn't have looked for without a push. And more than anything, remind us to appreciate what we have and to remember what is truly important in life.

Thankfully,

Virginia & Donna

http://deberryandgrant.com
http://myspace.com/twomindsfull
http://twomindsfull.blogspot.com
deberryandgrant@gmail.com
DeBerry & Grant
PO Box 5224
Kendall Park, NJ 08824

P.S. We enjoy meeting you so please check our website for our travel schedule, and updates on our movie news.

From: CCooke1044@aol.com
Date: Tue, 6 Jan 2009 19:55:45 Est
To: <mybrokestory@gmail.com>
Subject: Karolyn's Kloset, Ltd.

My story of making it through my "Broke Time" probably mirrors that of many other people. However, my strength was in my determination not to accept brokenness.

During the early 70s I found myself, at the age of twenty-eight, divorced with three children, with only an associate's degree, and receiving forty-five dollars per week in child support . . . that is, whenever it came. Lord, how I remember going to the bank with knots in my stomach, praying that the check wouldn't bounce. Already I was supplementing my meager income of $7,500 a year by doing small catering jobs, when I realized my growing children would need my help when they were ready for college.

It was about that time I realized I had to find a way to get my four year degree, while working full time. Then the idea came. I envisioned starting, *Karolyn's Kloset, Ltd.*

With absolutely no funds or experience, I approached my son's football coach, who owned a women's clothing store, and convinced him to give me clothing on consignment to sell. He agreed. Soon, I had racks of clothes in my government-subsidized middle-income housing apartment. My business plan began to take shape.

I recruited a few friends who worked in factories, hospitals, secretarial pools or any setting where there were significant numbers of women, as sales agents. I also carefully selected women who were, themselves "clotheshorses."

Each agent would arrive at my home every Saturday afternoon to turn in her receipts, pick up new stock, and shop for themselves (Even with their 30 percent discounts, they usually spent most of their earnings purchasing new clothes from me). My business began to grow, and I approached another shop owner who made it possible for me to gain entry into the market. This was a real stroke of luck because I was able to do business by simply paying cash for small orders, often choosing one or two items of a particular style. At 6:30 every Saturday morning, I could be seen in my little Pinto, dashing out of Westchester County to the garment district in New York City. I made friends with an attendant at a parking lot, and for a few extra bucks and an occassional gift of Johnnie Walker Black or Tanqueray, my purchases were secure as I dashed between suppliers, rushing to be home by noon.

In time my children were running their little businesses and keeping their own financial rccords. My two sons were selling men's socks, while my daughter sold pantyhose and handbags throughout the seventy units in our apartment building. The word began to spread, and soon my business had extended to the two additional buildings across the street as well as local beauty parlors, barber shops, and churches. *We had abandoned our broketime for goodtimes.*

Wow, is it possible we were thinking . . . "Yes We Can"?

From: "InPraize" <inpraize@allprovas.com>
Date: Wed, 17 Dec 2008 12:33:26–0500
To: <mybrokestory@gmail.com>
Subject: Contest Entry

The Best Broke Summer of My Life
By Stephanie L. Carter

In January 2000, my husband landed what we believed was the perfect job. He was making more money than he had in years and we could finally be comfortable. We were able to make rent without struggling; we purchased a new car and the bills were paid on a regular basis. This lasted for exactly *one year* until the company lost all their government contracts and my husband was without a job.

He fought to find comparable employment, but it just wasn't happening. Being disabled, I was basically of no assistance because his meager wages, while not enough to support our small family of four, were too much to qualify me for Supplemental Security Income. But we held on as long as we could . . . which was exactly seven months.

In June, we realized that we would have to leave our rental property because it was totally unrealistic to think our landlord would continue to let us stay there without our being able to come close to the monthly rent. But we had nowhere to go and no family that could offer us shelter. We attempted to reason with our children (my eleven-year-old son and twelve-year-old daughter from a previous marriage) and have them stay with their grandmother, but they didn't want to be separated from us.

As the deadline for our move grew closer, we prayed for an answer . . . and, as usual, God delivered. With a loan from my mother, we purchased a three-bedroom tent and some basic camping gear, and on July 4, 2001, we claimed our independence from fear of the unknown.

My husband, daughter, son, and I moved all our belongings into storage, packed up our personal necessities, and pitched our tent at the Groveland Oaks County Park in Holly, Michigan. We simply knew that God would act before it became too cold for camping. After three expensive weeks in Groveland Oaks (at twenty-three dollars a night), we became worried because funds were running low and another temporary job had gone bust for my husband. God still hadn't found us a place, but he did point us to the Holly State Park, which was only eleven dollars a night.

Yes, we were homeless, but we swam, barbecued, hiked, and enjoyed the peacefulness of being together the entire forty-five days we were there. I have to admit that we haven't been camping since, but we talk about it fondly even now.

Yes, God did deliver us from the camping experience, but there were still more trials we had to endure before we finally had affordable housing. There have been many struggles since, but the one thing we have always held onto was that if God saw us through *forty-five days* of living in a tent, He can see us through anything else that may come upon us in this life.

God bless!

What Doesn't Kill You

Seeing Thomasina "Tee" Hodges dancing the night away at her daughter's wedding, you might be fooled into thinking that she has everything life can afford: a magnificent dress with matching high heels, an elegant hairdo, a beautiful family, and even a handsome younger man biding time to be by her side. But this external image conceals a more somber truth, as Tee internally struggles with the reality of a lost job and a deepening debt just waiting to catch up with her. Choosing to lie to her closest friends and family rather than accept the truth, or share it, Tee allows herself to spiral down into a deep financial and personal recess. But with her strong and humorous voice to guide the way, we witness as Tee pulls herself up by her bootstraps—proving to us, as well as to herself, that women are nothing if not tenacious, and that the strong bonds that we create in our lifetimes will help us survive in the end.

For Discussion

1. The first chapter epigraph quotes, " . . . all you can do is mop up the aftermath, dump it in a giant personal hazmat container and move on." The topic of resilience is deeply woven into the fabric of Tee's story. Do you feel that it was her own strong character, the people around her or both that allowed her to pull through the adversity she faced?

2. How did denial facilitate more problems for Tee? She believes that you should "never let them see you sweat" (page 8), and acts accordingly, but that only deepens her debt and her troubles. Is this a common hurdle for people in distress?

3. What role does Olivia play in Tee's development? Does her idea of destiny eventually become part of Tee's religion as well? How does Olivia's parenting style differ from Tee's?

4. Both of Tee's important careers—at Markson & Daughter and To a Tee—help her make use of skills (label design and organizing) that she originally hadn't even considered marketable. What does this show us about jobs and careers? What are the authors saying about natural talents?

5. When Tee recounts her marriage, she distinguishes between the dreamy stage of love and the "reality portion that set in . . . The part about what's for dinner? Who's doing the laundry? And what time are you coming home?" Do you agree with this distinction? And how do you think that Amber and J.J.'s marriage managed to avoid that trap?

6. Discuss the Thanksgiving scenes present in the book—from the shared traditions of old to the addition of new members, like Ron and J.J. How was this setting important, both to establish a sense of time and a context for Tee's troubles?

7. When speaking of her parents, Tee comments, "We're all geniuses when it comes to playing the cards other people are dealt." Do you agree that it is easier to solve other people's problems than your own?

8. In one particular scene where Tee is trying to analyze all her problems, she says, " . . . ignorance is not bliss. It just means that when life slaps you upside your head you can say, 'Where'd that come from?' and halfway believe yourself." How do you interpret this thought? Do you agree that ignorance is simply an excuse?

9. Why do you think that Tee keeps the truth from her own parents, even when she urgently needs their help? What did you make of her parents' reaction when she finally tells them the truth?

10. Tee leads a very solitary life—she voluntarily isolates herself from her parents, daughter and son-in-law, and eventually even from Gerald and the Live Five. She explains that throughout life, she has been betrayed by her closest friends, and rhetorically asks, "How do you know whom to trust?" Do you think that she ever answers this question for herself?

11. Two of the toughest downgrades in Tee's life involve her car and her house. She speaks of these luxuries as the measurements of her accomplishments. How do you feel that this materialism led her into the deep recesses of debt? How did letting go of material things allow her to concentrate more on herself as the ultimate judge of her accomplishments?

12. Discuss Ron as an example of entrepreneurship. Why do you think that Tee first rejected Ron? What about his final speech in her kitchen made her realize that she was wrong to dismiss him? And what in his demeanor set him apart from Gerald?

13. *What Doesn't Kill You* clearly shows strong ties and resonances between the different Hodges generations: Tee's parents, Tee herself, Amber and—at the end of the story—a new grand-baby. Tee admits: "Somehow when you become an adult, and have children of your own, it's easy to forget you'll always be your parents' *child*—and that their radar is as tuned to you as it was when you *thought* you got away with sneaking in past curfew." How do parents play a role in our own personal development? And, likewise, how do they sometimes keep us from learning the lessons we have to learn for ourselves?

14. Tee sees herself as a voice from the past whose message serves as a warning to a new generation: "And I'm writing [my story] all down . . . so I can give my grandbaby a word or two of advice, not that they'll listen. Some things you just have to learn for yourself." What does this say about the chronology of life experiences? What do you think of this end to the story?

A Conversation with Virginia DeBerry & Donna Grant

The title of this novel is borrowed from a classic adage, as in many of your other books, including *Tryin' to Sleep in the Bed You Made, Gotta Keep On Tryin'* and *Far from the Tree*. Why do you use expressions to title your books? Do you seek to reinvent them and make them relevant to our current lives?
We like expressions because they are familiar—whatever walk of life you're from—and the words are always wise and sum up a situation perfectly. Of course most of us don't realize that until we experience that 20/20 hindsight for ourselves.

What Doesn't Kill You reads like a proclamation of independence. Although it's carried out by a woman, it seems like an important lesson for anyone—the lesson of living and working for your self-satisfaction. How do you feel that you've learned that lesson in your own lives? Are your careers as writers part of that self-discovery?

We think self-discovery is an ongoing process. It doesn't, or shouldn't, stop when you've reached a particular milestone . . . the eighteenth birthday, getting married, starting your career, having a child. Goals are OK, but life is not about the end game it's about all that happens before you get there; truly it's how you play the game that matters. We are on our own journey(s) of discovery, not only about writing but about as much other stuff as we can possibly experience.

In your books, you always explore the enduring relationships between women. In *What Doesn't Kill You,* you treat that topic in a different way—both giving due diligence to the bond between mother and daughter and acknowledging a woman's need to concentrate on herself. This is an especially important theme when it comes to financial well-being. Do you feel that it's an important message for women specifically?

Women must learn to take care of themselves—not just their families—because in reality, you are actually the only thing you can really count on.

Are any of the characters in the book based on people you know? If so, whom? Do you feel that the best characters are ones that the authors know in real life?

We actually try to avoid using people we know from our lives in our stories—it's not fair, and we mostly want to keep them as friends! But there's a lot of Virginia in Tee's personality and demeanor and way too many of Tee's experiences. Virginia doesn't have any children, so no, there was no sleeping with the best man at her daughter's wedding, but many of Tee's post-employment dilemmas are ones Virginia knows personally—so we had a great "in-house" resource.

Another important choice of words from Julie comes when she tells Tee, "You know, Tee, you don't know what's around the next corner if you don't turn it." Are these words that you have often had to say to yourselves? What is so comforting about a close friend assuring you that there will always be un-predictability to life?
It's hard to be brave all the time. Sometimes it is hard to be brave at all and, without your friends, to remind yourself that you have to keep putting one foot in front of the other, that "this too shall pass"—the journey would be so much lonelier and more difficult. We often quote the scene from *Butch Cassidy and the Sundance Kid* when they're on the cliff—the posse is hot on their heels. Butch suggests they jump. Sundance says no and is forced to admit he can't swim. Butch cracks up and says, "Are you crazy? The fall will probably kill us!" Then they hold hands and jump.

You don't conceal the fact that the friendship between the two of you began with competition, as you were both working in plus-size modeling. Eventually, you developed a successful co-authorship career. Does the strong friendship between Julie and Tee mirror your own? Is there a specific common ground that leads to strong bonds when two people share a competitive past and a common respect for one another?

Mutual respect and trust has got to be at the core of any thriving friendship, and that has always been the case with us. And we established early that although we were competition for one another, the contest would always be fair. Unlike Tee and Julie, professionally we were always on equal footing. Tee started off as more of a role model for Julie. We enjoyed allowing their friendship to grow, so much so that Julie later has lessons to teach Tee. The space to grow and change is a wonderful gift friends can give each other.

Toward the first surge of her new career, Tee mentions that she created a blog with ideas on organization where her readers could ask for tips, ask questions and make comments. Do you find that your own blog (twomindsfull.blogspot.com) is a place where you can connect with your own readers and reach your audience more directly?

We love having our readers connect with us via email, our blog and our MySpace page (myspace.com/twomindsfull)! We post topics that run the gamut from the serious to the ridiculously inane, but our favorite part is reading the comments—and frequently commenting back. We like the immediate, hands-on involvement. And yes, we do monitor our own blog and MySpace page—'cause we get asked that all the time. That's why we're sometimes slow to respond—it's all do-it-ourselves.

Why did you choose the end of the story to be dedicated to the future, the new generation created by Amber and J.J.? How do you feel that our own experiences help shape those of the next generation?

We have loads of readers that are a generation, even two, younger than we are. And we're always tickled when we hear from them, in great detail we might add, about the things they learn from our books. When you reach a "certain" age, as we have, you have attained a "certain" wisdom—but that's nothing new, it's what has been happening with human beings on the planet from the beginning. So as storytellers, we are doing our part in continuing a cycle that's as old as life itself.

Your books have a great following with women and especially with book clubs. Why do you feel that the lessons you exemplify in your stories speak so loudly to groups and to women? Are either of you in a book club?

We believe that the truth of women's life experience—family, friends, mates, children, jobs, struggles, joys and everything in between, is a universal experience, one that transcends age or race.

Are you two currently working on another book together? Can you tell us anything about it?

Indeed we are—all we can (will) tell you at the moment is that, like so many of today's headlines, politics and scandal will be at the heart of the story. Will the past cast its shadow over the present forever?

Enhance Your Book Club

1. This book is primarily about organization—physical, emotional and personal. Write a "diary" entry about the sector of your life that you'd love to have a Mess Master come and sweep into nice, compact cubbyholes. Are there any ways that you can help do that yourself?

2. Tee taps into a small but viral underworld of reality television, that of the home makeover and DIY organizing. Do you agree with the organization of the renovated rooms? Do shows like these help their "customers" find a good balance between cleanliness and style?

3. Much of *What Doesn't Kill You* deals with careers—those that change, those that serve as models to others etc. Are you looking for a change yourself? Check out such websites as LinkedIn.com and careerbuilder.com.